BREED

BREED

K T Davies

www.foxspirit.co.uk

Breed © 2014 K T Davies

Cover Art by Ewan Davies

conversion by handebooks.co.uk

ISBN: 978-1-909348-65-3

All rights reserved, including the right to reproduce this book or portions thereof in any form.

A Fox Spirit Original
Fox Spirit Books
www.foxspirit.co.uk

*To Ewan, Raven and Gabe,
the best rum crew a cove could wish for*

Acknowledgements

There are no acknowledgements it was all me! Me! Me! Muahahaha..haha...ha. *coughs*

Oh, all right then. I admit it I had help.

Thanks to Maureen Kincaid-Speller for her l33t early doors editing skillz, swiftly followed by the fab Darren Pulsford and his word wrangling wizardry, ably assisted by the amazing MadNad. Even more thanks to the scary wonderful Aunty Fox, Adele Wearing for taking a flyer on me and my scaly mate and also the redoubtable Gavin Pugh for fettling the whole thing into a neat and tidy package. May I also extend my gratitude to messrs. Colin Barnes, Alex Bardy and Kev McVeigh, beta readers extraordinaire and a team of right topping gents.

Prologue

There's nothing quite as exhilarating as headlong flight, when fear of the unknown is banished by the sure knowledge that whatever lies ahead cannot be as dreadful as that which is behind. It is liberating, like being a child again. Although, truth be told, as wild as my childhood was, this was the first time I'd ever been chased by a dragon.

Even though my situation was rapidly sliding from dire to fatal, every fibre of my being sang with the sheer joy of being alive. I let out a loud whoop! It was a challenge, an exultation. Not to be outdone, the dragon answered with an ear-splitting roar and spewed a mouthful of frosty bile in my direction. I dodged into a stand of knotted pines. A wash of ice glazed the copse, leaves shattered like glass, trunks and boughs cracked like old bones. I escaped all but the merest lick of cold fire but that slight splash was enough to peel the skin from my shoulder. I stumbled, arms windmilling, feet scrabbling for purchase. The second I regained my balance, I dug my claws into the ground, and propelled myself down the mountain. My thoasan father had blessed me with his race's superior speed and agility, alas; my human mother had cursed me with the stamina of her breed. The pace was hard and the furious dragon was devouring my lead with every beat of its coriaceous wings.

It seemed that, in this rare instance, crime had not paid. It was a sad state of affairs, but not one that I'd live long enough to regret if my chilly friend had anything to do with it. Thus disillusioned (although highly motivated), I sprinted from the snapping jaws of death. Provoked by necessity to exert itself, my mind began to race as fast as my feet. The thought occurred that if I discarded the sapphire I'd stolen, the dragon might let me be, but then the wise words of Mother leapt to mind. *'Hope is for fools, and only losers rely on luck—more wine!'* I could almost see her; slouched across the Rat Bone Throne, majestically drunk and sneering at my predicament.

Tossing the stone would be pointless, the act of a desperate cove. Why on earth would the great, flying turd-sack let me go when it could retrieve its treasure *after* it had turned me into a frozen smear on the mountainside? It wouldn't. Like me, the big ugly bastard was greedy, and even if throwing the gem worked, and I escaped from this particular pot of arse-pickle, I'd be leaping from the jaws of one monster into the arms of another. To return to Mother and the Guild empty-handed would bring a far harder death than any the dragon could mete out. My dear mama had elevated brutality to an art form.

Another roaring breath whipped snow and dirt into an icy shroud. Jagged fractures raced me down the mountain. I narrowed my eyes against the blistering glare and glanced over my shoulder. The dragon was tearing its way through the frozen knot of pine less than thirty feet behind me. It paused a moment, fixed its pale blue gaze upon me and bared its sabre fangs. The air was awed to stillness; the thunder of my heart froze. There stood my death, sharp and cold. While my eyes drank in the full measure of my doom, my legs kept running— trying to save with speed what I had failed to protect with wit. They were doing quite well, up to the point that I stepped into nothing.

I pitched forwards; the breath was hammered from my body as I rebounded off the rough sides of a deep fissure. As I fell, I clawed at rock and earth to try to slow my descent. Darkness opened beneath me but I managed to snag a wedge of stone and hang there, my legs swinging in the inky void. A steady drizzle of grit and snow rained from above. I adjusted my grip so that I could pull myself back up into the cleft but the rock came away in my hand.

My thoasan instincts trumped my human ineptitude and I landed prone with arms and legs outstretched, spreading the impact of the fall. Myriad stars exploded before my eyes, lighting the dark. I squinted through the fireworks at the grey eye of light winking above me. When the eye closed I had wit enough to roll aside. A torrent of icy vomit gushed down the hole. I laughed as I passed out, lulled to slumber by the sound of the dragon venting its impotent fury on the mountain.

I'm not sure how long I was unconscious: all I know is

that when I came round, everything hurt. My hair spines had saved my skull from cracking like an egg against the hard floor but the brain within was feeling somewhat scrambled. I pawed my face and traced tears of dried blood to a sticky gash on my forehead. As I flexed each limb to see what still worked, a chorus of aches and pains sang a song of cuts and bruises. My frost-burned shoulder stung like a bastard. I sat up and brushed the grit from my raw flesh. Considering that I'd just been chased by a *very angry* dragon, I think I got off rather lightly.

Eventually the world stopped spinning and I peered into the darkness. I was in a cave that a human might describe as 'pitch black' but if I concentrated I could discern variations in the many shades of charcoal that layered the darkness. I adjusted my initial appraisal; it wasn't a cave, it was a large chamber with several exits. Time had feasted on the room like a hungry dog, worrying the once beautiful sculptures and carvings into piles of half-chewed rubble.

I drew breath, tasted fetid air, the musty stink of decomposition and the sapid aroma of rain watered fungus, and… *something else.* There was another scent in the mix, something I couldn't quite place. I drew a deeper breath; let the smell roll over the buds where my breed-muddled tongue had decided not to bifurcate. It was an acrid-smelling taste; a mix of fear-sweat and anger.

I wasn't alone.

Shaking off the effects of the fall, I sprang up, drew my blades and scribed an arc in the darkness. It was my way of showing anything that might be sizing me up that it wasn't worth the pain of trying to find out what half human, half thoasa tasted like. Nothing moved, but the smell lingered like a nightmare, clawing at the edge of my senses. Now, as much as I enjoy playing 'stab in the dark', time was against me. I had to get out and get home with my prize before Mother unleashed the Guild.

I summoned the words of a spell to mind and a fist sized ball of light bloomed before me. With a thought, I sent the pale sphere towards the recess where the smell of anger was strongest. Sure enough, hunched beneath an arch of fallen masonry was... *a thing*.

No bigger than a malnourished human child, its skin was mottled grey and its wrinkled head was far too big for its spidery body. It was wearing a ragged shirt and breeches of an ancient design. It blinked a pair of large, pure black eyes, and scratched nervously at the cobweb of wispy hair that garnished its head and pointed ears. It was a pathetic looking creature; a cross between a very old human and a very young one, but I did not lower my swords just yet. I'd come across some dangerous coves prowling the sewers and back alleys of Appleton that looked just as harmless as this scrapling.

'Don't hurt me, I mean you no harm—I did you no harm,' it said and raised its hands to shield its eyes from the light. Its voice was little more than a hoarse whisper, as though it was unused to talking.

'What the fuck are you?' I demanded, holding it at sword point.

'Isn't it obvious?' it asked.

'No, why, should it be?' I didn't give a damn what genus of goblin it belonged to, I was more concerned with how I was going to get out of here and off the mountain without being eaten by an angry dragon. The thing took a small step towards me, still mindful of the steel between us. It scratched the tiny horn buds on its forehead.

It was something infernal then, a descendent far removed of the demonspawn that fought in the Schism War. It stared at me with its huge, dark eyes and folded its arms.

'You're an imp of some kind.' I ventured unenthusiastically.

It straightened up, puffed out its bony chest. 'I... am a demon.'

I snorted. 'Are you indeed? A demon of what, pray tell?'

It cleared its throat. 'I am a tormentor of scribes.'

'A who of what?' I wasn't sure that I'd heard it correctly.

It set its wizened face in what I suspected was supposed to be a righteous frown, and planted its bony little hands on its hips. 'I steal nibs, sometimes entire quills, and upon occasion, sealing wax and the odd scrap of vell...' I didn't hear what else it said as by this point I was laughing too hard. Not only had I almost been frozen to death by a dragon, admittedly, one that I had provoked, but I was now stuck in a subterranean… *somewhere*, with only a mad goblin for company. You couldn't make this stuff up.

'That's really petty,' I said when I finally stopped laughing and could breathe again.

It did its best to glower. 'I'm a specialist.'

'I thought demons were supposed to ravage and destroy, lay waste to civilizations, that kind of thing, not steal pens.'

'Have you ever seen a scribe hunting for a favourite nib? Or been there when one has discovered the ink has dried up because someone, *me*, has left the lid off, hmm?'

'No. I can't say that I have.'

It wagged a finger at me. 'Well, let me tell you, it can lead to a great deal of destruction when you steal the pen of a scholarly type. They are by and large, a highly strung breed and given to wild fits of temper.'

'Angry scribes, eh? I'll watch out for them. D'you have a name, or shall I just call you Destroyer of Pens?'

'Stupid human. Do you think I would tell you my name and give you power over me?'

'Human?' I gave myself an exaggerated once-over. 'Are you blind?'

My feet were covered in red and orange scales, and I had seven taloned toes on each foot. He couldn't see the scales on my shoulders and back because of the tunic I was wearing, but the liver-red stripes on my soft, human arms and neck were plainly visible. I smiled just enough to show him the tips of two of my four sharp canines. And even if it hadn't noticed my feet or hair or stripes, it had looked me in the eyes—my bright, yellow eyes—and must have seen the flicker of my third eyelid.

The demon shrugged dismissively. 'Mortals all look the same to me. What's *your* name, half-breed?'

'Mind your own business, imp.' I gave it my best broken-bottle glare and sent the globe of light to the ceiling. It hovered beneath the stopple of rubble and ice that choked the hole about forty feet above us. It would take days to melt even with the aid of magic and longer to dig through.

I needed another way out if I was to avoid a bounty being placed on my head.

'I came when I heard the dragon. That's when I saw you. I thought you were dead,' said the imp.

I was struck by a sudden, horrifying thought. I groped at my chest. After an agonizing moment I located the sapphire nestled in the folds of my tunic. Relieved, I chuckled. Some demon. Not only hadn't it cut my throat while I lay senseless, but it hadn't even bothered to search me. The youngest kinchin cove in Appleton would have had the wit to do that.

My stomach growled. I wasn't a natural when it came to sorcery. If I maintained the spell for much longer the hunger would really start to bite. I searched through the debris and found some wood dry enough for me to fashion a torch.

The imp sneered at my efforts. 'Real warspawn can see in the dark.'

'They also rip little shits like you in half. Do you want to go down that route?'

It didn't answer.

'No, I didn't think so.'

I sparked the torch to life with my flint and tinder and wafted it towards the imp. It leapt back from the wash of wavering light.

'That's better.' I said and gave it a knowing look. 'You never know when you might need to burn something and as I'm neither a real sorcerer or a real warspawn this'll have to do me.'

'The mage lords were too afraid to give the warspawn the ability to use magic. They were scared that their creatures might use it against them.' It snorted. 'Cowards.'

'That's fascinating, really, it is. You should write a memoire, get some use out of all those pens that you've nicked.' Although I didn't give two shits what had happened hundreds of years ago. I did get the impression that there was more to the little scutbucket than merely tormenting scribes. I might have delved a little deeper into its history but the pressing need to find my way out pushed all further thought on the matter to the far corner of my mind. I explored the chamber, it had four exits. One was blocked, and none of the others looked more promising than the next. I tasted the air. A full-blood thoasa might have been able to discern a thread of freshness floating amid the turgid air, but my human-blunted senses couldn't pick anything out.

While I pondered which way to go, I let my gaze roam over the heavily embellished walls. The sputtering torchlight sheened the drab stone with gold and lent a semblance of flickering life to the vicious demons marching towards an unseen foe. This was no ordinary dwelling buried under a rock fall, that much was plain. A knot of gloom tightened my gut.

'What is this place?' I asked the imp while not really wanting to know the answer.

It sat itself on the severed, stone head of a demon and drew its knees up to its chin. Its blank stare echoed the enigmatic vacuity of the statue's gaze.

'Shallunsard's Keep.' The imp's breath curdled the frigid air.

'What?'

'Shallunsard's Keep: the bright star of morning, the jewel that glitters in the crown of Helel.' Its reedy voice turned rich and resonant. It arched a feathery eyebrow, gave me the all-knowing wide eye, as though I should know what it was talking about and be impressed.

I wasn't. 'You mean *was* the bright star. In case you hadn't noticed, a mountain fell on it.'

'Ah. Yes. I remember the fall.'

'That's wonderful. Pray, sirrah, d'you also remember the way out? Only I have to be somewhere yesterday.'

'I do. And I will show you—for a price.'

I waved my sword at it, all casual like. 'Let me stop you there, shorty. My body and soul are owned by my mother, and she's one demon I will not cross.'

It made a sound akin to that of a cat throwing up a hairball. I think it was trying to laugh. 'I want nothing so… prosaic. I just want you to take me out with you.'

'You can't come with me. My mother, who is also my employer, wouldn't be at all happy if I brought an imp home. She has a strict 'no pets' policy.

'I have no wish to travel with you, breed. Just take me across the seal.' It wrapped its arms around its legs. 'Agree, and you'll be out of here in a matter of hours. Don't, and you can spend the rest of your life, short though it may be, lost in these ancient and labyrinthine halls.'

'*Breed*?' I laughed. 'Am I supposed to be offended? Because if I am you'll have to do better than that. I've been insulted by the best, and whatever happens, I'll wager that I'll last a few days longer if I spit-roast your carcass, *arseling*.'

'You think so, eh? The restless dead might have other ideas.'

I was about to reply with a stinging riposte but my attention was diverted by the sound of something shuffling behind me. I tilted my head and caught a whiff of decay. Without further prattle I dropped the torch, pivoted to my right, and rammed my blades into my unfortunate stalker before I'd given much thought as to what or who it might be. I'd apologise later if it was someone looking for directions, but where I come from sneaking up on a person is a declaration of murderous intent. Nobody plays 'guess who?' in Appleton, not twice anyway.

I knew something wasn't right when I felt my swords bite into flesh as hard and dry as rawhide. I have a good working knowledge of human anatomy and knew both blades should have been sticking in its gut or the transverse colon as the quacksalvers name it. There's a satisfying pressure to guts, a comforting suck on the steel, a bit like a warm handshake that tells a cove they've hit the mark. I'd hit nothing. My blades hung loose within an empty husk. The knot of gloom in my own gut tightened another notch. This was an entirely new experience and, truth be told, too much for my poor brain to keep pace with so I just gawped at the skewered corpse like a caw-handed cully.

While I stood there, goggling at the first walking corpse I'd ever seen, it grabbed me by the throat. I was somewhat perturbed by this and screamed like my arse was on fire until it tightened its grip and choked off my air pipe.

Shocked into action, I twisted my blades and ripped them through its desiccated body. The flesh was as tough as boot leather, but fear lent me an extra measure of strength, and I cut the bastard in half. The legs fell away, but the divorce of top from bottom didn't encourage it to loosen its bony fingers from my throat. Cursing, I sheathed my blades in its chest, took a firm grip on its hawser taut arms and wrenched the skeletal hands from my throat. Free from its deathless grip, I threw the damned thing to the floor, retrieved my blades and stomped on it until it was nothing more than an inlay of old flesh and bone.

'Neatly done.' The imp clapped. 'As you can see, this place is dangerous, infested with the restless dead. I know how to avoid them… most of them, at least.'

'I've a mind to make you one of the permanent dead for not warning me that thing was behind me.'

'What do you expect? I'm a demon, I don't do nice, helpful things; it's not in my nature.' The smug little shit picked a fleck of dry skin from its ragged shirt. 'You would also be wasting your time; nothing stays permanently dead down here. This place is cursed.'

'Of course it is.' I kicked a sliver of skull across the floor. 'Does it flood too? Is the air poisonous? Will blood drinking rabbits attack at midnight?' I sheathed my blades. 'Just my luck to be trapped in a fucking dungeon with an irritating, half-sized demon, and gods only knows how many walking corpses and if I don't get back to Appleton in the next few days it's open season on my head.'

The demon chuckled and steepled its fingers. 'As they say in the common argot, you're fucked, unless you agree to my terms, which I have to say are rather generous, considering your predicament. Now, do we have a deal?'

I sighed. 'Alright, alright. Just show me the way out.'

The demon grinned, displaying a neat row of tiny, needle-sharp fangs. It offered its hand. 'Remember, Breed, a deal is a deal. You promise to take me over the seal, alive and well?'

I didn't know much about demons, other than what I'd heard in the Nest when some lag wanted to impress their cronies. I recalled something about it being a bad idea to make deals with them, but I didn't see that I had much choice.

I clasped its hand. 'Deal.'

We walked for what felt like hours along lavishly carved corridors piled with mouldering furniture and heaped with bones: lots and lots of bones. After what felt like hours of trudging along the same corridors I was starting to think that the mad little skunkpizzle was leading me in circles.

Demon or not, if it was playing me false I'd skin the little bastard. My frost burned shoulder ached and I was running out of patience. I was also heartily sick of looking at the endless procession of grim-faced heroes and heroines battling snarling demons. Some of the rooms we crept past piqued my professional interest when I spied a glimpse of a chest or the gleam of something shiny hidden in shadow, but my demonic guide insisted that we press on. Even though I had a sapphire the size of a pigeon egg tucked into my shirt, it pained me not to steal everything of value that wasn't nailed down.

'So what are you in for?' I asked, bored of listening to my own breathing and the wet slap of the imp's feet against the flagstones.

It tilted its head to one side, and narrowed its eyes. 'What are you talking about, Breed?'

'WHY. ARE. YOU. STUCK. IN. HERE? WHY. CAN'T. YOU. LEAVE?' I said.

It scowled and ran a hand over its fluff dusted scalp. 'A sorcerer imprisoned me—something of an overreaction in my opinion—all because I stole her favourite pen: albino peacock, silver nib, very classy.'

'That's it? How long have you been here?'

'I was bound here in the year that Queen Halda the Red Witch and the Hammer of the North, united in battle against the Lord of Dawn.'

'Really? You do know how long ago that was, don't you?'

'Seven hundred and sixty seven years, six months, one week, three days and... nine hours,' it said and stomped off along the corridor.

'You've aged well, considering.'

When I got round to bragging about this adventure in the Nest, I'd leave out the 'small, insane demon' part. I would instead claim that my dread companion was seven feet tall with flaming eyes, wicked horns and great, leathery wings. I'd also tell my awestruck audience that I'd cut a far more cunning deal than just 'get me out of here'.

We passed more rubble-strewn chambers and the occasional pile of ancient corpses. Clad in rotting armour, they lay where they had fallen, names and deeds forgotten, their passing marked by none... *and their purses still hanging from their belts.*

Oh, sweet salvation but it was hard overcoming the habit of a lifetime and not filching their chink.

Eventually, after a couple more hours of walking in silence, I felt the lightest kiss of fresh air brush my cheek. I sniffed, caught a hint of pine sap and loam. It seemed that my little goblin friend was steering us right after all. I quickened the pace.

'So, what'll you do when you get out? Whores and ale, or is it straight back to business for you?' I asked, feeling much happier now that I knew we were going in the right direction.

It sighed. ''Tis not a *business*. A demon's wyrd—its nature—is written in its blood. 'Tis as strong an imperative as the suns' need to shine, the rain to fall, the seas to—.'

'Alright, I get it. You're a committed pen thief.'

Silence fell again and we continued on until we came to a junction. The imp raised its hand. We stopped. The passageway snaked off to the left, a pair of large doors hinted that some kind of hall lay before us.

'Which way now?' I asked.

'Through the hall. We're close now.'

I believed it; the scent of trees and taste of cold, fresh air oozed from under the doors. It was like nectar and I made to enter the hall, eager to be away. The imp grabbed my arm and pulled me back. It had quite a grip for something so small. 'What?' I said, and wrenched my arm from its miser's grasp. 'What is it?'

'You remember I said I could avoid *most* of the restless dead?'

'Urgh.' I handed it the torch, and cast a light spell.

The wavering globe banished the shadows in the hall revealing more than a dozen, shrivelled corpses lying on a black-and-white tiled floor. The ancient dead were wrapped in silken shrouds woven by countless generations of spiders. Some of the corpses were human but there were also warspawn as well as demonspawn locked in fierce combat. Why death had claimed them all at once was a mystery. That it had been sudden was not; hands were locked around throats, mouths were open, frozen mid-shout, swords were buried in skulls and chests. I dragged my gaze from the grim tableau and hoped that the cove with four arms and tusks like longswords was one of the permanently dead.

Despite the silvery radiance of the magical light, the furthest corners of the chamber remained cloaked in shadows. To my right, an obsidian throne stood brooding atop a raised dais. I half turned to speak to the imp when something on the throne caught my eye. Curious, I directed the light over to it. A sword was lying across the armrests of the throne. It was *glittering*.

The imp tugged my sleeve. 'The surest way to traverse the hall without waking these poor souls is—'

I stopped listening. The sword had captured my attention. The hilt glittered like frost in the moonlight. As vulgar as it was valuable, it was encrusted with diamonds which are an irresistible lure for rogues like me. Before I could stop myself, I was halfway across the room, eyes locked on the glittering prize.

Thankfully, not *all* of the dead were restless.

When the clamour of battle stopped ringing in my ears. I sheathed my blades and drew a deep breath. The imp was rolling around on the floor, laughing its skinny little arse off.

'What are you laughing at, you little bubo?' I had a scratch on my leg that stung a bit, but that was all. The dead might have been restless but they were very slow.

The imp's raucous laughter dwindled to a giggle. 'I have never seen something that wasn't under the influence of a powerful geas act so recklessly.' It shook its head. '*Thy* wyrd is greed, halfling.'

I snatched a verdigrised coin from the floor and threw it at the demon. 'Here you go,' I said. 'When we get out, find yourself a nice inn and buy a big, frothy pint of fuck off, on me.' Chuckling, it plucked the coin from the air and then idly toed a skull into the shadows. A moment later, the brain case skittered back towards us only this time accompanied by the dry clatter of bones.

'You missed one,' the imp sang.

I sighed. '*Why did you do that?*' I said and drew my blades *again*.

'Demon.' It shrugged, and settled its arse on the dais.

The restless dead lurched from the shadows. Creaking muscles worked its rotting jaw as though it was trying to speak but all I could hear were its teeth grinding.

Unlike the others, this one was wearing the remains of ancient plate armour and wielding a longsword. It wove its blade in a loop before launching an overhead blow. It was fast for a corpse, but nowhere near fast enough to catch me. When it was committed to the swing, I pivoted on my left foot and scythed my blades through its neck and torso. The head flew backwards and rolled into the shadows while the torso folded in half beneath the sternum. I sheathed my blades with emphasis and swept onto the dais without so much as glancing at the goblin.

The throne was carved from cloudy obsidian and decorated with a writhing mass of dragons that crawled across the seat, back and armrests. It must have been incredibly valuable but was far too big and heavy to move, unlike the sword. The blade was double-edged, deeply fullered and tapered to a fine, diamond-cut point. The pommel and cross-guards were thick with glittering stones. Time had been kind to the gaudy weapon and the steel was unblemished. I picked it up, gave it a swing. It was perfectly balanced.

'Do you see how it's been forged?' the imp asked. 'The metal has been smelted and reworked a thousand times, forming minute steel crystals within the many layers. The Shen call it star steel because of the way the crystals shine like stars in the night sk—.'

While the imp prattled on I took a firm, two-handed grip of the hilt and smashed the blade against the arm of the throne. There was a loud crack and the blade snapped neatly just below the rain guard. I let the now useless blade lie where it fell and stuffed the hilt into my tunic. When I turned round I was surprised to see the imp staring at me, wide-eyed and open-mouthed.

'What?' I asked.

'You— Tha...that was *Dawnslight*; the greatest sword of the age... It...it was priceless.' The little rat dropping scuttled over to the broken blade, picked it up like it was a sleeping babe, and gently laid it on the throne.

'Priceless, eh? And just where in the Empire d'you think a *breed* like me could fence a blade like that? I'd either end up doing the gallows jig or be vented by one of the Guild if I turned up with something like that and tried to sell it. Now, loose stones I can fence a few at a time without drawing attention to myself. Anyway, what's it to you? It's a sword, not a pen.'

The imp didn't answer; it wandered out of the hall with its head bowed.

After a few hundred feet the passage widened. Decapitated statues stood either side of a gaping wound where I assumed the outer doors must have once been. A cold wind howled a rousing greeting, carrying with it a hundred smells and tastes that I never thought I'd miss so much. Beyond the ragged arch, the rose-infused glow of the setting suns melted into the dark horizon. I ran outside, opened my arms, and embraced the racing air.

I was standing on the ravaged lip of a cobblestone promontory that ended abruptly fifteen feet from the entrance. Below, a scree slope stretched about fifty feet before giving way to a broad sweep of pines which in turn flowed into the vast, green sea that was the Arrak Basin. On the far side of the forest was Appleton, my home town. A thick pall of smoke from the calthracite burners marred the sky, marking its location. I turned to my companion who was lurking nervously in the shadows of the entrance.

'I need you to take me over the seal,' it whispered. It didn't look me in the eye; instead its gaze flitted nervously from one foot to the other as it shuffled from side to side.

'Oh, right, *the deal*.' I went over.

It held out its hand. I saw it was shaking, could smell the acid tang of fear and apprehension rising off its diminutive body. I picked it up and carried it into the sunlight.

'Put me down, breed!' it squeaked, kicking feebly against me.

Laughing, I put it down on the other side of the large steel ring that was set in the cobbles by the doorway. I guessed it was 'the seal' because of the arcane scribbles incised in the metal rim.

'Oh,' it said. It sounded surprised. 'I... '

'The words you're looking for are *thank you*,' I said and went back over to the edge to better plot my route down. It was steep but not a difficult climb. The imp didn't say anything; it was probably embarrassed for having misjudged me, or so I thought.

It wasn't the first time I'd been wrong about something very important and unfortunately not the last.

As ever, my body was quicker on the uptake than my brain, and so when I heard the soft implosion of air followed by a wave of heat and sulphur, I didn't spring into action and draw my blades. Instead I slowly and carefully turned around. For the second time that day I was grabbed by the throat, only this time I was lifted off the ground.

The demon was easily over seven feet tall and naked but for a few shreds of cloth clinging to the bony scales jutting from his dead white shoulders. He had long, curving horns like those of a massive ram, and fine, sharp features. His all-black eyes were the only things that hadn't changed and like all true demons, he had great leathery wings.

'You broke my sword, *Breed*,' he intoned in a voice that I felt as much as heard. 'Sorry,' I gasped.

His laughter sounded like a rock slide. 'Oh, Breed, there are some trivial imps and some petty demons, I'll grant you that, but a demon dedicated to stealing pen nibs? You really believed that?' He laughed again and squeezed a little harder.

'You are without doubt the most stupid creature I have ever encountered. Some might say, too stupid to live.'

'I... h...helped... you.' The growing pressure lessened, but I was still dangling by my neck over a precipice.

'Helped? We made a deal: I showed you the way out, and you took me over the seal.'

He took a step back and released me. I dropped, sucked in a huge gulp of air and coughed it straight back out again. The demon rolled his heavily muscled shoulders and cracked the fourteen fingers that terminated in gleaming black talons. I got ready to leap over the edge.

'So what *are* you the demon of?' I asked, trying to buy some time to come up with a plan.

'Oh. Ravaging, destruction, laying waste to civilisations, you know, that kind of thing. The more pressing question is, what am I going to do with you?'

'Let me go?' I offered, somewhat hopefully it has to be said. The demon reached a taloned hand towards the seal. A lance of white hot fire leapt from its fingers and engulfed the ring. The air burned black and bitter as the metal melted and ran between the cobbles.

'That's better,' he said. A curtain of steam rose between us. 'Let you go? That would be fair, I suppose, only I don't want everyone to know I'm back just yet. I'd like to surprise them.' He winked.

'I won't tell anyone anything, I promise.' Even as I said it I knew it was a lie, and so did he.

Before I could leap backwards and take my chance with gravity, he grabbed me again. Once more his iron-hard fingers closed around my throat and he swung me so hard into the rock face that I felt like I'd dented the mountain with my head. *Now* I fought like a cornered thoasa. Kicking and clawing for all I was worth, I made no impact on it whatsoever.

With the last hiss of breath I had left in me, I croaked 'Shallunsard!' The pressure lessened.

'That is the name the world knew me by,' he said and released me.

I slid down the wall and crumpled in a graceless heap, but I was saved. I had power over a demon lord. I was—

'Of course, that isn't my *true* name,' he said.

—fucked.

The demon threw his head back and laughed like thunder.

'What? You didn't really…? Ah, Breed, if only the rest of the world were as stupid as you. It held out its hand. 'Hilt.'

I fished the hilt of *Dawnslight* from my tunic and slapped it in the demon's waiting hand. The gems flashed crimson in the dying rays of the suns. He raised his other hand above me, the air crackled with energy.

'Let's make a deal!' I begged, cringing away from the blast of fire that I knew was coming.

His hand hung over me like a hawk's claw poised to crush a rabbit's skull. The suns haloed him in scarlet. I held my breath. After an eternity, the demon lowered his hand.

'Very well, Breed. I have a deal for you: Bring me the Hammer of the North.'

'Very well, but he's been dead for centuries,' I said, and then I realised what he actually meant. 'You mean the Hammer's *hammer*, don't you?'

He nodded. 'You owe me.'

'Funny, that's not a million miles from how I ended up being chased by a dragon.'

'Why doesn't that surprise me? Now, do we have a deal, or do I turn you into a cinder block?'

'Since you put it that way.'

The demon held out his hand. I gripped it.

'How long do I have?'

He grinned. 'A year and a day.'

'Deal.'

As soon as the words left my mouth, my hand began to burn. I tried to pull away but the demon held me fast. When he let go, I stopped yelling and looked down. A black sigil had been burnt into my palm, marking me out as the demon's own. I looked up, a salty oath on my lips, but the demon had vanished.

Chapter One

Appleton does not smell of apples. Appleton smells of shit and misery, which summed up my situation perfectly.

Thoasa are the toughest breed of warspawn, able to survive for weeks on nothing more than a few mouthfuls of brackish water, run for miles without tiring, and still fight like ten bastards in a sack at the end of it. So it's a shame that my mother is human. That much less hardy side of my lineage was desperate to add the contents of my stomach to the corrosive salmagundi of viscera pooling in the bottom of the honey pot I was hiding in.

As I slipped and skidded in the greasy waste, I tried to follow the thread of this particular enfucked situation back to where everything had started to unravel.

Stealing the sapphire from the dragon hadn't gone exactly to plan, I'll grant and then I'd inadvertently loosed a vengeful demon onto the world but what really irked me was that I had been forced to hide in a giant gong pot just because I was a couple of days late getting back to Appleton. Two poxy days and my own mother had put a bounty on my head.

The honey wagon slowed. A yelled greeting-cum-warning was followed by the creak of gates. We'd arrived at the city. I hunkered down out of habit rather than fear of discovery. Not even the most zealous greenshanks would think to search a honey wagon for fugitives, and why would they? Only a lunatic or a fool would hide in a shit pot. The team of urux pulling the wagon bellowed lugubriously when the driver encouraged them on with a few licks of the lash. My fragrant carriage jounced against its neighbours and I slid around the pot like an oily rag. After a halting five mile journey from the dump to the city I was covered in filth, and despite the best efforts of tear ducts and nictitating membranes the stinging fumes were blinding. My finely tuned sense of smell had also been bludgeoned to uselessness by the olfactory assault of the putrid effluvia.

After the last outbreak of plague all tannery waste and

night soil was required by law to be dumped at least five miles from the city. The Imperial Factors who ran Appleton didn't give a crusty scab about public health, but they did need a workforce to dig and refine enough calthracite to supply the Empirifex's Royal Cannoneers. So it was almost funny that a cove like me had benefitted from an imperial law. I would have laughed if I wasn't trying not to breathe.

As we rolled along the pots clattered hollowly against each other, much like the heads of the two Blades who'd waylaid me on my way back to the city. After a brief and pointy exchange with the pair of opportunists, I left them in the shallow grave they'd prepared for me. It was a bit of a tight fit, but where there's a sword there's a way. Their clumsy attempt had at least warned me that Mother had made good on her threat to put a bounty on my head. I wasn't surprised; she had a terrible reputation to maintain.

The wagon slowed almost to a halt. I carefully lifted the pot lid a finger's width and saw that we'd reached the crossroad of Pater Lane and Main Street. Seven-foot mounds of grey-dusted urux shit banked the busy thoroughfare. Everything in Appleton is grey, even the shit: height of summer, depth of winter; the soot that falls from the calth burners paints all seasons the same uniform shade of hopeless.

After we crossed the Silverlight River the urux gathered pace and channelled their breath through the hollow bones of their crests. Before long the beasts' ululating cries rolled through the timber and daub canyons of Old Town's shanties and dilapidated mills. Minutes later, the mournful cries of their stable mates flowed back towards us.

I didn't leap out as soon as the cart pulled into the gong farmers' yard; I lifted the lid a crack and waited for the dead-eyed driver to unhitch the urux. Unsurprisingly the yard was empty save for her and the animals. As she led them to their stalls I saw the locked bronze cuff on her wrist that marked her out as a self-indentured servant. It made sense given the job, pawning yourself to the state was common practice amongst the poor of Appleton. With the animals bedded down, she grabbed her coat and left the yard. I waited a short while before tipping the lid and vaulting to the ground.

Rancid fat oozed between my toes. It was times like this that having seven, clawed toes on each foot was a massive pain in the arse. I wished, albeit briefly, that I'd inherited Mother's human feet; little fleshy sausages that you could squash into a pair of shoes and not get covered in filth every damn day.

I squeezed a handful of arse-cranked alluvium from my hair spines. It did nothing to improve my appearance but I felt a yard less wretched without rotting viscera dripping down my back. My left hand itched; I scratched the black sigil of the demon Shallunsard that was embedded in my palm. I had a year and a day to find the hammer of the Hammer of the North, the weapon of the greatest hero the world had ever known that's if Mother didn't do for me first. I laughed at the absurdity of the situation and tore a strip of cloth from the lining of my jerkin to bind around my hand. No point adding 'demon-marked' to the list of reasons people had to kill me.

Despite my appearance and exotic aroma, nobody gave me a second look as I made my way along Tannery Lane. In this part of Old Town I'd have drawn more attention if I hadn't been covered in shit. I took a few random turns to make sure that I wasn't being followed before heading down Grinder's Snicket. Wedged between clapboard warehouses, at the end of the narrow passageway, a flight of steps led to the cellar under Blookmann's Grindery.

In a dark corner of the cellar, behind a row of storage racks that were never moved, used, or inspected, was a cunningly hidden sewer entrance that the Blookmann family and their employees were paid to ignore, along with the shady types who used it. I was about to congratulate myself for evading my brothers and sisters of the Blade when I saw something move under a piece of sacking crumpled by the cellar door. The suns hadn't quite set, but thuggish shadows mobbed the alley and fell heavily across the doorway. I tried to arrow my gaze through the murky depth only to find that it was a little *too* dark down there. Someone was using hedge magic. The spell to deepen shadows was a favourite among the stealthily inclined members of the Midnight Court. Scribed on blood-clay tablets, you used them once and then they crumbled.

They were a nice little earner for sorcerers of modest skill or those who wanted to stay on the right side of the paradox of power.

Whoever had cast it had used it in the right place, but they hadn't taken their smell into account. Free of the gong pot, my senses were my own again. I tasted the air and let the ambient funk of the alley wash over my tongue. The lurker was human, and either a male or someone who had been pissed on by a male. Whoever they were, they hadn't washed in a while and had recently dined on pickled onions. A rot-nosed poxmonger would have been able to smell the tang of cheap wine vinegar that cut through the alley's background perfume of cat piss, pigeon shit and grindstone dust.

It was an amateur mistake, very sloppy.

Outwardly I affected an air of nonchalance as I strolled towards the cellar. Inside I was drawn as taut as a bowstring, ready to spring into action. I waited until I was half a stride from the steps before I snatched my blades from their scabbards and leapt forward. As planned, I landed inches from my would-be ambusher, leaving him scant room to manoeuvre. He spat a curse and threw the sack aside. Like me, he was using two long knives; weapons of choice for the discerning back alley fighter. Unlike me, he wasn't very good. He swung his steel but I parried both blades—inside to out—and kneed him in the jewels. As he folded I butted him in the face. Gargling snot and blood, he took a seat in the corner. I rocked him off to sleep with a smack in the teeth and then had a quick rummage through his personals. The ghost of a familiar odour clung to the tumble of silvers that I found in his purse. I gave the coins a lick and a sniff. They smelled of failure and self abuse. They smelled of Sketh.

There are those who say that Appleton's sewers are nothing more than a shit-smeared, fat-calked labyrinth, a treacherous maggot burrow where only the desperate or the deadly venture willingly. *Here be monsters*, they say, which I know to be true for I am one of them, and this is my home.

The passage under the grindery isn't the safest way to get to the Nest and therefore seldom used, which was why I chose it. From here I could either take a long and time consuming detour or a shorter but more perilous route. I paused briefly to weigh the relative dangers of keeping Mother waiting any longer against the risk of taking the potentially fatal shortcut. The scale tipped decidedly in favour of taking the shortcut.

Nobody knew if Ludo had ever been a single person. Some speculated that it had been a sorcerer who'd pushed the paradox of power too far, others that they, he, she, or it had always been the way it was—just another freak birthed too near some old Schism-tainted battleground. The only fact about Ludo that was beyond speculation was that it was a deadly cove of the highest order.

I was hoping that the guardian of Mother's backdoor would be out fishing the flow for 'treasures' when I passed through its lair. I am often disappointed and today was no exception. I paused before the bloodstained door; it was swinging gently on well oiled hinges. Long before Mother had moved the Guild into the sewers someone, perhaps Ludo itself, had blocked all but two of the entrances to the collection chamber that lay between me and my destination. It had been Ludo's home for as long as I could remember and for the same length of time I'd known that if the doors were locked it meant that Ludo had a *visitor*, as it liked to call the victims it lured to their deaths.

'Come iiiin,' Ludo sang in an unsettling twine of baritone and falsetto. I sheathed my blades and entered. Previously when I'd gone to see Ludo to beg a favour for Mother or take the shortcut through its home, I'd felt a thrill of fear as invigorating as it was disturbing. I was therefore disappointed to find that after almost being killed by a dragon and a demon in the space of a week, the thrilling terror of a visit to Ludo was somewhat muted.

Thoasa hadn't been bred to be emotional; they'd been bred to kill demons for the Mage Lords. Even now, seven hundred years after the Schism War, the descendents of those mage bred warriors were known to be a coldly practical breed of warspawn. It was the human in me that enjoyed the spikes and troughs of stirred emotions.

I took in the room with a casual glance. A rusting walkway spiralled up the wall before tapering off beside a blocked up doorway. As usual it was piled with a huge variety of objects that Ludo had fished out of the sewer or taken from its many victims. Today I hardly thought about the coins and jewels lying scattered amid odd shoes, broken buckets and yellowing bones. I just wanted to get in and out in one piece although at a push, I'd settle for alive.

As usual, Ludo was dressed in a motley outfit sewn from mismatched swatches of fabric that the more ghoulishly inclined gossips swore had been cut from the clothes of its victims. It had artlessly posed itself for my benefit and was leaning against a broken alabaster column with a mildewed book held daintily (and upside down) in its giant, red claw. Belying Ludo's imitation of gentility and refinement was the collection of severed heads that had been nailed to the wall. In various states of decay from skull to still dripping, the gaps in their ranks were a reminder to be extremely wary of this cove.

Over the years there had been several doomed attempts by heroes and rogues alike to kill Ludo and plunder its hoard. Mother had never *officially* sanctioned any of those attempts, although I know she would have happily taken her cut of the loot had any of them succeeded. Ludo and Mother had an understanding: she didn't move against it or make too much of a fuss when one of the Nest's less cautious patrons vanished, and Ludo kept an eye on the back door to her territory. It was a pact between monsters which, thus far, had extended some protection to me as Mother's only offspring although I never took my safety for granted.

It flipped the book closed and beamed a wet-lipped smile with both of its lopsided mouths. Imagine taking two humans, sticking their eyes on stalks, replacing the right arm of one with a massive lobster claw and the left arm of the other with a flaccid tentacle and then squashing them together in a huge vice. That gives you some idea of what Ludo looked like. Its smell was equally unique, akin to a bowl of overripe fruit and maggoty bread, with a subtle hint of liquorice. Its gender was another mystery, as not even the lowest slubberdegullion in the sewer had dared a sniff of that hem and lived to tell the tale.

Ludo watched me intently, both pairs of grey eyes dancing merrily on the end of weaving stalks. Like a fleshy jigsaw; its vaguely human skulls were distended, flattened and bulging where nature had deemed necessary according its warped design. Greasy fronds of hair the colour of curdled milk clung to its sallow pate. Two extra legs unfolded from somewhere beneath its gaudy raiment and the two halves glided apart. But not the voice. When Ludo spoke, its voices remained in disturbingly perfect unison.

'Dear friend has come to visit! Dear friend smells *very* tasty; like a ripe skin fruit plucked straight from the flow. Mmm, luscious,' Ludo both rumbled and squealed. 'What pretty thing have you brought Ludo, what treasure?' Its eyestalks contracted and extended excitedly, both halves licked their rouged, too-full lips.

I took out the ambusher's purse and tossed it to the half of Ludo with the pincer. The claw snapped shut on the bag like a bear trap. It weighed the pouch appreciatively before tipping the coins into its human hand.

'Only coins for Ludo?' It sighed and deposited them somewhere within its motley. 'Ludo likes pretty things, likes eyeballs, and pigeon tongues, and sapphires as big as hens' eggs.'

'Alas, dear friend, I only have one of those and it belongs to Mother.'

The halves continued to slowly move apart, casually flanking me like a pair of wolves. I tried to watch both of them without looking like I was watching either.

Ludo pouted and teased a lick of hair behind its ear.

'Mother!' Ludo groaned, swung away from me like a petulant child. 'Mother has a bony soul, a heart of flint, a mind of knives and wasps. Stay with me, dear friend. I'll kill you for much better reasons than jealousy.' It licked its lips.

'It's tempting, friend Ludo, it really is, but I've already kept the old dear waiting and… what do you mean *jealousy*?'

Ludo tittered. 'You're a sharp-set cove, dear friend. You

know the grip is slippery on the greasy pole of power. Old hands lose their strength.' It fondled its nethers suggestively.

'Come again?' I said whilst trying neither to stare or avert my gaze.

'Mother fears you.'

I didn't get chance to answer, to say *with respect* that I thought it had dropped a maundering whid and should stopper up its bung hole. I didn't get a chance to say anything because one minute both halves of Ludo were casually gliding around the room and the next it apported.

'Here I is!' It breathed in my ear.

I didn't flinch. I didn't as much as twitch when the warty, red claw *clacked* an inch from my neck. Ludo giggled. The other half wandered over to the exit and clapped its hand and tentacle.

'Dear friend is *very* clever,' it said from over there, and next to me.

'I do try, friend Ludo, I do try.' I smiled at the eyestalks. Its clammy human arm slithered around my shoulder and it sniffed my neck. I stiffened, not because I found Ludo repulsive—who was I to talk?—but because the skin and scales on my shoulder were still a little tender to the touch.

Ludo giggled. 'Ice burn, hmm? Has dear friend been playing kiss-chase with a dragon?'

'Something like that.' I smiled through gritted teeth.

Ludo sniffed me like a boar hunting truffle snakes. It grabbed my hand, tugged the strip of cloth aside and sucked its teeth. 'Dear friend is demon-marked. Dear friend is fucked.'

Ludo apported. The part that had been beside me vanished and appeared by the exit where it cosied up with its other half. It opened the door, and urged me out with a flick of its claw.

I obliged without hesitation. The light behind me thinned to a narrow wedge. I glanced over my shoulder. The old villain was loitering in the doorway, eyestalks bobbing in thoughtful contemplation.

'Be well, dear friend,' it sang in tenor and bass. 'But don't come back too soon.' The door slammed, bathing me in echoes and locking me in darkness.

The booming wave of noise ran ahead of me rippling ever weaker as it spread through the tunnels. It was good to be back in the sludgy veins of the city. I knew this darkness, knew the way the shadows wrapped around flesh and stone, knew every nuance of every native stench and sound. I feared no evil. This burrowed corpse was the only home I'd ever known, and as far as I was concerned there was no better place to dwell. But then, worms like me, hooked into the arsehole of Appleton, had a habit of elevating the feculent passages far above their base purpose. I suppose I was a bit of a romantic at heart.

Not long after leaving Ludo's, a burst of tavern babble breached the silence, welcoming me home with raucous laughter and slurred curses. I had almost reached the Mouse's Nest. The Inn was the epitome of dump and proudly catered to the vilest scum and most dangerous flotsam that dwelt within or passed through Appleton. The queen who ruled this benighted kingdom was the most evil, ice-hearted monster I'd ever met, and I'd parleyed with a demon so I knew what I was talking about.

She was known as Mother Blake or just Mother to her gang which she had imaginatively named 'the Guild'. I was one of her Blades; that she also happened to be my actual mother was purely accidental according to the woman herself. I never met my father the thoasa. Apparently he went off one day to buy a goat and never returned. Mother and I did not get on but for the most part bore the burden of our relationship with stoical disdain. After the demon she was the very last person I wanted to see right now, but I had no choice if I was to save my neck. By way of encouragement, I promised myself that as soon as I handed her the sapphire and she cancelled the bounty, I was going to dive into a vat of cheap wine and stay there until I was entirely pickled.

My high-spirits lasted for about another four paces which was when I caught the unmistakable whiff of failure and self abuse. I flattened myself against the wall just before a spiral of air riffled past my face. The crossbow bolt whined like a mosquito as it sped into the gloom. I cut sparks from the bricks as I swept my blades from their scabbards and peered in the direction from which it came. About fifteen feet away, the skein of smells that were tickling my nostrils knotted themselves into a familiar lump that was pressed tight against the corner of the wall. I'd wanted a legitimate reason to make Sketh bones for a long time so in a way I was grateful that he'd opened the account, but I could have kicked myself for not spotting the little turdling sooner.

'When I catch you, *Sketh*,' I growled, 'I'm going to peel your balls like a couple of grapes.' That was an exaggeration: I didn't have the patience to peel his poxy fruits, I was just going to stab him a lot. My fellow Blade ducked around the corner. He ran, the slap of his feet receded at a pace. I followed at a walk because I knew where he was going. He kept running until he reached his destination. Soon after, a blast of conversation and the smell of stale beer billowed through the tunnels. Sketh had reached the Nest.

Chapter Two

There wasn't a sign above the door of the tavern, more a literal representation of the name. Sitting in a rusting cage was a half eaten human skull that had been carefully packed with rags by the now long dead and desiccated rodent curled within. Nobody had ever dared to ask Mother who the skull had belonged to, just in case she was in a mood to redecorate.

As well as being the only inn in the sewers, the Mouse's Nest had the dubious honour of being the headquarters of the Guild. Mother had built both from nothing with only her wit, powerful sorcerous skills, and efficient stock management. I sheathed my blades. There weren't many rules in the Guild, but few sane people entered the Nest looking like they wanted a fight.

Before entering I straightened up, cracked the bones in my neck with a quick head toss, and composed my expression to read 'cross me and I will stab you in the face'. I'd been away a while and the heady stench of piss, pel, and beer tickled my nostrils as soon as I opened the door. I wanted to sneeze, but stone cold killers don't sneeze. Instead, I swaggered through the crowded bar. For a moment, I thought news of my adventures had somehow preceded me, lags and bravos all but fell over each other trying to get out of my way.

Then I remembered.

I could tolerate the stink of the gong pots, but non-thoasa couldn't. Even down here, in a tavern in the sewers I must have stunk. Somewhat deflated I gathered the tattered shreds of my ego and hurried through the main bar.

Members of the Guild tended to congregate in the dimly-lit back room of the inn. Casual drinkers were allowed, but were often discouraged from staying with a polite smack in the teeth. This shady den was where deals were made, fates sealed, and the well-heeled—faces hidden behind masks—came to have awkward problems permanently solved. It was like a temple: silence ruled... except when someone came in smelling of rotted brains and fermented pigeon dung. A couple of the patrons gagged, several threatened violence. One shrank back into a curtained booth, quiet as a murderous little mouse.

'Evening, Sketh,' I said as I strode past the booth.

'Er… aye. Evenin',' he mumbled.

I had no intention of starting anything in here, not when I was already in Mother's bad books and besides, it was dreadfully rude to fight while people were trying to have a quiet pint but it didn't hurt to make Sketh sweat before I closed his account. It served the bastard right for trying to vent me. But before I could have a short, sharp word with my brother-in-arms I had to square everything with Mother.

The stairs down to her den were hidden at the back of the room, behind a faded tapestry of an imperial knight. The image of the armour-clad bastard was a warning to the Guild Blades of who'd come calling if they misstepped. I took a deep breath. The thrill of excitement I'd thought lost was now dancing light fingers up and down my spine. I pushed through the tapestry.

Lediss was slouching at the bottom of the stairs. The door guard's once muscular bulk hung like sacks of sodden wheat on his tired bones. The ogren glared at me, his solitary eye gleaming angrily from beneath his heavy brow. He snorted, rubbed his stomach with a grizzled paw. He'd been with Mother for as long as I could remember. The big oaf was slavishly devoted to her but hated everyone else, including me. Over the years I'd watched him slip from being Mother's red right hand to her doorman. The next step down was working behind the bar. After that it was sweeping the floors and emptying spittoons and then he'd be out on his arse, prey for those with long memories and axes to grind, which couldn't come soon enough for my liking.

'You stink,' he said, spittle flying from his broken tusks.

'I can wash; you, however, are always going to be an ugly, one-eyed bastard.'

He growled. So did I. It was good to be home. The ogren shoved the door open and tossed his head impatiently. I spared him a sneer before sauntering inside.

'Where have you been, you miserable, half-breed bastard?' Mother shouted.

'Hello, Mother,' I said cheerfully, even as the leaden surety of doom settled over me.

'Don't you fucking 'Mother' me.'

Imagine a room that has been decorated by someone with a lot of money but no taste *whatsoever* and that was Mother's audience chamber: an eclectic goulash of the most expensive and gaudy fixtures and fittings money could buy... in Appleton. Now imagine it upside down.

Upon my arrival Mother and I engaged in an unfortunate bout of bear garden badinage. Soon after I found myself disarmed and hanging by my ankles over the pit, suspended from a rope held by that grinning, rut-stuck barrel-fucker, Lediss.

The pit was a sheer-sided hole that Mother had dug down into the uncharted tunnels where the dog rats lived. It had taken her months of patiently feeding the dog rats juicy morsels of miscreant to train them to come when she called. The pit was now the centrepiece of her audience chamber, much like a fine crystal chandelier might be in the house of a less bloodthirsty noblewoman. Unfortunately for me there was nothing more than the whim of a madwoman and an arthritic, one-eyed ogren between me and an unpleasantly bitey-chewy end.

Mother sprawled across the Rat Bone Throne in her usual pose. One bird-thin leg was hooked over the arm of the glazed mountain of skulls and bones and a silver goblet hung from her bony fingers. She nailed me with a pin-sharp stare as I slowly spun to face her and her bodyguards. The Dumbrovski twins flanked her throne like a pair of malformed bookends. The identical goblin brothers liked to think of themselves as the killer elite of the Midnight Court. Killer elite, my arse. I didn't fear them, but I had a healthy respect for the hand cannons they were carrying.

One of the pair, Klaus I think, going by the stink of fermented fish drifting from him, tightened a sparkling zanthe crystal in the priming screw of his gun. That the hand cannons could blast a lead ball through imperial plate armour at fifty paces was why I was hanging upside down over a pit of massive rats, instead of stabbing the smug grins off their faces.

'Two days late.' Mother sneered. Flickering candlelight etched a deep v between her eyes. Neatly coiffured waves of dyed black hair shone darkly and framed her thin face. Like a lot of humans, she valued her appearance as much as, if not more than, her abilities. I didn't understand it. Her command of sorcery was exceptional but you couldn't tell that just by looking at her.

Next to the throne an incense clock smouldered on a cracked alabaster table. Another string burnt through and a tiny brass weight dropped into the boat-shaped metal tray, signalling the death of another hour and the approach of my demise. The next string began to smoulder.

'I lifted the fucking sapphire *from a dragon*, what more do you want?' I said indignantly, although I admit, it's hard to be taken seriously when you're upside down.

When I swung round to face Mother again, I saw that she was examining the stone in question.

'You also lost my fucking shipment of pel,' she said, and slammed the rock against the arm of her throne.

'The fucking guards weren't supposed to be there!' I snapped back.

A foot of rope slipped through Lediss's hands. Mother laughed. Some of the more sycophantic Blades joined in. A few of the bolder rats leapt at the tail-ends of my hair spines. Mercifully I was still out of reach. Blood flows almost to the tip of each leathery strand and it damn well hurts when they get bitten or cut.

'Cunting guards or not, you shouldn't have dumped my pel. This…' She wrinkled her nose at the huge rock like it was a turd, '… *bauble* will barely cover my costs, let alone compensate my clients for the inconvenience.'

'Inconvenience to your… Most of your *clients* don't notice when they've shit themselves.' I rejoined. What was really biting her arse was that they had gone and bought their drugs off Pork Chop Jing instead of her. Angry as I was I didn't

39

point this out or mention her rival's name, not with the furry masses staring up at me, eyes bright with hunger.

Muttering, Mother tucked the sapphire into her sleeve and took a slurp of wine. A dribble of scarlet ran down her chin and joined the widening stain blooming on the delicate brocade of her blue satin gown. She stabbed me again with another accusing glare as hard and sharp as coffin nails. I'd seen more warmth in the eyes of the dragon.

'If I'd have known what an utter and complete fucking lackwit I was growing in my womb, I'd have gutted myself with a rusty fork rather than give birth!' She spat. 'Useless! Just like that flyblown bastard father of yours. Two cocks and *you* are all he could produce!'

Nobody had the guts to address Mother's wilful ignorance of thoasan biology, least of all me. To emphasise her displeasure, she lobbed her goblet at my head. I easily dodged the improvised missile. Lediss didn't. The cup struck him on his blind side. He yelped which would have been funny had he not fumbled the rope as he pawed his face. I dropped another couple of feet before the fat-fingered idiot caught it. Grasping talons reached for me, I curled up to my knees to avoid the advances of the more athletic rodents. Backed against the walls by the force of Mother's anger, the Guild Blades all watched in silence, except one.

Wulfrun pushed through the ranks and approached the opposite side of the pit to Mother's throne. Square on, the northerner's stance showed a confidence just shy of confrontation; bold, but not arrogant, strong but not a threat. It was a fine, dangerous line, one I'd never seen any cove walk for long.

As I swung between them like a fleshy pendulum I could almost feel my skin burn from the intensity of their staring contest. I tried to look inconspicuous, which isn't easy when you're six feet tall and hanging from a rope.

'There's no need for this, Mo. The stone's worth twenty times what you lost,' said Wulf.

He had one of those voices that made you want to listen. A born leader, he was liked and hated in equal measure in the Guild. Nobody treated him with indifference. He'd only been a full member for a few months but in that short time he'd made his mark and proved he was as clever as he was big, something that had fatally surprised the Blade he'd replaced. The double-headed axe strapped to his back belied his talent as a cracksman but advertised well enough that he was a more than competent enforcer; something Mother hadn't missed. She liked him, and let him get away with more than many who'd been with her for years.

It was obvious that there was a strong, physical attraction between them from the moment they met over a pile of blood-drenched corpses and a consignment of stolen rum. He was just her type… big, muscular, and clever; although being human, I assume he only had one cock.

'What do you suggest, Wulf?' All trace of fury had left her voice, the snarl had been replaced by a purr.

'Timekeeping aside, Tails got you the stone.' He gave me a sly wink when I drifted between them on my slow, elliptical rotation. 'Didn't you tell me you had an awkward job that needed doing? Maybe it's something Tails could do, t' make up for being late?'

So, they not only shared a bed but she'd confided in him too. I felt no slight; she'd never told me anything but there were others in the room who I could sense were recalculating Wulfrun's worth and their relative positions in the Guild.

Mother's lips curled back in something like a smile. She clicked her fingers and Melpinin flip-flapped from behind the throne. The amphibane's moist skin shone like verdigrised copper in the tallow gold light that was dripping from the candelabra. He was wearing a powdered wig that was made for an entirely different shaped head balanced precariously on his warty pate. He filled another goblet and offered it to Mother on the platter of his wide webbed hand. She snagged it without acknowledgement and took a thoughtful slurp.

My fate was dependent on so many unfathomable and irrational factors that I'd already started planning how I'd get past the slavering pack of dog rats and out of the pit tunnel before they could tear me to pieces. As for Mother, I didn't have time to waste hating her, although it did cross my mind that perhaps I should at some point in the future, when I wasn't in imminent danger. The amphibane might have given me an encouraging double blink of his saucer eyes before he hopped behind the throne but it was hard to tell from my position. I couldn't remember how long I'd been upside down; all I knew was that my head felt like a blood-soaked sponge. My hair spines were rigid from the amount of claret that had pumped into them *and* I was still covered in shit. Much longer like this and I'd have to cut the rope with my claws and rescue myself.

'You might be right, Wulf.' Mother turned the stem of the goblet between her bejewelled fingers. 'But my furry friends—' She gestured to the dog rats with a languorous wave, '—will be ever so confused if they don't get their treat and it took an age to train them. You see my problem?'

The very next instant, the goblet clanged against the empty throne. A sharp burst of summer fruit soared from the spilled wine, momentarily distracting me from what had just happened. My body was much quicker on the uptake and was already twisting to face Wulf.

To his credit, the barbarian had started to turn and was reaching for his axe before Mother appeared behind him and shoved him in the pit. He didn't cry out as he fell; he wasn't the type. As soon as he landed on the writhing mass of hungry rodents he was back up, and laying into them with a fury that matched their hunger, mighty thews braced against the rapacious onslaught.

It was a mistake.

He must have realised that the tunnel leading from the pit was big enough to accommodate even his bulky frame, so why hadn't he run for it? I suppose Mother's surprise attack had thrown him. Whatever the reason; his choice to stand and fight was the wrong one. If I'd been in any position to make a wager my money would have been on the rats. The other Blades in the chamber didn't pass on the opportunity for a quick bet and as soon as coins were exchanged they began cheering and cursing, depending on where they'd put their money.

After a tense handful of minutes, Wulf let out an anguished cry as a rat tore the sausage of his guts through a bloody gash in his stomach. It was over quickly after that. The last I saw of the barbarian were the butterfly blades of his axe drowning in a spray of scarlet. Mother watched every bone-snapping, flesh-rending second, and I watched her; watched the play of light and shadow scratch frowns and chase smiles across her blood-splattered skull canvas.

I almost didn't blame her. As a sorcerer she was subject to the paradox of power: the more magic a sorcerer channelled, the less stable, physically and mentally, they became. The clever ones got round this by developing strategies to cope with and contain their abilities. Meditation, drugs, regular bleeding, and quite commonly limiting what they did and how often they did it. Mother handled the paradox by embracing murderous insanity, I would say 'like a lover' but it meant more to her than that.

Twenty minutes later, the feeding frenzy of the alpha rats gave way to the scrap-hunting of the pack. The spell of slaughter broken, Mother looked up and fixed me with her viper stare. If I was lucky, the bigger critters would be sated after eating their way through a mountain of prime barbarian and I'd be able to make good my escape through the tunnels. Ready for the drop, I waited for her to give Lediss the order to let go of the rope.

'In half an hour your fucking hero will be nothing more than a pile of rat shit.' Her voice was husky, thick with the iron blood scent that perfumed the room. 'There's a lesson for you in that. Fail me again and you'll learn it the hard way.'

The echo of her words died away until the only noises were squeals and the sharp crack of bones being splintered. She turned her algid gaze on the other Blades who were all trying to look less worthy of note than the next cove along. The air was thick with the hot metal stench of blood. It was powerfully intoxicating and made my muscles tremble and twitch in anticipation of a fight.

Mother spat into the pit then vanished. By the time I'd spun round, she was sitting on her throne as though she'd never moved. You had to respect skill like that. Only a master of her art could apport with such precision. It was why she was still queen of the Midnight Court after twenty-two years, probably why she and Ludo held to their little arrangement. The Dumbrovski twins cracked matching toothy grins, vicariously smug and no doubt relieved that someone they'd seen as a rival was now passing through the digestive tracts of fifty or so dog rats.

Melp flip-flapped from behind the throne again. His tongue flicked out and snared the dropped goblet which he duly filled and handed back to Mother. She drained it in one, her cheeks flushed scarlet, suffused with wine and murder. She slouched on the throne. Nobody spoke; the silence dragged on until, from below me, I heard the scrape of metal. I looked down to see a pair of smaller rats had the leather wrist strap of the axe clamped in their teeth and were dragging the weapon across the blood-soaked clinker towards the tunnel.

Other than a few wisps of sun bright hair and scraps of leather there was nothing left. Wulf the leader, the hero, was gone. My would-be saviour was rat food and I was still dangling arse over head, surrounded by Blades. Still, I'd had worse days.

'Let the lackwit down,' Mother ordered.

Dutifully, Lediss let go of the rope.

I rolled when I hit the sodden ground. Bright green eyes glowed in the darkness of the tunnel.

'Not like that, you fucking moron!' Mother bellowed at Lediss.

Before I could cut through the rope it was pulled taut and I was yanked off my feet and hauled from the pit before the somewhat sluggish rats reached me.

The audience chamber was cleared of everyone except the Dumbrovskis, Melp, Mother and me. The grille over the pit was replaced and covered with the orange and purple carpet.

'I suppose you think you're off the hook now?' said Mother as she held out her goblet for a refill.

'Er, yes. I rather thought I was,' I said. I tried to sound contrite even though I felt anything but. She smelled of wine, raw meat, expensive perfume and the tiniest hint of sweat, just a grade sharper than mere heat perspiration. It couldn't be fear—nothing scared her—but there was a subtle hint of… apprehension? If I didn't know better I'd have said she was wary of me, which was worrying as she'd been wary of Wulf. I suppose it could have been worse; she might actually have liked me.

'Well, you're not, and you stink. Why were you late? Never mind.' She snarled drunkenly and too quickly for me to do anything except open and close my mouth like a dying fish.

'I need you to kill that louse farmer, Pork Chop. Don't bother trying to work out why, just get your arse over there and do it. I don't care how, just do it tonight, now! I was going to send Sketh, but the vapid little turd-sack has vanished—'

'It wasn't me,' I interjected.

'What wasn't you?

'Nothing.'

I was in desperate need of a wash but I daren't risk visiting a bath house. Even one that catered to warspawn would probably balk at letting me in like this. Not only that, but if Mother found out that I'd stopped off for a scrub, she'd have fed me to the dog rats *again*. 'Misunderstanding', my arse. That cock stain Lediss was going to pay for dropping me.

I did stop off at the room I rented in the Nest to pick up my bow. Not even Mother would object to me arming myself for a job that I had no idea how I was going to accomplish. I knew it was the paradox that kept her dancing on the edge of madness. She threw a lot of power around and there was a price to be paid for that. Trouble was, I seemed to be the one who was paying it.

Now that I had a moment to breathe, I saw that my faithful jerkin, my *only* jerkin, was beyond repair this time. The back had been ice-burned by the dragon and it had half a dozen ragged tears from when I'd fought the restless dead in Shallunsard's Keep. That it had soaked up a goodly amount of… *liquor* from the gong pot was the final nail in its sartorial coffin. I'd never be able to sneak up on anything smelling like a rancid shit pot, not even in Appleton. I tossed it in the corner, regretting that I'd never thought to keep a spare.

Other than the mattress, the only piece of furniture in the room was an iron bound chest, and only then because it was bolted down. Despite what they say, there really isn't any honour among thieves. After disarming the needle trap I'd rigged on the lock, I dug out a spare shirt. It offered no protection but the mud-brown homespun would at least hide my orange stripes and pallid human skin. I also found a pair of fingerless gloves. They were old and speckled with mould but they'd do a better job of hiding the mark in my palm than the strip of cloth.

My heart did a drunken waltz that might have been akin to human dread when I thought about what Mother would do if she found out about the deal I'd made with the demon. I told her that I'd been late back because I'd run into a gang of ogren after escaping the dragon. It wasn't the most convincing story but as I was dangling from a rope at the time of telling, I forgave myself for the lack of bardic flair. As it was, she was so drunk and angry she barely heard a word I said anyway. I'd decide what to do about the deal I'd made with *him* later. Right now, I had to kill a gang boss for *her*. Dragons, demons, Ludo, and Mother. There were just too many monsters in my life.

I wrapped my bow and quiver in an oilskin and took a last look around my little corner of heaven. It was strewn with month-old rushes, and as damp as a sick rat's arse. I wasn't sure but I had a nagging feeling that there must be more to life than this.

Chapter Three

The Silverlight River crawled through Appleton and separated Old Town on the east bank from New Town on the west. Two gangs controlled the midnight economy that kept both halves of the city moving: Mother's Guild, the headquarters of which were under Old Town, and Pork Chop Jing's outfit, the Pearl. Jing and his crew fancied themselves as more upmarket thugs and had their den just west of the river, on the Street of a Thousand Lanterns. It was what you might call the entertainment district if your idea of entertainment was being robbed blind and catching the pox.

The street was named for the lanterns carried by the whores of every stripe who worked the long meander. They fished for customers with bright paper lanterns dangling on the end of gilded poles. The miners and calth smelters would take their meagre wages and head for the river end of the street. The fastidious amongst them might even visit one of the bathhouses located at that end of the strip before picking up a whore or falling into the inn that best suited their purse. The more affluent denizens of Appleton would visit the theatres and expensive brothels furthest from the Silverlight when they were out whoring. The rakehells would dare the bawdier backstreet establishments, hunting for cheap thrills and pel and the whole wild jig was orchestrated by Jing and the Pearl.

I swam the Silverlight to avoid Jing's lookouts on the bridge and climbed out downriver of the main street, near an inn called the Grinning Dolly. The ramshackle flop-house was slowly falling into the Silverlight. Canted towards the river at a jaunty angle, the Dolly catered to hard-up culls and was the last stop for many who went for a swim with their pockets full of stones. I emerged much cleaner for my little dip in the drink, which goes to show how filthy I'd been because there are days when the Silverlight is so stiff with garbage you can walk across it.

Jing's compound was in the middle of the street. Impossible to miss, the brazen scarlet and gold pagoda stood three storeys higher than any of its neighbours. Cleaned daily by nimble amphibane servants it was a spike of brightness in an otherwise dreary city.

Unlike Mother, Pork Chop wasn't a sorcerer: he was warspawn and therefore lacked the ability to use magic. It didn't mean that he couldn't hire hedge wizards and sorcerers when he needed a few fireworks but he tended to rely on a sizeable retinue of armed guards to enforce his will. Being as I was half human, Mother had managed to beat a couple of simple spells into me. Unfortunately, apporting wasn't one of them.

I strung my bow before threading my way through the maze of back streets, dodging pel-smoking sentries and bored city guards, until I reached the high walls of Jing's compound. The mournful peal of distant temple bells rang out the tenth hour. The suns had long since surrendered Appleton to night's charitable embrace. Unfortunately for me, Jing's pagoda was lit up like a fucking bonfire.

Climbing the wall of the compound wouldn't be difficult. Not being seen while doing it just about impossible. A burst of laughter rippled over the wall as though mocking my predicament. It was followed by the opening strains of a dolorous tune. The smell of succulent roast kitten and the sickly-sweet aroma of grilled pig wafted towards me and made my stomach growl. I sniffed, caught the undercurrent of tea, beer and brachuri blood mead. Curious as to the cause of the celebration, I made my way to the back gate of the compound.

Unlike the front entrance which was richly decorated with giant insects and gilded arrachid warriors, the rear gate was unadorned, iron bound and to my delight and surprise, wide open. *'Now, tonight!'* hadn't just been Mother raving. She must have known that Jing was holding a banquet. Security would be tight, it always was—people like Jing and Mother only survived by maintaining a ridiculously high level of paranoia—but it would be less focused on the dark and silent places, drawn as people are to light and movement. The influx of guests, the loud music, and abundance of pel and drink would wear down the senses of even the keenest sentry.

Born in darkness, I would slide into the shadows like a hand into a glove.

A little more enthusiastic about the job, I jogged down the street. Just before the corner of the block, I squeezed behind a stack of broken barrels from where I could watch the road unseen. Like my old friend the ambusher, I cast a spell from a bloodclay tablet to deepen the shadows around me and settled down to wait, snug in the magical folds of darkness. A fistful of minutes later, a pair of amphibane link boys hopped into view ahead of a couple of wheezing humans carrying a sedan chair. They staggered towards Jing's, followed closely by a nice big coach which was what I'd been waiting for. Although the fine rattler was unliveried it must have been owned by a gentry cove because it was being pulled by no less than four horses. Only one of the valuable beasts acknowledged my presence bestowing an imperious snort as it high-hoofed past. Despite their pampered existence city horses were as inured to the stink of Appleton and its inhabitants as any plodding urux.

The driver pulled on the reins and applied the brake as the coach wheeled round the corner. When it was three-quarters through the turn, I sprinted from my hiding place to the rear of the carriage, dragging shreds of shadow with me. Holding my bow tight against my chest, I gripped the rear axle and slid under the vehicle. Supporting my weight on one arm, I wrapped my legs around the brake beam and gripped the leather through-bracing with my feet. It wasn't the most comfortable way to travel but it was unquestionably better than riding in a gong pot.

When I'd scouted the gate I'd made a note of the two beady-eyed ogren guards. All I could see of them now were their big hairy feet and the butts of the firelances they both wielded. Substantially bigger than hand cannons, the firelances worked on the same principle: calthracite powder and lead shot were loaded into the barrel and a zanthe crystal was locked into the firing claw beside a pan filled with more calth powder. Firelances not only made really big holes in whatever was in front of them but, as their name implied, they more often than not set fire to it as well. The bloody things were as dangerous as a drunken sorcerer but thankfully still uncommon due to the cost of zanthe crystals and calth powder. Things were changing; the Empirifex had a taste for conquest and had recently decreed that more mines should be found. There was still work for sharp coves like me, but I sensed that the days of the blade were numbered.

The horses' hooves clattered against smooth stone as the carriage entered the compound. The driver pulled up outside the pagoda. I clung on, hardly daring to breathe. On one side, I could see a neatly trimmed hedge in front of several long low buildings. On the other, the footplate dropped. A pair of silk hakama approached the step. A moment later, a dainty, slippered foot descended before being engulfed in layers of brocade-edged satin. Whoever it was smelled of emerald water and tincture of pomegranate. The carriage rocked and a pair of long, brachuri hide boots followed the gown. Why some of Jing's guests chose the rear entrance perked my professional interest, but I pushed the thought aside in favour of concentrating on the task ahead, that of killing the host.

A door opened, light spilled across the courtyard. I tried to think small and inconspicuous thoughts whilst being very conscious of the spatter of gold that clipped the frame of the carriage and fell across my back and hip. All it would take was for someone to look, and understand what they were seeing; to connect the abstract shape to that of a living being and then, just for a change, I'd be in a right pot of arse-pickle.

I pressed myself as close to the underside of the carriage as I could and willed the driver to move off. Afore long, the reins snapped and the horses pranced away, drawing murmurs of delight and admiration from those present. The haughty beasts were unimpressed and shat a trail of steaming, partially digested grass across the impeccably clean courtyard.

What little I knew about the layout of the compound told me there wasn't enough room for all of the carriages to wait inside, this one in particular: horses and urux do not enjoy each other's company. When we were about fifty paces from the pagoda I dared a quick look round. This end of the compound was framed by a collection of single-storey buildings that crouched against the outer wall. The driver turned the rattler to face the gate, which I took to be the best time to alight. When the rear axle was facing into the darkest corner of the compound, I dropped, flipped, and scrambled from under the swaying belly of the carriage. Supporting myself on my claws, I scuttled over the hedge and wedged myself in the shadow-clad corner of the buildings like a six foot cockroach. I held my breath and waited for sounds of alarm. None came.

My bow was made for thoasa; it was long and flexible, which allowed me to bend it beyond the tolerance of lesser weapons. The quiver of arrows wasn't as forgiving and I'd heard a couple of horribly loud cracks as I crawled from under the carriage, luckily nobody else seemed to. I felt inside the quiver. Two shafts had snapped leaving me with twelve. Given the task I'd been set, I'd be lucky if I had time to use one.

The music drifting from the first floor of the pagoda changed tempo. The reedy agony of an arrachid ballad scratched the skin off the air like the dying cries of a cat being slowly eviscerated. That was where Jing would be. The gang boss fancied himself a cultured cove. He'd be sitting there, smoking pel and enjoying the feel of the scathing vibrations that were making my ears bleed.

The windows on that level were set high on the wall and partially overhung by the flaring skirt of the roof above. I quickly and quietly crossed the compound, climbed the wall and vaulted over the balcony of the first floor of the pagoda seconds after two of the four sentries disappeared around the left-hand corner. Without waiting, I reached up, grabbed the lip of the sweeping roof, and swung myself up and under the eaves. I was safely tucked upside down in the darkness before the next pair of guards rounded the right-hand corner.

Gripping the cedar lintel above the window with my feet, I braced my back against the underside of the roof. The space smelled of musky wood and cobwebs. Wedged as I was in the angle of the roof, I could see into the room and remain hidden in the shadows of the eaves. If the guards patrolling the balcony looked up they'd see me, but why would they do that? There were far more interesting things happening in the hall, the courtyard and the street beyond the compound.

Even so, I was momentarily tempted to enhance the darkness with a spell, but I changed my mind, just in case the rumours were true and the place was warded against magic. I carefully drew an arrow. The last thing I wanted, other than to miss was to spill the contents of the quiver all over the balcony. I licked the flight smooth and threaded the shaft between string and stave before searching for Jing among the gentry gathered within.

There's something deeply unpleasant about the smell of arrachids. It's like old shoes that have been left to marinade in lemon juice and earthworms. It's not a strong smell, nothing that a human would notice, but I did. Not all the jasmine-scented fountain water and eaglewood incense in the world could mask the smell of a nest of them. As well as being the dress of their adopted culture, the Shen silk kimonos that Jing and his five offspring favoured also concealed their six double-joined legs, which apparently made some humans feel uncomfortable. I watched Pork Chop's dutiful sons and daughters circulating among their father's guests, making polite conversation and laughing at unamusing jokes.

Old Pork Chop was content to sit on a pile of plump silk cushions, smoking a pipe, surrounded by his favourite dozen or so concubines. The gang lord's long black hair hung to his waist; his violet silk haori perfectly matched the colour of his two pairs of eyes. It was said that the best arrachid silk was produced by virgins. If that was true, the amount of the good stuff floating around in this room would have made a brothel keeper weep. Jing smiled politely as his guests paid their respects, favouring some lucky few with a word or two, but for the most part he sat and watched like an arrachid gang boss sitting in the middle of his nest.

I didn't go straight for the kill. I first made a note of the security that would blaze into action the moment I vented Jing. The ogren standing guard by the sliding doors was of particular interest, partly because she must have been seven feet tall, but mainly because she was carrying a very large bronze hand cannon, the barrel of which was cast in the form of a roaring dragon. Although the imagery was labouring the point, the beast slumbering in the ogren's arms was due serious respect. Like the creature it represented, the weapon breathed ruin. I counted another four sentries positioned around the room, and there were probably a few more out of my line of sight, but as they were only armed with halberds and spears, they weren't as much of a concern as the ogren with the cannon.

The main door to the banqueting hall was directly opposite me, but Jing's dais was against the wall on my right so I had to lean left to get a good angle on the King of the Midnight Court. I re-nocked the shaft and drew the bow until the stave was tight against the window frame and my elbow was touching the rafters. I could have got a few more fingers' width of draw but this would be enough to put a shaft through Jing's slender body. I took a deep, slow breath and was about to loose when, for some reason, someone else in the room snared my attention. Irritated, I relaxed the draw and took a proper shufty at them.

I couldn't smell much above the blooming reek of arrachid, pel, and incense so I had to rely on my eyes but there was no mistaking the grizzle-chinned, pig-nosed, tiny-eyed lackwit strutting into the room, arm-in-arm with one of the Pearl. It was Sketh. The miserable little snot-gobbet had turned traitor. That it was probably my fault was not the point. The little toad-gobbler looked right at home and was grinning wide as a cheese rind. They'd even dressed him in a fancy pair of hakama and coiffed his greasy hair into a top knot. The tomb-toothed puke must have spilled his guts to the roots to earn such pampering. No wonder Jing looked happy. My aim tracked from Jing to Sketh.

As much as I wanted to vent the traitor, I knew I shouldn't. I had my orders; Mother really would kill me if I messed up this time. I re-aimed at Jing. Sketh snagged a drink from a passing servant; he was laughing at something his new best friend had said. I drew the string to my lobeless ear. *Jing, my target is Jing.*

I've often found that it's one thing knowing what you should do, and quite another doing it.

The arrow entered Sketh between the pectoralis major, or at least between where chest muscles would have been, if the little turd-biscuit had any. A rose of deepest red stamped my fatal brand on his nice new haori. Mother was not going to be happy.

It takes a lot to *really* rile me, but Sketh had succeeded where a demon, a dragon and Mother had failed. It wasn't just that he'd tried to ambush me, or that he'd come close to putting a bolt through my head— that was just embarrassing. It was the gong pot. When I should have been strutting along Main Road, I'd had to hide in a shit wagon to avoid my greedy comrades and *that* was why Sketh was dying on his feet.

The ex-Blade, ex-Pearl member stared at the ever-widening scarlet bloom, confusion stamped across his rabbity features. The game was only truly up when his companion tugged the yard shaft out of the tatami behind him. She frowned at first and looked questioningly at Sketh, who answered by slowly pitching forward and crumpling into the folds of his silks.

'Guards!' she yelled.

One shot. That's what I'd promised myself, even if I'd missed Jing. So by the time the ogren had blasted the window frame and a fair chunk of wall and roof into flaming matchwood, I was already halfway to the ground. Almost on the beat of my feet touching the cobbles, a gong hammered alarm into the languid night. You can always trust some bastard to ruin a party and tonight that bastard was me.

I sprinted across the compound and leapt onto the single storey building before anyone outside the pagoda knew what was happening. Given that they were in the same business they caught on quickly and by the time I'd dashed across the roof and had my foot on the compound wall, I heard the heavy *thwunks* of crossbows being discharged in my direction. I felt a velvety ripple of air before a searing whip of fire lashed my left arm. It was nothing, the slightest brush that merely encouraged greater effort when I leapt.

Darkness flowed beneath me as I launched myself over the gilt-edged void. I laughed. Landing softly, I wound the energy from the drop into a roll that spun me across the slates, thrust me up, and set me off running. I knew that if I could reach the river I'd get away. A jarring impact behind me underscored the *if*.

The sagging roof beams creaked and groaned. I didn't slow or turn around, I didn't need to. The smell of old shoes soaked in lemon juice and earthworms rushed at me on a following wind hot, hard and angry. Arrachids didn't swim well but they were experts at tearing people into tiny pieces so I summoned an extra measure of speed and ran for my life.

I don't like to brag, but I've outrun dragons, which was a good thing to bear in mind with one of Pork Chop's broodlings inches from taking a chunk out of my scaly arse. Their species of arrachid had a pair of vicious sword-like foreclaws, tucked just below the abdomen. I know it might not sound like it, but being chased by *this* kind was preferable to being pursued by the kind who spat gobs of sticky, poisonous web-snot from their nethers. Of course, given the choice, I'd rather not be chased by any kind of arrachid.

Ahead of me the river gleamed invitingly; a shining rod of rippled obsidian framed by crooked chimneys. I vaulted the pots. My many-legged pursuer smashed through them. Who would have guessed that Sketh was so well loved? Thus encouraged, I surged forwards and was just starting to pull away from my ardent pursuer when the roof collapsed beneath us.

When you're falling you reach out for anything, it's an instinct common to every creature that has limbs. I watched, quite detached from the act, as my hands and feet groped at timbers and slates, until they eventually found something substantial and latched onto it. Turned out it was the arrachid. She had a similar idea, and so, like boon companions, we fell together, briefly visiting a grimy, rat-infested loft before crashing through to the next floor… and the next.

By now I wasn't sure which were my limbs and which were hers. There was a mass of flame-red hair in my face and her arms were locked around my waist, but as luck would have it I was sitting on her pincers so she was unable to fulfil her screamed threat and stab me to death and beyond. In truth we both did a fair bit of screaming and cursing as old plaster, dead pigeons and roof rained down around us. Finally, we hit a floor that didn't break.

I landed on top of the arrachid, the air umphed from her bellows. Two pairs of angry, green eyes shone from amid the mass of hair, giving me a general target to aim for when I headbutted her in the face. She groaned, her grip on my waist loosened. I disentangled myself and sprinted for the nearest exit. Floral wallpaper, paintings, and bemused faces peering from doorways flashed past. The sound of three pairs of feet charging after me spurred me on. I hurtled along the corridor and through the door at the end without stopping to open it, which quite surprised the occupants.

A red robed human male with a black beard glared at me. He had another human pinned by the throat against the wall opposite the door. In his other hand blackbeard held a slender bladed knife. The other human was wearing rough brown robes and was struggling ineffectually against the bigger man. I leapt at the bearded cull and knocked his head against the wall. While he decided to have a little sit down, I relieved him of his pig-sticker which I then threw at the arrachid just before throwing myself through the window— again without bothering to open it. The arrachid yelled and crashed to the floor in a tangle of limbs.

I was prepared for a hard landing and so was surprised when my fall was broken by a passing group of late night revellers. With nary a scratch, I untangled myself from the skirts of a pleasantly doughy cull and was about to leg it when one of her foppish friends had the suicidal urge to draw a blade on me. I say blade, it was more a hairpin with a hilt.

'How dare you! You... you... what the devil *are* you?' The fop stared down the barrel of his bony nose, and quirked one of his plucked eyebrows. 'You should have stayed under your rock, lizard,'

A rouged, 'punch me' smile gashed his powder-pale face in response to the laughter of his friends. Playing to the crowd, he whiff-waffed the hairpin and took some kind of stance that I assumed a dancing master must have taught him.

I'd never had the patience to bandy words with halfwits so I snapped the blade and slapped his face for fear that a punch might kill him. He sprawled. Alas, the distraction was enough to give the arrachid time to join us and for a sizeable crowd to gather. I don't like crowds, especially when I'm the subject of their attention, and I certainly didn't like the arrachid who was aiming a murderous glare in my direction.

I drew my blades. She advanced, kicking a couple of the fop's friends out of the way with casual disdain. She'd definitely come off worse in our little roof dive and her arm was bleeding where I'd caught her with blackbeard's dagger.

'What the hell?' Another of the youths gasped indignantly. 'Is it raining demonspawn?' He and his companions drew an assortment of glorified toothpicks.

'Who are you calling demonspawn, you little shit-stain?' the arrachid snarled, pincers twitching.

Emboldened by his friends, the aforesaid shit-stain puffed out his fashionably thin chest. 'You, you four-eyed grotesque!'

The arrachid reared up on her hindmost pair of legs.

I'm not sure exactly what happened next as something akin to an anvil hit me on the back of the head. I dropped, stunned but only distantly alarmed. Pretty purple flowers of light burst into bloom before my eyes. My blades slipped from numb fingers, I fell. The last thing I saw before the press of fighting bodies closed around me was the brown-robed human. He was leaning out of the ragged hole we'd put in the inn, he was staring at me, his brow knotted in concentration.

What happened next is hazy, but I get the impression that the entire Street of a Thousand Lanterns decided that right then was the perfect time to have a riotous brawl. The night erupted in shouts and screams, accompanied by the sound of breaking glass and splintering wood.

Chapter Four

I woke up, face down on a hard floor. Pockmarked flagstones burnished by constant use swam into focus. There was something vaguely familiar about them and the wet metal stink of the place. Before I had chance to ponder my location further, I was grabbed under the arms and hauled to my shackled feet. Now I knew where I was. I tested the manacles around my wrists and got a slap across the head for my troubles.

'Stop that,' ordered the greenshanks. Coves like me called the city guard 'greenshanks' on account of their green uniform breeches. This one was short and her beady eyes were set deep in a flat, expressionless face. She had the heavy build of a mountain goblin, but must have been human because warspawn weren't allowed in the city guard.

I'd lodged in the cells under the law courts once or twice when I was a kinchin cove, but this was my first stay since I'd become a fully-fledged Blade. Other than the guests, nothing much had changed. The rows of cells looked and smelled the same. Those on the right-hand side, where they put humans were warded against sorcery. The left side was heavily reinforced for warspawn but bore no sigils. Warspawn—true warspawn, not half-breeds like me—couldn't use magic.

'What are ya?' the greenshanks demanded. Her breath smelled sickly sweet, like something was rotting inside her. It was probably cancer. She coughed. If she didn't already know she was sick, she soon would. 'Well, what is it? Thoasa? Do you understand?'

Before I had the chance to earn another slap by telling her that I didn't speak dolt, the door behind me opened and another guard came in. He looked tired and was sporting a week's growth of facial hair. I don't know how humans can stand all those bristles, they must itch something terrible, and then there's the lice. An old scar running across his cheek and nose spoke of past battles. Like a lot of the greenshanks in Appleton, he'd probably served on the front, fighting to gain the Empirifex another acre of nothing much at all.

He gave me a cursory once-over. 'S'just another breed, Tori. Put it in four.'

The guard called Tori grunted and prodded me towards cell number four on the warspawn side. Such a pity that the most dangerous spell I knew was how to boil water. Mother had taught me the spell when she was going through a phase of drinking hot chai. There was a chalk board nailed to the outside of the door. The guard looked at me expectantly.

'What? You're not going to give me a test, are you?' I asked.

Neither smile nor smirk marred the unleavened perfection of her pasty face. 'Name?' she asked, fingering the stylus that was chained to the board.

'Breed,' I said with a smile. If she got the joke she didn't let on. She invited me to enter the cell with a toss of her head. She patted the butt of a cudgel hanging from her belt, implying divers punishments should I not comply. If there hadn't been an entire garrison of greenshanks hanging around, I'd have taken the tickle tail off her and shoved it where the suns don't shine. As it was, I acceded to her invitation without argument. In truth, I wasn't in any particular hurry to get back to the Nest. I needed some time to come up with a plausible lie to tell Mother as to why I'd killed Sketh instead of Jing. 'Because I was annoyed' would lead straight back to the dog rats, if I was lucky.

The cell smelled no worse than anywhere consistently used as a toilet. I slumped against the door, grateful for the chance to sit down. Now that the excitement had passed, I was starting to feel the various cuts and bruises I'd earned during my recent adventures. The cells sounded busy, which told me it was still night. They'd empty in the morning when all the 'guests' were sent before the beaks. While I sat in the shadows, listening to rats crunching through cockroaches, I briefly regretted killing Sketh instead of Jing. But then I remembered sitting in the gong pot and the feeling went away. One thing I could be sure of was that nobody would finger me for killing the little bung-hole. The Guild and the Pearl had few agreements, but it would be a dull day in hell when either went to the authorities seeking what passed for justice in Appleton. I closed my eyes, tried to get a little sleep for the first time since I'd got back to town.

I shouldn't have been surprised that the sleep I snatched was far from restful. The thunder of a dragon chasing me down a mountainside accompanied by the laughter of a demon resolved into the sound of someone banging on the door and shouting at me to get up. It didn't feel like more than a few minutes had passed since I closed my eyes, but it had been long enough for the guard to change. A skinny cull with a cauliflower nose and weeping acne unlocked the door.

He squinted at the slate and snorted. 'Right... *Breed*, it's your turn in front of the magistrates. C'mon, look lively; they're in a hanging mood this mornin'.' He laughed, no doubt like he did every time he made the joke, which was probably every time he unlocked a cell.

I was stiff and thirsty and in no mood for light-hearted banter and I didn't have any coin to pay a fine, but that was the least of my concerns. By now Mother would know where I was. I'd delivered enough bribes for her to know how the wheels of justice were greased and just how much sway she had with the *official* government in town. Whichever of the magistrates she owned would pocket a nice sum of gold, set a low fine, and make sure that I was sent off with a stern warning not to transgress again. I didn't for one moment consider that Mother might leave me to rot. Even if she was angry, she'd pay to get me out just so she could kill me herself.

Me and a dozen other coves were chained together and taken up through the barracks to the City Hall, where the official if only *slightly* less nefarious business of running the city was conducted. Burghers and merchants, sycophants and toadies congregated in the lobby to exchange bribes, gossip, and backhanders. As our not-so-jolly band of resigned ruffians, penitent drunks, and tired whores shuffled past, the honest gentry squinted at us through spectacles, monocles and lorgnettes in order to properly turn their noses up. We were shoved into the holding pens outside of the courtroom just off the main lobby. I claimed my place in the cramped cage and watched the great and the good of Appleton go about their *very* important business. Ugly little pet dogs, smaller than your average sewer rat, pissed on the grubby marble floor and barked incessantly at everything. Bedraggled jadewings squawked mournfully from tenuous perches on the limp wrists and sloping shoulders of the more fashionable pillocks of society. The birds were the current 'must have' amongst what passed for the social elite of Appleton. Mother preferred to deal in pel, murder, and larceny rather than smuggling exotic pets. She didn't have the patience to peddle anything that needed gentle handling. She tried it once, but when the first twenty birds died of suffocation, she gave up.

'Oi, Breed! You're up,' The greenshanks crossed my name off the slate. I eyed the hand cannon in the crook of her arm and shuffled out as ordered.

The court's sickly yellow walls were bare save for the Empirifex's gaudy crest painted above the magistrates' bench. The leaded windows looked out onto Four Gallows Square, as if anyone needed reminding. Three periwigged magistrates sat on the bench above the court, shuffling papers and muttering amongst themselves about proceedings and the tiresome preoccupations of their day-to-day existence. A bored-looking scribe sat beneath the bench sharpening his quills. My palm itched. An image of the demon Shallunsard sprang unbidden into my mind. I thrust it aside. I had to try to think innocent thoughts and see if I could push them through the naturally sardonic set of my face bones.

I was shoved into the dock and the door was locked. A sorcerer's sigil etched onto the heavy bolt was there to ensure no magic could be cast from inside the cage. A couple of guards stood either side of the door, fingers resting on the triggers of their hand cannons. It did my professional pride no harm to know that they weren't giving me the benefit of the doubt.

Unusually for morning court there was quite a crowd in the public gallery. Several of them had cuts and bruises, others had torn and blood-speckled clothing. Almost all were staring daggers at me. I guessed that they must have been the rakes that I'd landed on the night before. What with deals with demons and inadvertent assassinations I'd hardly given them a second thought. For their part they seemed delighted to see me, in an angry mob sort of way. Sitting behind them, knitting furiously was an old human I knew well. Martha Ferney, or *Mattie the Drop* as she was known in the Guild, looked like your average grandmother, but you turned your back on her at your peril. She didn't look up when I came in, but I knew she'd clocked me.

Her presence was reassuring. Despite Mother's constant admonishment never to hope, seeing Mattie meant that Mother probably wasn't too angry and that she'd sent the old mort with a bribe for the judge. I relaxed but tried to look contrite, which isn't easy with a face like mine.

The Chief Magistrate cleared her throat and cast a bulge-eyed glance in my direction. 'Case the fifth on this 10th day of Messidor by Empirifex, Dunstan the Seventh's grace, Year of the Pantheon, 766. The court will rise.'

The court obeyed. A lawyer in a black gown swept in and bowed before the bench. I was touched; I didn't think Mother would go to the trouble of hiring an attorney.

As it turned out, I was correct.

'Council for the Prosecution begs leave to proceed, Magistrate Ornlably,' quoth the daughter of prattlement I had briefly mistaken for my defender.

'Yes, yes, go on,' said the magistrate.

I very much wanted to object, struck as I was that I might be getting stitched for killing Sketh after all. My mind raced; had Jing turned barley? Had he ripened into a yellow-backed coward, broken all the laws of hell and actually *gone to the authorities?* Such a thing wasn't entirely unheard of; lesser members of the Midnight Court had committed slow suicide by going to the catch-poles, but no one of Jing's stature had ever stooped so low as to get the lurchers involved. It was downright dishonourable. I was shocked.

'Thank you, Magistrate. I'll hurry to the quick, as the Court's time should not be spent lingering over such overt miscreancy. I would be so bold as to say this is a—'

'Just get on with it, Councillor Cheams,' said the magistrate. At this point I was inclined to agree. I was *very* keen to find out just what I was being charged with.

'My client,' the lawyer indicated a skinny cull in the public gallery with a black eye and swollen lip, 'was the victim of a vicious assault, and I therefore ask that the savage responsible...' Cheams pointed at me '... feel the full force of the law. Death! Is too good. This gutter scum should serve the Empirifex in the calthracite mines for no less than twenty years!'

Cheams was shaking with bought and paid for indignation by this point. The magistrates exchanged weary glances. 'How very thoughtful of you, Cheams, but we're more than capable of coming up with a sentence. All we ask is that you present the evidence.'

'As you wish, Magistrate.' The prosecutor straightened her wig. 'Would the first witness, Sir Mathory Walmster, please take the stand.'

It turned out that Mathory Walmster was the razor-nosed fop who'd pulled a blade on me.

He swaggered over to the witness stand and bowed to the magistrates. 'Lord Harringhay, Lord Reevis, Aunt Gwendolyn.'

My heart didn't sink; it dived majestically into the pit of my stomach, dragging my hopes down with it.

The chief magistrate—A*unt Gwendolyn*—whiffled into a sheaf of papers and waved him to silence. 'Yes, alright, go on, Councillor.'

Cheams strutted before the witness, hands clasped behind her back, no doubt contemplating the easiest conviction she'd ever won. 'In your own words, Sir Mathory, before the seal of the Empirifex, his duly appointed magistrates, and this court,' she intoned. 'Pray tell, what befell you and your companions last night on the Street of a Thousand Lanterns?'

He cleared his throat. I rested my elbows against the bars, keen to hear what fantasy the simpering dung peddler was about to spew.

'Thank you, Councillor. My friends and I had just enjoyed a tolerable supper at Fausto's on Garrotte Street, and were on our way to Tremlaynes when that... *thing*,' he chinned in my direction, 'Leapt upon my companions and attempted to accost Lady Juliet.' He indicated a pinch-faced froe I wouldn't tup with borrowed nethers. She simpered; the gallery made a unified rumble of displeasure and threw facefuls of hate in my direction, though I noticed not one of them had the cods to look me in the eye.

The fop continued. 'As a gentleman, I stepped in to defend my friend from the amorous advances of that... creature, who, with its vile accomplices, proceeded to attack me and my comrades. I'm happy to say, we were more than a match for this gutter-scum and had gained the upper hand by the time the city guards arrived.' He dusted himself down, puffed out his chest. 'And lucky for this creature that they arrived when they did.'

I noticed that the greenshanks guarding the dock exchanged wry smiles at that. I was interested to know why the arrachid had been left out of the account, and indeed why the rank virago wasn't in the holding pens, and then it struck me. Jing might have outbid Mother in the bribery stakes.

For the next hour a long procession of ill-used ladies and gentlemen limped from the public gallery and took their turn on the witness stand. I was accused of all manner of grievous crimes, from beating the fop and his crew to attempted murder. Had I been conscious I probably would have done what I'd been accused of, far worse in fact, leaving a damn sight fewer of them to point their waggers at me today. The arrachid wasn't mentioned at all, not once. It was as though she'd never even been there. Eventually the Chief Magistrate looked at me.

'Do you have anyone to speak for you, any defence council?' She asked.

I shook my head.

'Do you have anything to say in your defence?'

'Yes, as a matter of fact, I do' I said. My words drew a startled murmur from the gallery. 'This is a travesty!' I tried to mimic the tone of the councillor. 'I wasn't even conscious for most of the fight. I'm the victim here, Your Honour—'

'Alright, that's enough. The defendant's evidence has been duly noted by the Bench.'

As unfair as it was, I knew better than to argue. You never beat the law, especially if you looked like me. Once the beaks had you fast, you weren't going to encourage them to go easy by haranguing them. It was better to submit and get it over with as quick and as painless as possible. I'd been done up tighter than a corpse's arsehole and no mistake, but there was no point bleating; who'd listen? I looked over to Mattie; she shrugged and cast another stitch onto the formless mess she was knitting. After a whole two minutes of thoughtful deliberation, Aunt Gwendolyn rapped the table.

'The court will rise,' she intoned, barely stifling a yawn. 'The defendant is hereby sentenced to seven years' hard labour in the Empirifex's calthracite mines. Case closed. Send in number six.'

The magistrate set her seal to some documents, the court sat. I stood there a moment, trying to work out how the hell I'd got into this mess, how the hell I was going to get out of it, and what the hell was going to try to kill me next.

While these various thoughts jostled for my attention my gaze was drawn to the public gallery; not to the smug fucks busily congratulating each other, or Mattie, but to a brown-robed cove who I recognised as the same whey-faced cull from the inn. He shuffled awkwardly past the spindle-shanked gentry but didn't leave the courtroom as I'd expected. Instead, he made his way over to the bench and, to my surprise, beckoned the chief magistrate down from her perch and even more surprisingly, rather than having him thrown out or flogged or sent to the mines, Aunt Gwendolyn, complied. Not to be left out, the pettifogging lawyer stuck her neb in.

In the gallery, Mattie packed away her knitting and gave me a look that told me I was on my own. Meanwhile, whey-face was heads down with the magistrate, locked in a heated argument over I knew not what, save that there was a lot of gesticulating and headshaking by both parties. It was then I noticed that the brown robed cull's left hand was missing, the wrist being tidily sheathed in a leather cup.

After a hissed exchange between the lawyer and wheyface, the magistrate shooed them away and returned to the bench where she knotted heads with the other two magistrates. Both cast slit-eyed glances at me and wheyface. Eventually, after much debate, Aunt Gwendolyn brought the court to order.

'Order! The court will come to order or I'll throw you all in the bloody mines.'

The chatter stopped immediately. The magistrate fixed her dull-eyed gaze on me. I smiled and shrugged, neither of which seemed to please her.

'Due to… *mitigating circumstances*,' she rearranged her face into an expression of resigned disbelief and glared at wheyface. 'The court has decided to show leniency in this case, and commute the sentence to five years' indentured servitude to Brother Tobias of the Sacred Order of Scienticians of Saint Bartholomew.' The priest smiled and sketched a bow.

'Case closed.'

Chapter Five

Somewhat begrumpled by this final downward turn of events, I cursed all the way out of the court, laying all manner of vile imprecations upon the heads of my accusers, the magistrates, and the greenshanks who dragged me back to the cells.

Being condemned to the mines had been an excessive punishment for falling onto a bunch of over-privileged popinjays but I could've escaped from the mines. Extort some coin, use it to bribe guards, grease the right palms: I'd have been out within a month with no one the wiser. Judicial indentured servitude reinforced by a sorcerous geas was an altogether different proposition. Although I *know* there's no point fighting the catch-poles when they have you, I often rebel against my own wise council. It's like a disease. Very kindly, the greenshanks tried to cure my affliction by administering a dose of steel-shod boots as soon as I was out of sight of the ruffs and ribbons.

I woke in a cell, manacled to a ring set in the floor. My nose was crusted with blood and my jaw ached like I'd been repeatedly kicked in the face which, I blearily recollected, I had. As I lay there, contemplating the righteous vengeance I was going to wreak on the bastards who'd put me here, the peephole in the door slid open. From my position on the floor I could just make out a pale face peering in at me. I forgot about the manacles and lunged at the priest. He recoiled despite the three inches of steel between us.

'I mean you no harm,' he mumbled. 'I just want to talk to you.'

'Well, there you go, you've talked to me. Now fuck off.' I was in no mood to chat with someone who'd helped condemn me to magical slavery.

'I saved you from the mines!' he countered as though he'd done me a favour.

'I could get... Oh, never mind. Just leave me alone.' I couldn't be bothered arguing with the one-handed lackwit. I had to focus on how I was going to get out of here. I'd given up on Mother; if she'd been going to help she'd have done it by now.

'It was all I could think of at the time. I used what influence I have. I'm sorry,' he said.

'Why? Why the hell did you try to 'help' me? What's in it for you, priest?' I think he looked confused, it was hard to tell. He had one of those soft, book-bathed faces—pale and smooth from lack of sunslight or kiss of the wind. It was the kind of face that begged to be slapped... repeatedly.

'Because you saved me.' He shivered. 'What happened after you went through the window was an accident. I was trying to help, but I was disorientated... and the spell went awry. I honestly didn't mean to knock you out, but with hindsight it's probably a good job that I did because—'

Again I forgot the manacles and, snarling, I lunged at him. The chain snapped me back to the cold stone flags. The moon-faced bastard loitered awhile, staring at me with a look of pity and guilt written across his milky features before he eventually slunk off into the ragged shadows of the lock-up.

It was night when they came for me. I hadn't slept; I'd lain in the darkness, listening to doors slamming and inmates proclaiming their innocence, cursing or weeping, sometimes all three. I was trying to decide if I was going to make the guards do this the hard way or if I was just going to submit, like a lag of the highest mark. What was churning my vitals was not knowing if the geas of servitude would dominate my survival instincts, something I guessed would come in handy given the apple carts I'd upset lately. I didn't know how much of my free will would be curtailed and that worried me. I can't say I was scared. Thoasa were bred to be fearless and although I was only half thoasa, I don't think I'd ever really felt that emotion as powerfully as humans seemed to.

What I did know for certain was that I'd been given five years, but had less than one to find the Hammer of the North before my life, and possibly my soul, was forfeit to Shallunsard the demon. Not to mention Jing, who would most likely send the Pearl after me and of course, Mother would undoubtedly want to know why I'd disobeyed her. As nice as it was to be wanted, I couldn't afford to be bound in servitude to the milksop priest. I needed to go to ground, preferably in another country, until everyone forgot all about me.

Before I could formulate a brilliant plan to escape, the door was thrown open and a lantern was rudely thrust into the cell, half blinding me as I'm sure was the intention. The barrels of a pair of hand cannons were thrust into the circle of light.

'So you're a Guild Blade, eh? Don't look much from where I'm standing,' said one of the cannon-wielders from the darkness.

'Spoken like a true hero… from the brave end of a barking iron. Come out from behind the brass and we'll go tap for tap, see how ye fair then, eh, greenshanks?' I grinned. The greenshanks declined my offer.

A less blustery guard unchained me and I was dragged from the cell. The two gunners stayed behind us as I was shoved down to the lower levels. I didn't know anyone who'd been down here. All I knew was that it was where confessions were extracted and indenturing by sorcery was carried out. Any cove down on their luck could sign up for regular indentured servitude and sell their labour in exchange for work and food but *punishment* indenture was another fish altogether. I should have felt honoured. Not just any lag got indentured by sorcery; only those for whom chains were not enough of an impediment to making mischief suffered this fate, and then only rarely as it was an expensive spell from what I'd heard. Soul-binding, anything to do with dominating the will of a person, extracted a high price from the sorcerer.

My stomach rolled. I've been stabbed, shot at, lashed, even burned by dragon breath, but this was something much more worrisome. Pain only hurts. Losing my free will filled me with a greasy feeling of dread.

At the end of a blood-splattered, flame-scorched corridor was an iron door inlaid with alloys of a dozen different metals that had been hammered into overlapping sigils. It hummed with magical energy; the air grew stiff with power the closer to it I got. I stopped a few paces from the door. One of the greenshanks behind me stumbled. If I spun round now I could take his cannon and torch and have a quick dance in the dark with his gun-wielding companion. I might even get the better of them with surprise on my side, but the chances of fighting my way out of the barracks were slim even with a pair of irons to back me up. When I was shoved onwards I relented, my stomach twisting like a sack of snakes.

On the other side of the door a passage split right and left. A strong smell of dried blood and giblets emanated from the right. I was taken to the left. At the end of the dimly lit corridor I was thrust into a room that was little more than a rough-hewn cave. There were no other exits. A half dozen rancid tallow candles spilled a dim light across the floor and wreathed the low roof in oily ribbons of smoke. Unlike the building above, built to emulate the architectural fashion of Valen of the last twenty years, this place looked ancient and reeked of old magic and primitive rites.

The floor was obsidian, variously inlaid with groups of concentric and overlapping rings of copper, bronze, steel and iron. Each ring was scribed with arcane sigils. I was invited at gunpoint to stand in one of a pair of overlapping steel rings, where I was duly shackled. The smell of strong incense 'blinded' me to all but the overpowering scent of attar of roses, camphor, and the sour undertone of knotweed.

After a few minutes the door opened and my saviour shuffled in. The one-handed bastard swallowed hard when he saw me. He was followed by the sell-spell or as they preferred to be called, Court Appointed Sorcerer. She cast a sharp-eyed glance in my direction and frowned before instructing the priest to stand in the ring beside mine, luckily for him it was beyond my reach.

'Sweet Saint Bart, what happened to you?' the priest asked me.

'Juris impudence,' I said. The greenshanks stationed by the door chuckled.

The sell-spell shushed everyone. Stooped and grey, she looked well past her prime but must have been good at her job given the gold trim on her robe. She obviously dealt with her paradox through pain, as every sagging wrinkle on her face was pierced. Lips, nose, eyebrows cheeks, every inch of pliant skin was either scarred or hung with tiny silver rings.

She made no announcement; nobody gave a speech or read out the sentence. The sorcerer merely lit a censer and began to pace the perimeter of the circles, muttering the incantation that would bind me to wheyface. In her other hand she held a thick silver wrist band inscribed with sigils. My palm itched to the point of burning.

'I… I'm really sorry about this. I honestly never intended to—' the priest muttered, his eyes imploring like those of a beaten puppy.

'You better hope this works, priest,' I hissed. 'Because if it doesn't, I'm gonna skin your pasty hide and wear it while I fuck your grandsire's worm-infested corpse.' It wasn't the most imaginative curse, but I was starting to feel lightheaded. The priest flinched as though I'd slapped him.

For a second though he'd looked like he might grow some stones and give me some stick in return, but he didn't. The fire that had briefly kindled in his eyes died and he shrank into his robe. I felt no sense of triumph; the room was starting to spin and I was struggling to stay on my feet. The sell-spell's voice bored into my skull, made my bones hurt. The room spun faster; the inscriptions in the floor began to glow, the world blurred, the ground rushed up and kissed me into oblivion.

I woke to find myself lying on an unpleasantly yielding mattress somewhere that didn't smell of piss or mildew. I forced my eyes open. Hard sunlight streamed through a pair of gauzy curtains. Fastened seamlessly around my left wrist was a bright silver cuff. I sat up and promptly puked my guts up.

After emptying my stomach of everything but the lining, I lay back on the bed, shivering despite the warmth.

'It will pass,' said a familiar voice. I raised my aching head. A few feet beyond the end of the bed, the priest was sitting at a book-buried desk. His hood was down, revealing closely cropped yellow fuzz, set above watery grey eyes and a soft-chinned face ill-defined by age or character. 'The sickness is due to the magic. I felt awful for a few hours after, but... I think it's worse for...for...'

'The victim?' I offered. It came out less angrily than I'd intended.

'Would you have preferred seven years in the mines?' he snapped.

I sat up and swung my legs off the bed. 'Yes, I would, as a matter of fact. Hard labour is preferable to slavery.' I felt a spike of anger. The sharp note of defiance reassured me that I hadn't been turned into an entirely spineless drudge. A terrible thought occurred to me; I looked at my hands and was relieved to see that I was still wearing my gloves. At least the demon mark hadn't been discovered.

'You wouldn't have lasted seven years; nobody does,' he said quietly.

I grinned at him. 'You're right there, priest.'

'Brother Tobias of the Sacred Order of Scienticians of Saint Bartholomew, actually. You may call me Brother Tobias, or Father or...'

I snorted. 'My scaly arse, will I call you *Father*.' I stood up, lights danced before my eyes. I was pleased to see him shrink back in his seat. Pleased to taste a faint whiff of fear sweat above his watery musk.

'Then Brother Tobias will suffice, or sir.' He tapped the desk with his leather wrapped stump. 'You are my servant, *my property*, for the next five years. You might as well get used to it.'

Like fuck, I thought and pain blossomed in my head like a flower made of nails. It felt like I'd drunk a pail of the cheapest, sot-brewed, back-alley rum and had then proceeded to headbutt rocks.

'Yes, *sir*,' I intoned. The pain lessened. 'You dumb-armed muff-fumbler,' I whispered. The pain spiked again; I stumbled.

'What did you say?' said the priest and rushed over, his face knotted with concern. He looped his arm around my waist and eased me back onto the bed.

'Nothing of import,' I said when the pain gave me leave to speak. It had hurt like hell, but the pain helped me feel my way around the geas, allowed me to get the measure of my bonds. I'd sprung a fair few master-crafted locks in my illustrious career; I'd find a way to unlock these chains, magical or not.

'So, what shall I call you?' he asked, all nice like we were newly acquainted friends.

'Breed,' I said. He nodded, as though it was a perfectly acceptable name for someone like me. I cracked a smile at his ignorance.

'Have you ever been outside of Appleton, Breed?' Tobias asked.

'No, sir,' I answered humbly, ignoring the hammer tapping in my skull. I knew his type. Barely out of puberty but wanting to be thought venerable, to be called Father. As if reading a pile o' books conferred wisdom as well as knowledge, as if the robe he wore was something more than clothing. The flash of contempt squeezed another pinch of pain from my noodle.

The priest left the room. An icon of a platter-faced human with a yard stick in one hand and a staff in the other glared down from a plinth on the wall. A moment later the priest returned with a mop and bucket which he handed to me. He flicked his gaze towards the yellowing puddle of vomit.

I started mopping. 'Is that Saint Bartholomew?' I asked.

'Aye, may his name be praised,' he bowed towards the icon. 'Ours is a relatively new order, though by His grace, it is gaining prominence and followers with every passing year.'

'How nice.' I said and finished cleaning up the puke. I offered the pail and mop to the priest. He frowned and pointed to the door.

I took it outside. An unadorned corridor stretched right and left. Long and low-ceilinged, the sandstone walls and floor had been scrubbed to the colour of old bone. A strong smell of incense tickled my nose. It must have been one of the monasteries in New Town's temple quarter—not a place I'd ever had much cause to visit, not during daylight at least. Of the hundreds of saints and gods in the Pantheon a few dozen had opened up shop in Appleton. They were mostly obscure or poor, scammers and sharpers hoping to find soft-headed culls, lacking in wit but not wealth, to swell their ranks. There were a few of the true believer kind who'd take the poor, exchanging a hot meal for a sermon, a bed for a lifetime of unquestioning devotion.

By the plainness of the cloister and the homespun garb of the pew-bashers creeping about, I guessed this wasn't one of the most affluent orders, which was a pity as I didn't have so much as a clipped penny to my name. A few of the brothers and sisters cast fearful glances in my direction as they passed. As I had a mop in my hand instead of a sword, they continued, offended but unalarmed by my presence. Those I saw all looked human, which was nothing unusual; humans and warspawn rarely shared anything, least of all religion. Thoasa had their gods, but I preferred to believe in that which I could see, smell, and hear, rather than otherworldly beings—except for the Annurashi, they made their presence felt from time to time although I'd never seen one.

I handed the mop and bucket to one of a group of shave-pated priestlings shuffling by, and went back inside. Tobias was at his desk, stuffing books into a backpack and stacking sheaves of paper which were covered in elaborate diagrams and elegant scrawl. Though I kept it quiet, I could read imperial as well as Shen, Guldistani, Vrok, and a smattering of a dozen more. Mother believed that education was important and had learning beaten into me from an early age. My tutors were mostly scholars who'd fallen on hard times and had a desperate desire to work off their drug or gambling debts teaching me, rather than lose their fingers. Given Mother's reputation, they needed little encouragement to make sure I remembered what they taught me, and I still had the scars to prove it.

'I must shortly return to our temple in Valen,' said the priest. 'I'll need you to carry my belongings and help with cooking, that kind of thing. Should we encounter any undesirables on the road, I give you leave to help me fend them off.'

'With a mop?'

'What? No. Just your… hands, er… claws. Just, you know, do what you did the other night.'

'I had my blades when I was *saving your life* the other night. Do I get them back?'

He laughed nervously. 'You didn't use them as I recall, so no, they won't be necessary.'

'Now, you say that, but there are some dangerous roads between here and the capital—haunted by all manner of scum that will not be discouraged by fists and feet alone.' I knew this to be absolutely true as from time to time I'd been the scum that haunted them, and very lucrative it was too.

'No, it wouldn't be right, and besides, in his wisdom, Saint Bartholomew has seen fit to gift me with certain abilities that allow me to… calculate both defensive and offensive angles of reality. Blades will not be necessary.'

I shrugged. I had no idea what he was talking about and neither did he judging by the flush in his cheeks. 'Remember you said that when you're being slow-roasted alive by some meat-starved ragabash.'

He frowned. 'Don't you mean when *we're* being slow-roasted alive?'

'Nah, thoasa don't make good eating, it's the scales.'

'Oh, I don't know.' He grinned and made a show of sizing me up. 'Other than a few patches of scales here and there, you don't look to have too hard a shell to crack. I'm sure you'd make a perfectly excellent meal for some varlet, should the situation arise.'

'If you let me use my blades, the situation won't arise. But if it does, they'll eat you first. Soft, white meat is a delicacy, after all.'

'If I thought you were being insolent, I would have you flogged.'

I shrugged. 'It wouldn't be the first time.'

His pinked cheeks darkened to scarlet, according me the victory. 'I shall pack my books myself. Please don't touch them.'

He curled his left arm into his sleeve, a practiced, defensive habit by the look of it. If he hadn't bound me to slavery I might have felt sorry for him. Only *might*. I knew some dangerous coves who were missing the odd appendage. In my experience, it's not what you have, it's what you do with it that counts.

The rest of the afternoon passed in near silence save for a few begrudging exchanges. The quiet suited me well enough; I had a lot to contemplate. Mattie would have told Mother what happened in the court, question was, what would she do about it? The priest sent me on various errands within the monastery which gave me the chance to explore the limits of my bond while I recovered from the ill-effects of the indenturing. Although not painful *as such*, the longer I was away from the little piss-streak, the more a nagging itch grew in the back of my skull. I wasn't sure if it was a real feeling, like someone tapping me on the head or if it was just my imagination searching for some sign of the magic that bound me.

Away from prying eyes, the cuff proved invulnerable to several surreptitious attempts to smash, lever and saw it off. All I succeeded in doing was giving myself a headache. I didn't so much as scratch the metal. After I gave up trying to remove it, the horrible realisation dawned on me that I hadn't really being trying as hard as I might to get it off. My heart, my *will*, wasn't in it and it didn't really bother me.

After a few hours' running errands, the dizziness wore off and I stopped jumping at every noise that might be a Blade or angry arrachid come to settle my account. The brothers and sisters of the Order of Saint Bartholomew were wary around me; some flinched when they came upon me unexpectedly, a few actually squeaked. That these timid culls survived in Appleton was the best and only proof I'd seen that they had any kind of divine protection.

That night, drained from the indenturing, I fell asleep outside the priest's room within minutes of putting my head down. The corridor floor was pleasantly cool and dry, the swept flagstones smelled of lavender, shoe leather and clean, garden soil.

A few hours later, I was woken by the sound of light, shuffling footsteps. I didn't leap to my feet because assassins don't shuffle. I opened one eye a crack but lay as still as a corpse. The smell of wool, sweat, and old human piss wafted past my face as someone swirled the hem of their robe away from me. Whoever it was knocked quietly on the priest's door and entered without invitation. I'd heard the bells chime midnight probably two hours before, so I was curious as to who was visiting the priest when all goodly, godly folk should have been long abed.

The priest and his visitor were too talkative for this to be a simple lovers' tryst. A wise Blade knows well enough that it's better to keep ears open and mouths shut, something neither of the prayer peddlers seemed to ken. I put my shell against the door. They started their conversation whispering and I struggled to make out much of what they said, but they quickly forgot the precaution. A couple of minutes in and they were chattering like a pair of excited children. Their naivety made me smile; I found it charming, in the same way that a hawk finds a pair of conies a delight to behold.

'I have no doubt the binding geas is powerful, but more powerful than... *that,* Toby?' As I'd guessed, the shuffler was old. His voice rattled and was occasionally lost to breathy, wheezing coughs.

'With all due respect, Benedict, I know what I'm doing,' said the priest with more sureness in his voice than I'd heard before. 'I've prayed and I've done the calculations. You have to trust me; the Order has to trust me.'

'Marius has already tried to kill you. Sweet Saint Bart, just saying that makes me feel ill, that it has come to actual violence.'

'He wasn't trying to kill me, just scare me. Trust me; it's not the first time. But that's in the past, now.' The priest paused, something rattled. 'No, try turning it the other way.'

The old man grunted, straining against something. My mind jumped to all manner of prurient conclusions.

'I'm not convinced. Oh, right, I've got it,' said Benedict. There was a pause and the rustle of what sounded like waxed paper. 'Oh, these are rather nice. Thank you, Toby,' said Benedict. He was eating something; I could smell sugar. 'But about Marius, I think you underestimate his ruthlessness and that of his order. This isn't about religion to them, this is about politics—power, albeit temporal.'

'Glad you like them; Mother sends me a tin... every

month. No matter where I am, her care packages find me.' He laughed. 'The blackbell cherries are particularly good, very sweet. And since when has there been a difference between politics and religion?'

'Oh yes, these are lovely,' said Benedict through a mouthful of cherries. 'Careful, Tobias, you're starting to sound like those jaded old sots in the Synod. But yes, it's a sad fact that the two things are oft entwined, or should I say *entangled*, to the detriment of all. But back to the matter; if you're right about *that thing*—and I'm not convinced you are—then malevolent forces could be rising as we speak; forces that are beyond the power of the Synod to contain. Please, for all our sakes, be wary of it. We do not want another Schism War.'

Although I couldn't see, I was pretty sure *that thing* the old piss-sack was talking about was me. I can't deny that he was right. People should be wary of me, especially those who've landed me in a pot of arse-pickle or talk about me behind my back, they should really watch out.

'I know what I'm doing, Benedict. No, please, take them; I don't have much of a sweet tooth.'

'Very kind of you, my son. I'll do what I can to calm the situation, but I have little influence in Valen these days and Augusta is looking for any means to garner support for her challenge. If she can rally the orders behind a cause, *any* cause, even one as vile as this... Oh, Tobias, if only you hadn't given her the reason she needed.'

'I couldn't lie. This is too important. I had to report what I'd found.'

'But what you found is open to interpretation and abuse, as we're seeing now. You should have waited, or better yet, not told the Synod at all.'

'No. I'm sorry, Benedict, but I cannot legislate for the evil in people's hearts. The truth had to be told, the world must prepare. It will happen; *that thing* is proof.'

'If you fail, hundreds, nay, thousands will perish.'

'I know. Enjoy the sweets.'

'I shall. May Saint Bart guide you, my son,' the old man sighed, defeated.

The latch rattled. I lay back down before the door swung

open. A curl of warm air blew the same pissy perfume of old human across my face. The smell of sugar and cherries added a little finesse to an otherwise depressing odour. When the old man shuffled round the corner, I rolled onto my back and stared at the whitewashed ceiling, a cold nugget of discontent lodged uncomfortably in my gut. They were scheming and I was involved and, worse of all, it didn't alarm me overmuch.

By the time I drifted back to sleep, dawn had begun to wash night's shadows from the walls. I dreamed of the demon Shallunsard; saw him sitting on his obsidian throne, toying with the broken hilt of Dawnslight. He looked at me and shook his head.

The call to morning prayers didn't wake me; instead what roused me was the frantic clamour of alarm bells ringing out across the city. Bereft of anything approaching a sense of emergency or purposefulness, priests and priestesses stumbled into the corridor and clumped themselves into babbling knots of confusion.

The air was tinged with smoke from bakery ovens lit hours earlier, but the smell quickly thickened into something more sinister than baking bread. My first instinct when trouble called was to absent myself and yet, here I was, guarding the priest's chamber door like a faithful cur and wondering why. When he finally showed himself, I bundled him back inside, followed him in and locked the door behind us. He floundermouthed something incomprehensible, his words dictated by a sleep-fugged mind. I propped a chair behind the door, hands twitching for blades I didn't have.

'What the hell is going on, Breed—what are you doing?'

'Looking after you, your priestness. Now stay away from the door until I've had a look-see out the window, there's a good fellow.'

I noted, albeit dispassionately that I was genuinely concerned for his welfare. While I grappled with the unfamiliar feeling of giving a shit about someone, I picked up a bludgeon-sized plaster effigy of Saint Bartholomew from the priest's desk and went to the window to see what the hell all the noise was about. The monastery courtyard was filling with bewildered-looking devil-dodgers but my attention was drawn beyond the walls to what I assumed was the root cause of the alarm.

I have no idea who named spew maggots, but whoever it was had a dark sense of humour, or a poor grasp of scale. These demonspawn were between six and eight feet long. True enough, they were maggot-like in that they were eyeless and as pale as a bled corpse, but there was no spewing; quite the opposite in fact. Their mouths were lined with three rows of serrated teeth, able to chew through the rocky earth where they made their subterranean burrows. How they'd come to be in the streets of Appleton instead of miles underground was a mystery as well as a surprise, but there they were, dozens of them.

The priest joined me by the window. 'Sweet Saint Bart and all the angels,' he said and tugged the improvised club from my hands.

'Miners must have delved a nest of them or flooded their tunnels. Look there's more coming up.' I pointed out where two more were breaking through the cobbles.

'It can't be just one nest, or one mine, come to that.' He pointed into the distance to where a cloud of dust was rising over a collapsing building. 'They're coming up all over.'

I grabbed the lintel of the window; the wood creaked but felt sound. 'Do you mind?'

He shook his head. I swung myself out and up onto the roof. It was good to feel the cool rush of wind against my scales. I looked across the city, across the tiled rooftops that spread in rolling red waves to the rim of the horizon. I could go anywhere in the city from up here, one leap and I'd be free, but I didn't take it. The magic anchored me to the priest.

To get a better look, I climbed onto the shoulders of a statue worn to an anonymous lump by wind and rain.

'What can you see?' the priest shouted.

'You don't want to know.'

'Actually, I do.'

'More spew maggots, all over the city. They're eating everything, everyone. Buildings are collapsing into tunnels. It's chaos.'

The cry of 'demon!' rang through the streets. Spew maggots were said to be demonspawn, created by infernal magic in much the same way that the warspawn were created by the high mages and for much the same purpose: to fight the battles the humans and the demons didn't want to fight themselves. That had been over six hundred years ago. Since then spew maggots had bred and lived relatively peacefully deep underground. They weren't harmless and were feared and avoided by miners, but I'd never heard of them doing this.

Why they were here, eating the citizens of Appleton like it was the good old days of the Schism War was a mystery… at least I hoped it was. It occurred to me that it might be my fault, given it had been just over a week since I'd released Shallunsard. I felt a stab of guilt when I thought about my comrades of the Blade in the sewers and what they must be facing, but the feeling passed when I recalled how none of them had tried to spring me from prison. Down below, the monastery gate cracked like kindling under the assault of a couple of maggots that were smashing their chitin armoured heads against it like a pair of living battering rams. A sense of alarm rose within me as I realised that the monastery and the Order of Saint Bartholomew were in grave danger.

'If I had my blades I could do something to help them,' I shouted to the priest. And then it struck me. The concern I was feeling wasn't mine. I didn't give a damn if my own blood kin was being choked down by the maggots, so why did I care about these sanctimonious geese? I didn't, but the priest did. His anxiety was infecting me through the bond we shared, filling me with all manner of unwanted and hitherto unfamiliar emotions. And what was worse, it didn't even make me angry, just dispassionately aware.

'Get inside, everyone!' Tobias shouted. 'Dear gods, why are they just standing there? Move, damn you!'

'Can't you do something?' I asked. A maggot reared up and bit a chunk out of a grey-haired sister. 'Sweet salvation, they're so fast.'

Perhaps summoned to the feast by its kin or drawn by the blood soaking into the earth, another maggot burst through the cobbled courtyard. The smell of burning bloomed in the air, smoke ropes uncoiled into the lightening sky.

'Give me my blades and I can help them.'

'I can't!'

'Then you do something. They're dying down there!'

'I can't! The angles are wrong. There's nothing I can do,' the priest shouted over the clamour of bells. Those members of the order who were able ran inside while the maggots feasted.

'What? Fuck the angles!' I shouted. 'Those things will go through this place like... like giant flesh-eating maggots. You have to do something.' I'd never heard me sound so concerned for anyone except myself. It was strangely moving, a bit like indigestion.

'Didn't you hear me? I CAN'T!'

I snorted. 'Won't more like.'

He craned his scrawny neck and glared at me as though I'd just called his mother a cunt and then with a yell, he turned and gesticulated at the courtyard.

There was a moment of utter silence. Time held its breath, hushed the world and stilled the very beating of my heart. The next moment rushed in with the fury of a storm, whipped the air to splinters as sharp as glass and turned the night into fire. The backwash of heat knocked me off my perch and onto the roof. My third eyelids flashed closed a moment before flames engulfed the courtyard and utterly consumed the maggots. The smell of cooked demonspawn was... unique.

The priest sagged against the window sill. I grabbed the edge of the roof and swung back in through the window. He was out cold, drained by the spell. If that was what happened when the angles were wrong I'd love to see what happened when they were right. The milksop had power.

I picked him up and tossed him on the bed. The courtyard, several outhouses, the remains of the gates, and a cart in the street outside the monastery were all blazing merrily. The fire would have spread to the monastery proper had not a dozen or so of the order rushed out and doused the blaze with a variety of small spells and a good quantity of water. By the time they'd finished, the suns were over the horizon and a fair portion of Appleton had been reduced to smouldering rubble. In truth, the city didn't look much worse, a little blacker where a day earlier it had been grey.

While he was unconscious the priest's anxieties didn't reach me through the bond we'd been forced to share, so I could enjoy watching the god-mongers in the courtyard stumbling around in the bleeding light of dawn. As amusing as it was, I couldn't help wondering why the maggots had attacked the city. I looked to the west, beyond the black line of rooftops, towards the distant shadow of the mountains where Shallunsard's lair lay buried.

The priest moaned in his sleep. I slapped a damp cloth on his forehead and although I'd resisted temptation for almost a full hour, I finally gave in and searched him. He had a sweet rum-bung, which didn't surprise me as I'd never met a poor priest. I took a couple of the crowns and some pennies and put the still healthy pouch back where I found it. Taking the coins hurt. I felt a stab of pain like a hot needle being driven between my eyes, but it was nowhere near as bad as the pain I'd felt when I'd given him a bit o' lip after the bonding. This pain settled into something akin to a hangover, and I'd had plenty of those. Of course, I had to go and spoil the moment by fantasising about smothering the whey-faced bastard with his pillow which caused an instant and blinding pain that dropped me to my knees.

The priest woke up about an hour after he'd cast the spell. Not long after he came round, there was a timid knock on the door. Still groggy, he motioned for me to open it.

'What d'you want?' I asked the handful of slightly singed and pensive-looking heaven-peddlers.

A skinny little woman looked up at me. 'Oh... I... I,' she stammered, and clutched the little yardstick pendant around her neck. 'We... we would like to speak to Brother Tobias. Is he, that is, is he—'

I got bored with listening and closed the door.

'Damn it, Breed. Let them in,' said the Priest.

I shrugged and did as he bid. They shuffled inside.

'Ah, Tobias—' said the woman. I slammed the door behind them, put my back to it and folded my arms. The weak-kneed culls jumped in unison. The priest shot me a warning glance.

'I've spoken to Benedict' the female stammered. 'He... er, he asked me to... that is, he'd like me to...' Her tongue bound itself in a knot of nonsense.

'... Say thank you? I suggested.

The woman dared a scowl in my direction. '... to ask you when... only, er... well...' One of the other priests, a portly fellow who looked as bored listening to her as I was, stepped in as she chewed over another mouthful of words. Tobias rubbed the bridge of his nose, dark circles ringed his eyes.

'You destroyed the whole courtyard, Toby, not to mention the damage to the monastery. It was pure luck that you didn't kill anyone. Such a regrettable lack of control.' The fellow smiled sadly. 'We've already had the city guard pay us a visit. They are less than happy.'

'You're right, Alph, I... I don't know what came over me.' Tobias scowled at me.

Alph softened. 'It was probably shock. Nevertheless, it has left us in a difficult situation with the city guard.'

'I'm sorry. I'll go and explain what happened.'

'Oh, no need. Benedict managed to placate them, for now.' The group exchanged guilty looks. 'He, that is, we, were wondering when you were thinking of leaving? Only, sooner might be better than later, given what's happened today.'

Tobias sat on the edge of the bed. An uncomfortable silence fell over the room. Alph went over to Tobias and put his hand on his shoulder.

'I'm sorry, Tobias, but I'm sure you understand. Your use of the spell was—'

'Impressive?' I offered. I was only trying to be helpful and speed up the painfully slow eviction.

'That's enough, Breed,' said Tobias. His voice was gravelled with weariness. 'Sister Lillian, Brother Alph; *everyone*. I did what I thought I had to do, but yes, I panicked. I knew the angles were wrong, but I did it anyway.' He again shot me an accusing look. 'I made a bad calculation. I'm sorry.'

Rather than give him a kicking, which is what would happen in the Guild if you screwed up, the group closed around him and offered their deepest sympathies. Bad angles, my arse; they were jealous and afraid. He had power that would make most sell-spells weep, and they were making him apologise for using it to save their hides.

After an hour or so of turgid theologising and the recitation of many, *many* trite aphorisms, Sister Lillian led the group in prayer. When they were done the sorry crew filed out. Exhausted and downcast, Tobias sat and stared at the icon of Saint Bartholomew.

'I told you the angles were wrong,' he said.

'They looked damn fine from where I was standing.'

The greenshanks finally cornered and slaughtered the last maggot just before midnight. The booming rapport of firelances heralded an end to the menace, but the damage had been done. The priest half-heartedly packed a few bags while I watched the city burn.

The next morning, after a breakfast of thin gruel we departed, waved off by a tired Father Benedict and a guilty-looking Sister Lillian. The three of them exchanged a few whispered words and said another prayer before we could finally be on our way. I was loaded with the pig-pizzle's baggage but I didn't mind. Although wheyface was in a sombre mood, I was happy that we were getting out of town and heading to Valen, which was exactly where I wanted to go. I didn't know a lot about imperial history. It was dull; just a list of dates and the names of dead human gentry, but I *did* know that the Hall of Heroes was in Valen and that the Hammer of the North and his blasted hammer were buried there.

I kept my head down and my eyes open as we made our way through the carnage. After Sketh's killing and the maggot attack I was betting Jing and Mother would be too busy to worry about me. Of course, as soon as they had a grip on the situation one or other of them, both if I was unlucky, would come after me. Crime lords, like nobility, were a vindictive breed and never let a slight go unpunished; it was bad for business. Until a few days ago I'd have been fighting with my fellow Blades against Jing and the maggots and whatever else fate threw at the Guild. Now the only family I'd ever known was lost to me. I can't say I missed them.

A curfew and order for summary execution for looting had immediately been put in place, and judging by the crop of makeshift gallows that had sprung up along the main roads, the law was being enthusiastically enforced.

We fought our way along crowded streets, past the burned out wrecks of buildings and massive yawning pits. A column of bull-shouldered miners, candle lamps tied to their caps, passed us on their way to the mines. Today, instead of resigned misery, their grimed faces were rigid with fear. The boss of their crew was an ogren with a limp. She cursed and kicked those who dawdled, but didn't seem overly enthusiastic about her work. I didn't blame her or them. Who knew what was waiting for them in the dark, miles below ground.

'Why are they going to the mines today?' the priest enquired. 'Surely it's too dangerous?'

'They don't have a choice. Look at their wrists. D'you see the jewellery?' I pointed out the bracelets marking them as indentured servants.

'The mine owners' will make them earn their freedom even if it means sending them to hell. The Empirifex needs his calthracite.'

The priest blanched. 'It isn't right. Someone should stop this.'

I laughed, I couldn't help myself; he was ridiculously naïve. How this cull had survived to adulthood was a marvel. 'You should go tell the patricians who own these poor culls' debts, then. I'm sure they'll take heed of your council, and while you're at it, you can spring me, seeing as how you're so set against forced labour.'

He stopped and glared at me. The miners filed past. The tide of refugees heading in the opposite direction flowed around us. My head started to pound.

'How can you, how *dare* you make light, when you…' He flailed his arms. 'When you've seen what those things have done?'

'What am I supposed to do? Cry? At least they're only

bound by contract. They could do a runner if they wanted, unlike me.' The veins in my temples throbbed.

'Nobody made you break the law.'

'In point of fact they did... sort of.'

'Enough! You've said enough.'

Steel flashed in his eyes. I fancied a moment that he might forget his meek manners and burn me to a stump but I stood my ground. Let him do it, I had little to lose. He shook his head and stomped off. Perhaps like me he was getting a taste of how the other felt. Perhaps his flaring temper was mine. I did hope so. I hoped my anger was causing him as much confusion as his bleeding heart was causing me.

As we made our way out of the city, all manner of grisly tale floated through the thronging crowds. Wild-eyed street preachers lamented the end of days, drunks gave gory, unabridged accounts of what the spew maggots had done. Ordinary citizens bleached pale by fear told of entire streets that had been swallowed by sinkholes and their hapless inhabitants devoured by the beasts crawling below. Demons had apparently come to Appleton. My palm itched. I kept my head down.

Flooding in the calth mines had probably driven the maggots to the surface. Damn mine owners, scraping every last crumb of calth out of the ground. It was a surprise this hadn't happened before, was what I kept telling myself as I forged a path to the gate. While I beat my guilty conscience into submission, I kept us moving. I was carrying almost all of the priest's belongings as well as dragging him behind me. Occasionally he insisted we stop and help some unfortunate cull whose cart was stuck in the mud or who needed a penny to buy food for their sick infant, blind mother, one-legged, crippled aunt twice removed. The priest was soft for all manner of con trick and sob story and slowed our progress considerably.

The closer we got to the Old Town gate out of the city, the more crowded the streets became. It seemed like the only folk not trying to leave were the bondsmen and women and their families. Huddled groups of the indentured watched as the tide of people flooded from the city, leaving them behind to clean up the mess with the greenshanks who'd enslaved themselves with oaths of loyalty instead of debt.

On Main Street, an urux had sunk up to its shoulders in a pothole, miring the huge, over-laden wagon it was pulling up to the axles and blocking the road. The animal wheezed pitifully as its lungs were slowly crushed and its frustrated owner lashed and kicked it in a futile attempt to get it moving.

The damage the maggots had caused was immense and still taking its toll on the city and its inhabitants. All over town, buildings were still collapsing, undermined by the maggots' furious burrowing leaving both sides of the city a wreck. If they'd survived, the Midnight Court would do well out of this.

We reached the gate just after midday. The greenshanks on duty there were in an ugly mood. Many had the ghostly ash-blasted features of those who'd been using firelances. The backblast from calthracite and zanthe crystal dust tattooed the skin of cannoneers with tiny silver-white pockmarks. The greenshanks eyed the crowd with the cold detachment of people too used to killing but we passed beneath their dead-eyed gaze without drawing attention.

Bursting from the city on the desperate tide, we joined the wave of dispossessed rolling north. I looked back once, just to make sure we weren't being followed. As we walked, we fell in with a group that swelled and contracted by turns as people joined or left the road. Anxiety and tension permeated every conversation. Every knot of travellers was tied together by the fearful rumours that demons had returned.

'Off t' Shadowspike!' a wide-eyed beggar barked at the priest. The maunder couldn't have been as old as he looked, given the vigour with which he was scratching his nethers and skipping along the road, but he was grimy, withered as kindling, and stank of pel and cheap drink.

'I'm sorry?' Tobias looked up for the first time in ages. He'd been quiet since our little argument. That he'd torched the monastery courtyard was probably also weighing on his mousy little conscience.

'Them demons!' The old man gestured at me with shit-stained fingers. 'They're heading t' the mountains. Mark me! This is just the beginnin'.' He rasped a phlegmy cackle.

'And you'd know, would you?' I said. 'Did you divine the truth in a ha'penny dram of bucket brew?' I made as if to backhand him. He skipped back, just enough. Beggars are good at gauging how much, and from whom, they needed to run. He hopped around, just out of arm's reach.

'Don't like the rub o' truth, eh, *demonspawn?*' The old tosspot shot me a gap-toothed grin.

The proclamation caused several of our fellow travellers to give me the fish eye of suspicion. There was not a blasted thing I could do to allay their fears, not now that the old fuck had planted the seed of distrust. To deny the claim, to so much as shrug it off would have been an acknowledgement. That acknowledgement would have been read like chicken guts and, given what I look like, most probably taken as an admission of guilt. People were afraid and looking for something tangible to hang their fears on. Not to mention, they would have been, in part, correct.

The demon mark in my palm itched or perhaps I just thought it did because my conscience was pricking me. Whatever the cause, I ignored it and set my face in a mask of neutrality. I didn't let on that I'd heard the whispered conjecture about my heritage, or that I could smell the pungent aroma of fear that bloomed like a swampy miasma whenever the old pel-head stirred the travellers' doubts about me with his drug-fuddled insinuations.

That night, when the group we'd been walking with stopped to make camp, the unofficial leaders of the motley crew: a retired soldier and a baker, asked for 'a quiet word' with the priest. If I hadn't seen him turn the monastery courtyard into a furnace I'd have been concerned for his safety. As it was, I just hoped the angles were right.

'... people are afraid.' I overheard the baker say; a pouty expression of worry stamped into his haggard features.

'This is ridiculous!' the priest retorted when the baker ceased his prattle. He then proceeded to argue my case. It was a worthy, but ultimately futile effort.

The debate went on long after suns' set. If nothing else, I

had to admire the priest's tenacity, but why he even bothered to argue with them was beyond me. They'd made up their minds before they'd come over to speak to him the only surprise for me, was that in this case, they were right, I was part of the problem. Not that they knew it, they were just afraid of me because of what I looked like. I was dangerous to be around; trouble in tooth and claw, and on some level the mad old beggar had sensed it.

In a purely practical sense we were better off without the rest of the group. I knew that if I was hunting this road, I'd go for the fat and slow before anything that looked like me. Add to that the priest's explosive gifts and we were far more likely to travel unmolested by brigands than a bunch of old folk, children and merchants.

When tempers began to fray and voices grew louder, the priest walked away. I guessed that he was used to losing by the way his face fell so easily into the sad little frown I'd seen so often in our brief association. It was the same look I'd seen on his face when blackbeard was about to close his account. The acceptance of inevitable failure, despite all the power he could wield, was baffling.

'I don't know why you bothered,' I said as we set off, leaving the camp of scared refugees behind us.

'Because it's safer for everyone if we travel together,' he answered, restoring my lack of faith in humanity. '*And* because their ignorance had to be challenged, now more than ever.'

He had to go and spoil it.

'I'm not exactly a saint, you know.' I shook my left wrist, the silver cuff gleamed.

He rubbed his chin with his stump. 'No, perhaps not, but neither are you a demon.'

I'm used to keeping a straight face, but I was sure I could feel the prickle of a blush touch my cheeks; it was always the human side that let me down.

'Oi! Wait!' someone shouted from behind us. We stopped. I was surprised to see the old tosspot who'd caused the trouble, skipping along the road, waving his spindly arms. I set off walking. The priest stayed put.

'I'm coming with you,' the beggar announced.

'I don't fucking think so,' I said and hunted around for a rock to throw at him.

The priest shook his head. 'Why would you want to come with us? You all but accused my servant of being a demon.'

The shit rag scratched his bony crotch and leered at us. 'Better t' run with the wolves than the sheep, eh?'

'Oh, no—' I began, but the priest waved me to silence.

'Very well, you may come with us.' The priest smiled benevolently. 'Perhaps when you get to know Breed you'll reflect on your mistake and revise your opinion.'

The old man slapped his thigh and danced on the spot. 'Ha! I doubt it.'

'So do I,' I said. 'Now fuck off.'

It would do no good; the beggar was smart enough to know who was in charge. He grinned at me, his bloodshot eyes bright with mirth.

'D'you have a name?' the priest asked him.

'Tosspot,' I offered.

The beggar laughed and danced about some more. Like most pel-heads he struggled to stay still when he wasn't using his drug of choice. 'Tosspot! Aye, I've tossed a few pots.' He cackled. 'Tossed in a few, too. Tosspot! Aye, *demon.*' He winked at me. 'That'll do.'

Chapter Six

When it became too dark for the priest and Tosspot to see, Tobias called a halt near a roadside shrine to the Pantheon. The All Seeing Eye, the symbol that represented the dozens of *officially* sacred gods and hundreds of honoured saints, was painted on a badly carved stone that was surrounded by piles of rotting fruit, bread and jars of dead and dying flowers.

After the priest had prayed and tidied up the shrine, we made camp; that is, *I* made camp. Tosspot and the priest wandered off in opposite directions to void their bowels while I built a fire and prepared some food for Tobias. I wasn't hungry—I'd eaten my fill the night before at the monastery which would see me right for a day or so. Humans were constantly eating, drinking or shitting; it was a wonder they ever got anything else done.

Tosspot came back first. I could smell him before his grimy little monkey face emerged from the bracken. The fresh, smutty brown streaks on his ragged breeches confirmed his complete lack of hygiene or self respect.

'Go wash yourself before you sit by this fire, you fucking cockroach,' I growled. Humans struggle to growl and talk; I have no such problem. He looked around for the priest, but he wasn't back yet. The grin faded.

'There ain't no rive—' he began.

I shot out my arm and pointed in the direction of the stream that I could hear burbling in the woods about sixty feet north of where we were camped. Grumbling, he trudged back into the undergrowth. If I hadn't been stricken by a severe case of 'fuck it' I would have followed him in and drowned the disgusting old bastard.

When he got back, Tobias mumbled a prayer then, without further comment, ate the burnt bread and cheese I'd prepared. At a time like this, I'd normally clean my blades or wax my bow. I felt lost without them. When he was finished the priest took out a notebook and pen. He cursed.

'What's up?' I asked.

'I've lost the nib.' He rummaged in his bags.

I laughed.

'Something amusing?' he asked. He gave up looking through his bag and resorted to using a pencil for his scribbling.

'I met a fellow who specialised in stealing nibs; least, that's the story he told me. Quite the rum cove.'

'Oh.' Now he looked up. 'Do you know anyone who makes an honest living?'

'Plenty. Why, priest, d'you want to meet some?'

'What? Are you implying that priests are dishonest?'

'Certainly not, master,' I smiled.

'It doesn't work on me, you know.' He closed the book.

'What doesn't work on you?' I asked, genuinely curious.

'Showing your fangs like that. I'm not intimidated, or impressed.'

You fucking well would be if I wasn't bound by a geas. The thought, and accompanying mental image of me ripping his throat out, was immediately followed by a spike of pain that made my eyes water.

The priest's attitude immediately changed from scolding to concerned. 'Are you alright, Breed? He moved over to me, rested his stump on my shoulder. 'That was my doing, I'm sorry. I shouldn't be angry at you.'

I blinked away the purple lights, almost laughed, but managed to catch myself. The idiot didn't understand the nature of the bond as well as he should. 'No, I deserved it.' I said, as contrite as a beggarly cur.

'No, no you didn't. I'm sorry. Sorry for everything.'

'No need, master.'

'Don't call me 'master'. Call me Tobias, or priest, anything, but I am no one's master.'

Sharpest thing he'd said all day. I smiled, close-mouthed. He went and sat back next to his pile of bags and picked up his notebook.

That he felt guilty was good. It was something I could exploit, work it to my own end, which was to get as far from Appleton as possible and as close to the tomb of the Hammer of the North as this fool could bring me.

'Your hair, it isn't like human hair,' said Tobias, changing the subject.

'No, not really.' I resisted the urge to comment on his startling powers of observation.

'Does blood flow to the end of each shaft? Only, I notice some of them are pierced.' He tapped the pencil on his stump.

'Almost to the end. They don't bleed much when they're torn.'

I got the feeling he was making notes about me—studying me like one of those things kept in the jars of vinegar that mouldered in the apothecary's window. A dull headache pulsed in the back of my skull.

He nodded and scribbled something in his book. 'You have a third eyelid?'

Again I resisted the urge to congratulate him. 'Yes, very useful it is, too.'

'But no tail at all?'

'No, more's the pity: thoasa tails make excellent weapons and give them superb balance.' I scratched my nethers, sat back and grinned. 'Anything else you want to know about?'

The tip of the pencil snapped on the page. He shut the notebook. 'I, er…'

The undergrowth stirred. I could smell Tosspot before he emerged, spackled with loamy detritus, looking for all the world like a withered tree spirit. He smelled less of shit than he had, but that smell had been replaced by another equally unwholesome aroma which explained the flush in his cheeks and the length of time he'd been away. He reached for the bread I'd left by the fire.

'Touch it, and I'll break your arm.' I said. His hand froze mid-air. He looked at Tobias who shook his head at me before turning to the beggar.

'Please, take it, eat your fill,' said Tobias.

Tosspot snatched the bread and tore a chunk off. Uncharacteristically for a pel addict, he put half back.

'Don't feel that you need to ask if you want to eat anything, Breed,' Tobias nodded towards the bread.

'Not hungry, thanks. You eat it, before it goes stale.' The

priest finished the bread by which time the suns' red halos were being cut to ribbons by the saw-tooth spikes of the tree tops.

We'd camped near the road. Carts and wagons, people on foot passed by late into the night, all heading away from Appleton. I didn't sleep. I didn't need to, which was handy because I didn't trust that self-abuser Tosspot. I'd work out watch shifts with the priest on the morrow if he still insisted on letting the mad old fuck travel with us.

The priest rolled himself up in a blanket, Tosspot curled up beside the dying embers of the fire. Cheeks dusted with ash, he looked like a penitent on pilgrimage.

'One o' them maggots came up near Steel-Eye Square,' he said. 'Right under a big, old bull urux.' His rheumy eyes shone in the firelight. 'It ate right through it, came out its back and that old bull still alive.' He shook his head, dislodging bread crumbs from his matted beard. 'Hole the size o' the suns right through it and it still standing, eyes wide as dinner plates. Took an age afore it realised it was dead. Now that's stupid, eh?'

'Speaking of stupid, how come you didn't get eaten when they attacked?' I asked.

He tapped the side of his rum swollen nose. 'Could ask you the same, eh?' He rasped a chuckle. 'I'm quick, used to be really quick—quick as you!'

Now it was my turn to laugh. 'No human is as quick as me.'

'Not now maybe, but once, a long time ago,' he said.

'Before you got a taste for pel and cheap booze?'

'Oh, aye, back in my glory days.' He chuckled. 'Back when the road was scattered with rose petals and every step was marked by a ballad, back when we were heroes.'

I laughed. Deep in the forest, something howled.

We'd walked for four days and had barely made it a hundred miles from Appleton. At this rate I'd die of old age before we even reached Valen. I needed to put more distance between me and the Blade and the Pearl. If they'd a mind, Mother and

Jing could afford to send an assassin to just about anywhere in the Empire. I wasn't the praying kind but I very much hoped Jing had been eaten by a spew maggot. It was simply too much to hope that a giant, carnivorous demonspawn had done for Mother.

We came to an old, pre-Schism bridge where the road split north and east. I knew it was pre-Schism because it was massive, and decorated with grim-faced human warriors. Centuries of neglect and robbery had taken its toll, and the once magnificent example of pre-Schism engineering was slowly crumbling into the gushing torrent. Even in its dilapidated state it was far grander than anything I'd seen that had been built after the war.

The priest informed me that we'd be heading east to Valen. The more direct route was over the mountains unimaginatively called the Dragon Spine that ran north to south. We could have taken the road north, through the foothills and up as far as the coast. From there we could either follow the coast east or take ship to Valen. The easiest, but longest route was the one the priest had decided upon. We'd take the road east, go around the mountains before turning north to Valen. If I'd been on my own I'd have gone over the mountains, but I was shackled to a one-handed priest and a stray lunatic. The priest could blow the giblets out of just about anything nasty we might encounter but I wished that I was carrying something sharp and pointy instead of a pack full of books and a skillet. I ask you, books instead of blades? Pointless. My comrades would, quite rightly, burst their bladders laughing if they knew what I'd been reduced to.

That eve, as twilight dimmed the day and tinted the world in sombre shades of mauve, we came upon a village, and not a moment too soon. I had been forced to walk at a snail's gallop for hours while the spoil pudding blathered godly nonsense at the capering madman. The endless sermonising made me wish I'd been born without ears.

According to the boundary stone the village was called Little Lea. I couldn't see a lea, just a dusty gash of road and a three-legged dog sitting by the sign, licking its nethers. If it had been named appropriately it would have been called

Dusty Shithole by the Roadside, which I'll grant was less lyrical than Little Lea but a touch more honest.

The inn wasn't hard to find. Other than a scatter of one-storey dwellings strung out along the North Road, there were only a few other buildings of note in Little Shithole. Standing back from the road was what looked like the village hall. It was near a rundown guard tower that was marked by a tattered standard. Across the road, down by the river, was a mill, and beside the mill's tailrace was a turf-roofed forge, judging by the rhythmic clang of metal on metal ringing off the cobble walls. The mill's water wheel churned monotonously, each revolution marking the passage of time with a sodden creak. If I'd been given the choice of living a single day in Appleton or living somewhere like this for a hundred years, I'd choose Appleton in a heartbeat.

'There's no temple,' said the priest like it mattered.

'There's a shrine over there.' I chinned in the direction of a roadside shrine that was hung with faded prayer ribbons and piled with tattered offerings. The priest went over and knelt before the badly painted image of the All Seeing Eye. Tosspot pulled a broken pipe from his shirt and licked the sticky pel residue from the bowl.

'You're not going t' pray? Beg the gods to save you from your miserable existence?' I teased Tosspot, not just because I was bored, but also because I didn't like him.

'After you, Breed.' The idiot grin was replaced by a facial tic. 'Don't suppose you've got any coin have you? Only...'

He didn't need to go on. He was an addict who spent every penny he got on pel or gut-rot booze. I had what I'd stolen from the priest and under normal circumstances wouldn't have given him so much as the stink off my shit, but perhaps if he got drunk the priest might cut him adrift. I tossed him a penny.

Despite the twitching he snatched the coin from the air with the practised deftness of the desperate. 'Ah, yer an upstanding cove, Breed,' he said and scuttled over to the inn, knuckles bleaching around his prize.

The priest spent the next half hour with his head in the dirt before the All Seeing Eye. I spent it eyeing the traffic and getting the lie of the land for want of something better to do. There seemed to be a lot of business going on between the guard tower and the village hall, even though it was the time of day when all respectable types should be sitting down to their dinner.

Three uniformed greenshanks ambled back and forth between the hall and the tower. I doubted that there would be many more of them stationed here, perhaps two or three and maybe a captain or a sergeant. Although we were on a main road, the village didn't warrant any more protection than a handful of greenshanks. If there hadn't been an inn it wouldn't have had an outpost at all. Places like this usually deputised the locals to swell the lurchers' ranks when need arose. I'd had to leg it once or twice from the odd posse of pitchfork-wielding bumpkins, though I can't say they filled me with terror.

The priest eventually stopped praying and came over. 'Thank you for waiting, Breed. I sometimes lose myself in contemplation of the holy scriptures.'

'It's not like I have a choice, is it? If I wander too far, my brain'll melt like tallow.' I spoke without thinking. He frowned, I immediately regretted snapping. Not only did it hurt, but I had to win this cull's trust, and being sharp with him wasn't going to keep him sweet.

'No. Quite.' He brushed past me and stomped towards the inn, shoulders hunched. I sank a fang into my tongue until I tasted sweet iron to remind myself to stay focused. *A year and a day*. It wasn't long. If I was to get the hammer for the blasted demon or get hold of enough gold to pay a sell-spell to break the bond I'd need to stay on the priest's good side.

The inn was even less inspiring on the inside than it was on the outside. A string of pipe-smoked hams were hanging above the bar, out of reach of what would have to be extremely hungry patrons. The cloying, sickly sweet smell of partially cured, partially rotten pig was overlaid with the odour of stale beer, piss, pipe-smoke, pigeon shit and dried urux dung. It was the same olfactory tale told by every backwater tavern in the empire. Bubbling on the hearth was a large pot of mutton fat and turnip stew. A dog was licking the oversized ladle propped in the inglenook. It was all very homely and utterly wretched.

'We don't serve your kind,' the one-eyed innkeeper barked as she burnished a tankard with a spit rag. I looked around; it was hard to tell where the one eye was aiming. Out of habit rather than anger I reached for the ghosts of my blades. The priest strode over to the bar. Before the woman could open her mouth again, he flipped a silver half crown onto the stained planks.

'Don't be ridiculous, that is my servant. I require a room and food, for both of us.'

The barkeep frowned, and rubbed harder at the tankard. She was obviously thrown by the sureness of the priest's demeanour, the absolute, 'do not question me' tone of voice he'd produced from gods only knew where. I was impressed; it seemed that the pissweed had some orchids after all.

The 'we don't serve your kind' wasn't anything I hadn't heard before; even in Appleton it was a common refrain and had lost its sting years ago. Under normal circumstances I'd either teach whoever it was some manners or, if there were too many witnesses, I'd leave and return at a later date and rob them blind. I thought of it as an arsehole tax. This was a first: having a human speaking up for me. If it hadn't been his fault that I was here I'd have been touched. Placated by the coin we were shown to a booth. While we waited for our food and ale to arrive we were surreptitiously scrutinised by a handful of bacon-faced and dead-eyed yokels. Happily, Tosspot was nowhere to be seen.

Eventually, the barkeep came over and slid two plates of congealing slop across the table, along with two tankards of grease spotted ale. When she caught me looking at her stitched-down eyelid, she turned her head away. I caught a whiff of something fishy, and a subtle undertone of overripe peach. It was her. The lank, greasy hair, the pasty complexion livened by cheap rouge; it all added up now.

I gave her the smallest of nods, an imperceptible acknowledgement that said, 'Your secret is safe with me,' which it was—so long as she played fair. She wasn't warspawn nor was she like me: a hybrid of two distinct species. She was probably one of the many poor culls spawned a little too close to an old Schism battle site.

The shame of being 'touched' meant good business for shankers who, for a price, would remove a touched babe's less than human feature with a snip here and a stitch there and no one would be the wiser save dear old mother and father. Eyestalks were a common 'touch', so many a child grew up one-eyed or blind, but it was better than being an outcast. Some of those who couldn't afford the discreet services of a shanker tossed their ill-favoured offspring into the nearest river rather than live with the stigma. So it was no surprise that the innkeeper didn't serve warspawn; she didn't want anyone with a sense of smell like mine to rumble her. That she could 'pass' for human with just a few minor adjustments had probably saved her life. She didn't let on to me, she hurried away, taking her peachy-fish smell with her.

'What's the matter?' Tobias asked.

'Nothing, well…' I chased a lump of gristle around my plate. 'It's just that I've never been so far from home.' I looked him square in the face, didn't blink, didn't blush. If there was one thing I could do well other than fight and steal, it was lie. He manoeuvred his bowl with his stump and stirred the broth.

He looked down. 'I… I'm sorry. I never intended this to happen. You must believe me when I tell you that everything I do is because I have to. So much is at stake, so much depends on me.'

'I understand,' I said, the bile rising in my gorge. 'Fate has conspired against us.' I wanted to grab him by the back of the neck and drown him in his stew. A swift, blinding stab of pain followed the thought. My eyes watered, which was good. I'd never cried in my life, but he wasn't to know that.

The priest put down his spoon and reached out, almost patted my arm with his stump, but paused mid air before awkwardly withdrawing. 'I promise, I shall endeavour to make our time together as easy as I can. I'm not a tyrant unlike… unlike some.' He'd left something unsaid, but I didn't dwell on it. I had the soft cull on the hook.

Sometime in the early hours I woke to find myself sitting on top of Tosspot with one hand around his throat, about to smash his brains in with a chamber pot. Someone nearby was shouting. Sleep-fugged, I forced my brain to work back from there.

I dimly recalled that the door had creaked open while I was sleeping on a palliasse beside it. The priest had been snoring fitfully on the bed. Someone crept inside and I'd instinctively grabbed their ankle and dragged them to the floor. At the same time, I'd leapt on top of them and picked up the first thing that came to hand, ready to beat them to death with it. Then I'd woken up. Just in time to not brain Tosspot, which was regrettable.

'Sweet Saint Bart, Breed. Let him go!' the priest commanded.

Reluctantly I stopped squeezing the old scrote's neck and got off him. 'Knock next time,' I said and returned to my mattress. Tosspot made an unnecessarily dramatic show of coughing and gasping for breath.

'If that's how you greet a friend, I'd hate t' see how you treat your enemies,' he mewled.

'You're no friend of mine,' I said. 'What did you think you were doing, sneaking around in the middle of the night?'

'I've been busy. I've been scouting the lay of the land.' He got up close to the priest, and whispered breathily in the poor cove's face, spittle flying from the blackened stumps of his teeth. 'I've been exploring the criminal underworld—for your safety, mind, and this is the thanks I get!'

I had to laugh at the idea that Little Lea could possibly have anything even approaching a criminal underworld.

'Well, er... thank you,' said the priest, trying not to recoil from the old sot's mephitic breath. 'But there really is no need... For Bart's sake, what is your real name? I refuse to call you Tosspot.'

'Rubin, your holiness, and mark me; places like this can hold nasty surprises for unwary travellers, eh?'

'I don't think we're in any danger, Rubin but thank you for your concern.'

'Twat,' I said. The priest looked shocked. I pointed at Tosspot. 'I meant him.'

Tosspot chuckled, breathed rum fumes and the stench of decay into the air. 'Ah, well you're right there, Holiness... but yon Breed might be, eh?' He sneered at me.

'What do you mean, Rubin?' the priest asked. This was a waste of time. He should have just tossed the old scrote out, and let us get back to sleep. Without him around I could keep working on softening up the priest.

'Well, as I was about my business earlier on, I happened across a couple of bene coves—'

'A couple of what?' the priest asked.

'Reliable types,' I offered. 'Although I very much doubt it round here. Mark me: he'll have been pissed out of his skull the minute he left us.' I beat a few lumps out of the mattress and lay down. 'He's probably been sleeping in a ditch 'til now. You should have a word with old one-eye; you paid for privacy.'

The priest waved me to silence. 'Go on, Rubin, tell us what happened?'

'Well, I went with these fellows to a more humble establishment, where the price of vittles is more suited to my pocket.'

'He means a backroom bawdy-hole where you'll be lucky if the bucket-brew doesn't make you blind or where the owner doesn't cut your throat when you're in your cups.'

'While I was there,' the old sot scratched his orchids, 'I heard that they're fixing to try and hang one o' *them*.' He chinned in my direction. 'On the morrow, so they say. They're making out that the cove is a demonspawn an' has been bewitching livestock, curdling milk, and cursing the locals. But my contact,' he tapped his nose, 'says that it's all a set up to snatch a claim to some land where calth's been found. That's cold work, if you ask me, hanging a cove for the price o' some rocks, even if it's only some misbegotten, by-blow like Breed here.' He looked expectantly at me.

I shrugged. 'So?' Even if it was a thoasa I felt no bond of kinship.

'So, I'm sayin' people get a taste for this kind of thing, eh?

You best be on yer uppers, less they nab you for hexing their chickens, or whatever it is you demons do.'

'Hexing chickens? Not I, Tosspot. I'm more your beggar-strangling type of demon.'

'That's enough, Breed,' the priest ordered. 'Tell me exactly what you heard, Rubin.'

It was a long night.

The next morning, instead of leaving Little Shithole, the priest insisted that we follow the crowd of locals to the village hall, which was being used as a courtroom for the purposes of the 'trial'.

'So what are you going to do?' I asked the priest. 'Demand they let this cove go or you'll burn them to a crisp with your sorcerous might?'

Tobias pulled up short, and turned on me. I felt a lecture coming.

'What I do is *not* sorcery. It is, as discovered by Saint Bartholomew, the manipulation of latent energy contained within the angles and planes of existence. And no, I am not going to threaten anyone. The Empirifex's law is all that is required to ensure justice is done,' he said, without a whit of irony.

'So it's not sorcery, and imperial law is the epitome of justice?'

'Correct.'

'My arse.'

'How dare you…!' he spluttered. His cheeks pinked. If he hadn't been capable of frying me in my own juices I would have laughed in his face. 'You know nothing, nothing of the enlightenment of Saint Bartholomew.'

'I know sorcery when I see it. I also know there's nothing as bent as imperial law. Trust me; I've bribed a lot of greenshanks and magistrates in my time.' A little voice in the back of my head was quietly suggesting that I shut my pie-hole, but I couldn't help myself. I was annoyed that we weren't leaving.

The priest was shaking. I could feel his anger raging below the surface. 'I am not a fucking sorcerer,' he said quietly.

And then I tumbled it. Curse me for the halfwit I was, but it took until right then to realise that all this sciencian waffle was how he handled the paradox. Using powerful sorcery put him on his arse, but his delusional belief in all this angles bollocks saved him from exploding or turning himself into a pool of living slime when he overreached himself.

I recalled a sorcerer who'd done just that about three years before. Story goes he'd been hired to kill Countess Orkazny, the Empirifex's cousin and lover at the time. She'd come to Appleton to inspect the calth mines. Apparently, the Grundvelt Separatists had sent the sell-spell, but as he was channelling enough power to wipe out Appleton, he lost control and the paradox got him. Rumour had it that the Empirifex had the still-living slime he'd turned into poured down his co-conspirators' throats until they choked to death. Mother laughed about it for days. Whatever the truth, I felt it was time to heed the little voice.

'Alright, alright, whatever you say, but imperial law's put a lot of high-minded dissenters in the calth mines as well as coves like me.'

'Traitors,' he said, with little real enthusiasm. How could he have? Everyone knew the truth.

'Call 'em what you like. But if what Tosspot—'

'—Rubin. His name is Rubin.'

'If what *Rubin*, says is true, you'll need more than the law to spring this cove. People have skinned their own grandsires for shares in calth mines. There's a lot of coin to be made from powder.'

'Enough. We're going to the trial, and if I suspect there has been any underhanded dealing, I shall step in, as is my right as… as a citizen of the Empire.' He fixed me with a watery stare. Pain needled my brain. It seemed that even thinking about punching him into unconsciousness and dragging him away before he got us hung was also against the rules of the geas. He strode off towards the village hall.

'Aren't they expecting you in Valen?' I called after him. He stopped, turned and narrowed his eyes at me. 'Won't your order be expecting you?' I pressed hopefully. He looked like he was about to say something but instead turned and marched resolutely towards the hall, Tosspot in tow. 'You whey-faced fuck.' I muttered, somewhat foolishly as it turned out.

When I recovered, I got up and followed them, mindful to direct my curses at the gods rather than the priest.

The hall was an unimposing, double-height, one-room affair, tied together by smoke-blackened beams that had probably been hoisted into place by the ancestors of the locals now gathering beneath them. The inheritors of this architectural marvel were elbowing and shoving each other, fighting to get a place at the railing that partitioned the chamber.

After listening to the gossip in the gallery it seemed that, in the opinion of the learned farmyard advocates, it was a stitch-up. Few seemed to care because from what I could make out, the accused was a freak and an outcast. *Ratface*,— the alleged demonspawn—was by all accounts as good as hung.

'Why are we here again?' I asked the priest, who'd also been ear-wigging the general chatter. 'I mean, I like a good hanging as much as the next citizen of the Empire, but we're supposed to be going to Valen. Saint Bartholomew will be waiting…'

'Don't be facetious, Breed,' said the priest as we pushed our way to the front of the crowd.

'Aye, don't be facetious, *demon,*' said Tosspot, loud enough to draw the attention of those nearest to us. A half dozen potato-faced locals glared at me. I smiled; they made the triangular sign of the holy eye. I made a silent vow to strangle Tosspot as soon as I got him alone.

The accused was led into the courtroom by a bored-looking greenshanks. Ratface, unlike the town, was well named. I got a good taste of her smell as she was led past the gallery. She was probably no older than eleven, pre-pubescent for certain. The long dress she was wearing made it impossible to tell if she had a tail, but she certainly had the face, if not the physique, of a mostly shaved rat.

Her eyes were small and dark and set either side of a long, broad nose over a mouth of over-large teeth, and her enormous ears stuck out at right angles to her head. Nobody in Appleton would have given her a second look. I looked around the spectators crammed into the hall. They were all human and within the arbitrary limits of what passed for 'normal'. In Little Lea the girl must have stood out like a turd on a pillow.

'What kind of warspawn is she?' the priest whispered.

'I don't think she is; probably just like Tosspot said, a by-blow of Schism magic, a lucky accident.' I winked. 'Kids like her are usually done in when they're born. I s'pose Mummy and Daddy must have—'

'Hold your tongue!' the priest hissed, with such vehemence I again found myself reaching for blades I wasn't carrying and was immediately lashed by a crushing pain for my troubles.

'Fuck's sake!' I jammed the heels of my hands into my eye sockets in a bid to crush the pain that was trying to rip its way out of the front of my skull. 'This relationship will not end well, priest,' I growled.

A grumble ran through the crowd and a space cleared around us. Tosspot cackled and hopped around like a frog on a griddle.

'All right, quiet down everyone, let's get this over with,' A self-important little burgher ordered as he pushed his way through the crowd. 'I said, shut up you lot!' He squeezed behind the bench and claimed the centre chair. There were ink stains on his lace-trimmed cuffs and fingers that marked him out as a nib-tickler. He was probably a tax collector, some sort of crown actuary for certain; he had the overblown airs of an imperial lackey.

He nodded to the greenshanks, who motioned for the girl to get into the rusting cage that stood in the corner of the room; no doubt it had been dragged in to make the place look more like a courtroom. The chickens pecking through the rushes undermined that effect somewhat. Caging the girl seemed excessive, given she was less than five feet tall. I could tell the greenshanks thought so too. He was looking everywhere except at Ratface and an old woman who was giving him the evils from the public gallery.

For her part, the girl seemed blissfully unaware of the danger she was in. She sat on the stool provided, kicking her legs, dark eyes inquisitively scanning the crowd. When her gaze fell on me, she smiled. I looked around to see if anyone had noticed, which of course they had. The space around us got a little wider, the stares a little more pointed. I would have killed for a weapon—probably have to before the day was over.

A couple of other worthies joined the nib-tickler on the bench. One was evidently the miller, given the light dusting of flour on her best Gods' Day smock. I guessed the other was the blacksmith given that he stank of charcoal and fire, and had a wiry cast to his skinny frame from days spent pounding iron.

'These are a fine bunch to judge if the girl's demonspawn: A smith, a miller, and a money-grubbing coin-counter,' I said to no one in particular. The priest didn't answer; he was too busy scribbling in his notebook. Tosspot was leering at anyone who happened to glance in his direction while scratching his nethers.

The earthy musk of the dung-dusted crowd was threaded with anger and fear, a heady mix and no mistake. Our little crew were making quite the impression. Another couple of greenshanks muscled into the room, rust pocked halberds in hand. They closed the doors, the crowd fell silent.

The three cronies on the bench put their heads together and had a quick confabulation. When they'd finished nodding sagely at each other, the nib-tickler rapped on the table. It was an unpleasant reminder of my own time before the bench and set me very much against anything they might have to say.

'In view of the statements and evidence we've already received, it has been decided by the council—' he nodded to his colleagues, '—that we shall proceed directly to sentencing the accused, Clary Bolliver, to, er, death by hanging, sentence to be carried out immediately. Costs incurred in the prosecution of this case to be paid by the family of the defendant. May the All Seeing Eye look kindly on her soul.' The miller elbowed him. 'What? Oh. Case closed.'

'Well, that's that. Shall we go?' I asked the priest.

Before he could answer the old woman who'd been glaring

at the guard screamed as though she'd been run through. The girl woke from her daydream at that and thrust her scrawny arms through the bars in an effort to reach the old woman who was likewise straining towards the girl.

Some of the crowd looked away, ashamed perhaps. A few actually looked upset, but most were nodding, mouths set in troutish frowns of grim approval. It seemed the good citizens of Little Lea were as quick as their city bred counterparts when it came to gilding the nevergreen tree. As someone who lived in a rough old world, where justice was summary and almost always fatal, I was unmoved by anyone's plight, save my own.

'Just a minute,' called the priest. The mouthy burgher tried to ignore him, but Tobias ducked under the rail and strode over to the bench, bold as you like. 'Councillors, a moment of your time, if you please.'

The councillors looked at the greenshanks. The two by the door didn't move and the one by the cage had his hands full trying to keep the old woman away from the bars.

'This is most irregular, er, Father,' said the burgher.

'I hope it is. I would hate to think that trying children for their lives is a regular occurrence in Little Lea.'

'That, Father, is not a child… that is *a demon*!' the miller exclaimed, while making the warding sign of the eye.

'That remains to be seen.' The priest rested his stump on the table. The gaze of all three of councillors flicked to where his hand should be. 'I was led to believe that this was the first, and only sitting of this court, am I correct?' They nodded in unison. 'In that case, and with the greatest respect for your rank and office, I must draw your attention to the fact that witness testimony must be given in *any* capital case, brought anywhere in the Empire, as stated in imperial law.'

The nib-tickler pushed out his chest. 'Ah, well, we've heard the evidence informally; there seems little need to go over it.'

'Never the less, imperial law states, quite clearly, that you must. Sergeant!' The priest marched over to the soldier by the cage. I never would have guessed he had this much mettle in him. It was likely to get us killed, but I had to admire his brass.

'Fetch your commanding officer, if you'd be so kind.'

'I must protest, Father,' said the miller. 'Priest or not, you've no right to come barging in here, laying down the law.'

The blacksmith, who had until this point kept his mouth shut, piped up. 'Neither you nor yer robes carry weight here, priest.'

'I'm afraid you're wrong on both counts.' The priest straightened, seemed to grow in stature. 'As first son of the Patrician house of Vulsones, I am within my right to demand that this trial be conducted in accordance with imperial law. Furthermore, as an ordained brother of a sacred order of the Pantheon, it is within my remit to act as defence council for the accused. I take it nobody objects to imperial law?' He looked at the girl who was oblivious, but the old woman wasn't.

'Please, save her, save my granddaughter!' she cried.

'That's settled, then,' said Tobias. 'I need time to review the evidence and prepare a list of witnesses so I suggest a short adjournment. Shall we say until the morrow?'

The nib-tickler looked at his colleagues. 'I... er... no. I mean yes, that would be fine... I think... er, court adjourned?'

The priest's little announcement made a marked and immediate impression on the citizens of Little Lea, and well it might. Everyone had heard of House Vulsones, one of the wealthiest noble houses in the Empire and a power in the Senate. I looked at the priest in a whole new light; the hypocritical little bastard.

By the time we returned to the inn with a bundle of court documents our bags had already been moved to a better room—one with a fire burning merrily in the hearth, well-fitting shutters and fresh rushes. No sooner had the priest sat down than the captain of the guard was shown in by the suddenly more deferential innkeeper.

The captain was unshaven and wearing a uniform made for a younger and fitter version of himself. The silvery flick of an old duelling scar marked his stubble-roughed cheek.

He saluted. 'Patrician Vulsones, my name is Nestor

Reynard, acting captain of the garrison.' He smelled of cheese and had recently splashed himself with rosewater to try and mask the odour of stale sweat. It had failed.

'You are aware of the trial, *acting* Captain Reynard?' The change in the priest's demeanour was as remarkable as it was sudden. Even Tosspot was stunned into silence. Tobias Vulsones had adopted the indolent weariness of a noble forced to deal with inferiors; as though breathing itself was beneath him. I wasn't sure if this was an act or if I was seeing the real Tobias and the scholarly priest was the mask. Either way, it occurred to me that I'd been gulled for the second time in recent weeks.

Reynard looked uncomfortable. 'Yes, my lord, of course. These are dark days, evil is—'

The priest cut him off. 'Why weren't you present for the hearing, Captain Reynard?' Tobias faced the fire and clasped his stump behind his back. This pose didn't suit him, it looked contrived, but Reynard was too busy staring at his boots to notice. 'Indeed, why weren't you sitting on the jury, Captain? Surely, as a representative of the military it's your duty, particularly in a capital case?'

As much as I liked seeing a greenshanks sweat, I hadn't missed the dagger-eyed stares from some of the locals when the priest had spoiled their little party. He probably ought to throw the guardsman a bone, just in case the yokels got a taste for hangings. Killing a priest, a thief and a madman probably wasn't the worst of what went on in a place like Little Lea.

'I... Yes, you're right, but I had other matters to attend to and, well, it seemed a straightforward case.'

'That remains to be seen. I will, of course, give a full report to the Knights Imperial as well as to the Imperial Magistrates when I return to Valen. I'm an old friend of Commander Pretorius.'

He was a pale human to start with, but at the mention of the commander of the knights, Reynard turned as white as a bled pig.

'Commander Pretorius? I see. Well, I came to let you know that the garrison and I are at your service, my lord.'

The priest half turned from the fire; the flames cast his face in bronze, and I could imagine that profile on a coin. 'That's good to know, Captain and I'm sure from now on everything to do with this trial will be run in accordance with imperial law.'

'Of course, my lord, I'll see to it. Now, if you would excuse me, I have to organise some patrols. We've had reports that there have been attacks on some of the local farmsteads.' Reynard looked pointedly at me. 'They say it's demonspawn.'

I grinned. '*They* talk a lot of shit, greenshanks.'

'Greenshanks? Only criminals call guardsmen 'greenshanks'.'

I waved my cuffed wrist at him.

He narrowed his eyes and tightened his grip on his sword hilt. 'Until the morrow, Lord Vulsones.'

'Captain.' The priest nodded.

Reynard spun smartly on his heel as though trying to prove he still could, and marched out.

When the latch dropped, the priest sagged into his usual slouch-shouldered stance. He went over to the table and began sorting through the court documents.

'You really shouldn't antagonise the local law. I might need his support,' Tobias muttered, his gaze fixed on the ink-stained pages.

'*Me* antagonise? If you hadn't put your dainties in it there'd be no need to worry about upsetting the local ironsides and we'd be on our way to Valen, *Lord Vulsones*.'

'And an innocent girl would be dead. And why are you so keen to go to Valen?' He'd dropped the patrician tone when the greenshanks left, but it returned with a vengeance now.

'Why do you care so much?' I said, the force of his anger bearing down on me. 'Innocent girls, boys—household pets—get hung every day. Why is this little ratkin so special?

'She's a child, damn it! She's just a child. And I will not ignore any injustice if it is in my power to prevent it.'

'And what if she really is a demonspawn, what then?'

'I do not believe there is such a thing.' He didn't sound convinced to me, whereas I knew for certain that demons, and therefore demon*spawn*, were very real. I just couldn't argue the point too forcefully without getting into dangerous waters—waters that flowed straight to the pyre. 'You're in a minority, then,' I said. 'Because those spew maggots are infernal; everybody knows it.'

'A lot of mistakes were made during the Schism, but that was centuries ago. Time has passed. We are what we do, not what we were born.'

'Is that right... *patrician?*' I grinned. 'Even I know that which is born of infernal magic is demonic, and that which was created by the High Mage Lords are warspawn. I have a soul; according to the Pantheon, demonspawn are soulless and damned.' I folded my arms. 'I didn't make the rules; your lot did.'

The priest shook his head as though he was arguing with a child. 'There has been interbreeding and six hundred demon-free years since the Schism. Everything has changed. What would you call yourself, Breed?'

'Unlucky. But I'll tell you this: I'm not infernal.'

'You show me your soul, Breed. Tell me in which organ it resides. I have seen all manner of creature inside and out, and I have never yet seen a soul.'

'I'm no theologian, but that sounds like heresy to me.'

'I am a scientician, it is my job to question. Knowledge and learning are divine gifts.' He sounded sickeningly sincere.

'It's a good job that you're a Vulsones,' I said. I'm not sure what kind of look he gave me, something halfway between pained and angry.

'What's that supposed to mean?'

'I mean, if you were a common cove you'd have talked your way to the gallows long before now. I don't know why you're bothering with all this; you could be living like a king.'

'If we let this girl die undefended, word will spread, and every Schism-touched *by-blow*—everyone with so much as a snaggle tooth—will end up burned or hanged by ignorant peasants or those with axes to grind. You know what people are like, particularly when they're afraid.'

I laughed. 'Oh, I know alright. It strikes me that it's us freaks who should band together; seems you humans are the real danger, not us monsters.'

'That is also another reason why I, a… a human, must stand up for this girl. You're speaking in jest—which, by the way, is an irritating habit—but you don't know just how many powerful factions are searching for an excuse to wipe out everything they deem 'unholy': everything that isn't human.'

His words washed over me, I was already bored with the conversation. 'You haven't won yet, patrician. These yokels are keen to hang someone. Tread carefully or it'll be us.'

Chapter Seven

At dawn, the priest dragged me over to the guard tower so he could speak to the girl. The court was due to convene at ten, which apparently was when milking finished. A heavy rain hammered home the promise of a miserable day as the peasants gathered outside the hall. Despite the inclement weather there looked to be more spectators than yesterday. News of the priest's antics must have spread to every den of clod-hoppers for miles around.

The priest had ordered me to go with him; Tosspot had disappeared the night before with a penny the priest gave him and hadn't returned. If the miserable old piss-sack kept leeching off the priest we'd be as broke as a whorehouse pisspot before we even got to Valen.

Tobias knocked on the guard tower door and entered unchallenged. An old greenshanks was snoring in an armchair by the stove. The grey-beard spasmed awake when the door creaked and stumbled to his feet. Rain splashed into a bucket in the corner, socks and long johns steamed on a line slung above the stove. It wasn't exactly the epitome of an elite military headquarters.

'Ah, I didn't hear you, sir… Father. Come in, come in.' He waved us in as he buckled his sword belt over his patched tunic. 'Early morning shift's always the worst, can't seem to keep my eyes open these days. If you've come to see Captain Reynard, you're too late. He's already gone over to the hall to, er, get things sorted.'

'Actually, I came to see Clary. If you wouldn't mind?'

The guard shrugged and fished a ring of keys from his trouser pocket. 'Her Nan's with her so watch out; she's a mean old goat.'

'I'm sure she won't object to me visiting. I'm here to help her granddaughter.'

'Aye, so I've heard. You're wasting your time, but I s'pose it's yours to spend as you see fit, Patrician. I'd leave well alone if I was you. A lot of folk have an interest in Halla giving up her place.'

'Is Halla the grandmother?' Tobias asked.

The guard nodded. 'Aye. It's this way, mind yer heads when we get down there.' The guard led us out of the room and through a galleried hall, at the end of which was a short flight of steps leading down. A couple of off-duty greenshanks peered over the balcony as we passed. It was reassuring to know that if the priest got himself locked up, busting him out would be easy. I'd seen more secure chicken coops.

'There's not been a hanging in…' The greenshanks paused as though thinking and walking was a taxing matter. 'Nine years. There isn't a lot of crime in Little Lea; bit of cattle theft, drunks, the odd fight. That sort of thing, nothing serious. All this talk of demons has just blown up out of nowhere; people using it as an excuse, if you ask me. Ah, here we are.'

'I heard you,' a trembling voice called from the darkness, thick with emotion. I could taste the salt of tears. 'You know what they're after! They just want my land, that's what this is about; they're threatening an innocent child for the sake of what's under my farm, the greedy, spineless bastards.'

The guard unlocked the door. 'Alright, Halla, that's enough. The father isn't here to listen to your theories…'

'Actually, I'm very interested in what you have to say,' said the priest as he ducked round the guard and offered his hand to the woman. She pushed the girl behind her and looked at Tobias like he'd offered her a bag of eyeballs.

'If you've come to tell my girl to repent, you can be on your way. She's done nothing, d'you hear me? *Nothing*. Go tell that bastard Sandison and his cronies.' She hugged the girl, who didn't seem like she was in need of comforting; she wasn't giving off any odour of fear. The tang of tear salt and anxiety that permeated the cell belonged to her grandmother.

The cell was more of a storeroom than a place of incarceration. It was piled with sacks and barrels of supplies, a small cot bed had been crammed into the corner.

'Leastways, we don't have to worry that she'll go hungry, she can just help herself.' The greenshanks chuckled, nobody laughed. 'Right, er, just knock when you want out.'

'Thank you. You might as well go with him, Breed, but don't go far.'

'If they attack you, just scream and I'll come running.' I winked at the girl, who gave me a shy grin.

When we were back in the entrance hall the greenshanks put the kettle on the stove. 'Do you want a cup of chai?' he asked.

I looked around, surprised to find that he was talking to me. 'There are only two other guards here, the rest have gone on patrol. I'm too old for running around in the wilderness. Did you say you wanted a drink?'

'Aye, thanks.' I didn't, but it was such a novelty having a greenshanks offer me anything other than a beating, I felt I had to accept.

He shoved a stool in my direction and poured a couple of mugs of chai that smelled like it had been stewing for a week. I sat and took the offered drink.

'I fought all through the Spice Wars. For the last six months my unit was in with a company of your lot,' the greybeard said.

'My lot?' I didn't think he meant Guild Blades.

'Aye. Thoasa, isn't it? Although... I can tell you're not *just* thoasa are ya?'

For a horrible moment I thought he was going to shout 'Demon!' and try to attack me with his kettle, but then I realised what he actually meant. 'Ah, no. My mother's human.'

He smiled. 'Human? I thought so. That's unusual; thoasa are... Well, they're big folk, as you know... Your mother must be quite a woman.'

If only he knew. 'Yes, she's a singular individual, very special.'

'One o' them liz... thoasa saved my life when our ship was rammed by a Shen war galleon. I thought I was a goner. I was trapped below decks when the mast fell, an' the ship was going down fast. One o' them lads shifted it and swam me t' shore. I'd broken my leg, see? No way would I have made it on my own, not with the brachuri swarming about the wrecks looking to pick off stragglers, the dirty sea scabs. See that.' He tugged up his trouser leg to reveal a silver scar running down his grey fuzzed shin. 'Bone came right through.' I nodded appreciatively, as that seemed to be what he wanted. To be honest, as scars went, it wasn't that impressive.

I spent the next hour listening to him tell me how terrible the Spice War had been and how much he missed it. I nodded when it seemed appropriate and drank his awful chai. Eighteen years after the Spice War, I was the beneficiary of his gratitude to the thoasa who saved his life. Funny thing was, he could remember dozens of tedious little details about the battle but he didn't know the name of the person who saved him.

When the priest called for the guard he sounded as angry as all hell. He stormed out of the cellar and over to the door without saying a word. His writing scrip was pinned under his dumb arm and he was carrying a fistful of papers in his right. A wave of simmering rage rolled off him.

'What's up? She didn't have a go at you, did she? I told you to shout if...' I said, and tried not to laugh.

'Enough. A child's life is in danger. Doesn't that bother you?'

'No, not really,' I said.

He gasped like I'd just hoofed him in the nut-sack and flounced out. I caught up and we walked to the village hall in half-arsed silence. I say half-arsed because priests, despite what you might think, aren't very good at silence; they like the sound of their own voices too much. Tobias punctuated the short walk with huffs, tuts and sighs—hints of the sermon he was aching to give. I could care less what he thought of me but I was annoyed at myself. I had once again managed to alienate the person who could probably gain me access to Valen's holy of holies and the Hammer of the North's thrice-damned tomb. I had to try and make amends.

'Thoasa just aren't as...' I wanted to say *soft*. '...as compassionate as humans.'

He snorted. 'You're not a thoasa.'

This wasn't working. Every time he opened his mouth I wanted to punch him. 'No, but I'm not a human either, thank the gods.' I muttered through gritted teeth as hot barbs dug into my brain.

*

Across from the gawping masses, the three members of the council took their seats joined today by Reynard, who looked uncomfortable, buttoned up in his patched and moth-eaten uniform.

The honest oak table they'd sat behind yesterday had been replaced by a much grander piece of furniture. Today they sat behind an elaborate, Shen-style monstrosity that had been inexpertly painted to look like leopard wood. I'd lay money on it that the ugly thing didn't purr when it was stroked. If whoever had donated it to the noble court could have afforded the real thing they wouldn't have been within a hundred miles of this dung-burgh.

My money was on the nib-tickler, one Hubert Sandison. He'd been the mouthpiece yesterday, though it would be interesting to see who was in charge today, now that the greenshanks was in attendance. Sandison looked particularly smug; he'd gone to extra effort and had dressed in what must have passed for finery in the provinces. The garish ensemble of screaming-blue velvet and cheap foil braid made him look like a sack of expensive shit tied with a bow. I didn't like him. Not only did he smell wrong, possessed as he was of a sour body odour, but he was a bully, and nobody likes bullies. His gaze met mine; he narrowed his eyes. I bared my fangs. He looked away.

The priest had been given a small table near the council's bench, opposite the cage. He was busying himself sorting through the notes that he'd made, his face a study in concentration. After another twenty minutes or so the accused was escorted into the court. Her grandmother wasn't allowed to be with her, which the old woman complained about as she pushed her way to the front of the crowd. The blacksmith gave her a polite if embarrassed nod of acknowledgement. The girl appeared oblivious to everything that was going on.

'Er, right then, if you would be so kind, Captain Reynard,' said Sandison. The blacksmith looked pale and sweaty, the miller likewise. I focused on them, tried to taste what they were feeling, but there was too much going on to filter out their particular smells, especially as they were sitting next to old sour sweat. Perhaps, like me, they were anticipating the priest giving them a lecture that they'd never forget. He certainly looked like he meant business. I folded my arms. I was looking forward to the show. And then something familiar and altogether unwelcome brushed my elbow.

'Don't turn around, and don't say anything,' said the old greenshanks from the guard tower.

He rested the tip of a blade between my elbow and my ribs. As soon as it moved, I would most likely be stabbed. I didn't move, I waited. The old guard had made the mistake of announcing his presence and his plan. I just had to pick the right moment to make him pay for it. My fingers tingled.

Captain Reynard stood up, tipped a nod to a couple of greenshanks. They pushed their way through the crowd and stepped up behind the priest who was oblivious. When the crowd hushed he looked up.

'It has come to the court's attention that this man—' Reynard snatched a piece of paper from the desk and pointed at the priest. 'This man is an impostor! Guards, seize him!'

'What's going on...? How dare you!' Tobias shouted as he was grabbed by the greenshanks. In the one-sided struggle the table went flying. The neat pile of notes scattered and swooped in slow, diving arcs across the floor. My hair spines bristled.

Any minute now.

'You, sir are an impostor, sent to aid the demonic forces at work in this town by those who would see decent humans thrown down. You are a traitor to your own kind!'

'Lies!' shouted Tobias. 'This is all because Halla found calthracite on her land and she won't sell it to y—' Tobias didn't get to finish what he was saying as, on a signal from Reynard, one of the greenshanks punched him in the gut. The priest doubled. I became an island of stillness amid the jostling crowd as partisan feelings were aired and scuffles broke out. The blacksmith stared resolutely at the table, the miller's dusty face bloomed scarlet with guilt and Reynard nervously fingered the tarnished hilt of his sabre. Only the nib-tickler was grinning like the world wasn't about to turn to shit. He nudged Reynard.

'Clear the court!' Reynard ordered.

'No, not yet, you fool, the witness!' Sandison hissed.

One of the greenshanks encouraged the crowd to get back with a few swipes of his halberd; many fled the building. The priest sagged in the grip of the other guard. The one behind me kept his hand steady and his blade poised. Halla scrambled under the barrier and locked onto the bars of the cage. Clary was at least paying attention to what was happening now. She leaned close to her grandmother and whispered something to her.

'Bring in the witness!' Reynard ordered. The crowd surged like a wave in a washtub. The greenshanks with the halberd barged past me, I didn't turn to see where he was going; I didn't want to provoke the old bastard behind me before I had to. With any luck he'd fall asleep before he got the order to finish me.

'This is a sham. Whoever you produce is a liar and you know it,' the priest said to the council.

'You should have kept your nose out of our business,' the miller offered. The blacksmith's jaw tightened but he kept his gaze fixed on the table.

A few minutes later the greenshanks came back. Even before I saw him, I could smell Tosspot.

'Why are you even bothering with this farce?' the priest asked. 'We all know the truth of the matter.'

'Silence!' Sandison bellowed. 'You are not the law in this court; I... er, we are. You, sirrah, will hold your tongue or lose it. Now, the witness will stand forward.'

Tosspot staggered before the bench. He was obviously in his cups but, with the fortitude of a well-seasoned sot, managed to stay on his feet after no doubt drinking enough gut-rot to kill a bull urux.

'What's your name?' Sandison asked him.

Tosspot leered at me. 'Tosspot.'

The miller and the blacksmith looked at each other, shared the shame of a guilty conscience between them. Bloody amateurs.

'Hmm. As you say. Pray, tell the court what you told me.'

'I don't remember telling anyone much of anything, but thanks for the grog.'

'This very morning, you told me that this man,' He pointed to the priest, 'was in league with demons!'

'No, I didn't. You told me he was in league with demons, and I said I wasn't surprised.' Tosspot belched. I could smell the hot, gingery fire of cheap brandy from across the room.

The priest folded his arms. '*He's* your witness? A beggar who'd sell his mother for a sniff of pel. Who are you trying to convince with this ludicrous charade?' He raised his voice, no doubt for the benefit of the crowd pressed against the greenshanks' halberd. They didn't care, they had their own scores to settle.

The rat girl let out a low, keening wail, as though finally aware of the danger she was in. Her grandmother tried to comfort her through the bars of the cage.

'Now see what you've done? You gutless bastards!' she spat at the council.

Sandison surged to his feet. Reynard clamped his hand onto the pig-eyed fool's shoulder and pushed him back down. The piss-and-iron stink of adrenaline filled the room. The air sang with the promise of violence. Sharp work was afoot.

Reynard looked at Sandison with undisguised contempt. 'Clear this fucking room.'

The guards shoved everyone out and barred the door. When it was done, Reynard turned on the priest. 'You're right, my lord Vulsones, it was a poor plan, badly executed. I'm quite embarrassed.' He smiled apologetically and drew his sword. 'How about this: When they were unmasked, the impostor and his…' he cast a daggered side stare at me. '… demonic minion attacked the council, and the hapless witness. In the ensuing battle, the brave guardsmen and women defeated the servants of evil. Alas, they were unable to save the witness, who was struck a cowardly blow by the demon. Is that more convincing, Vulsones? Oh, and by the way, it was Commander Pretorius who had me sent to this venal little shit-hole in the first place—seems she took a liking to my lover. Suffice it to say, I will not be sending her a report regarding this incident.'

'You mange-faced bastard!' Halla bellowed. 'I'll tell her! If I've got to walk to Valen, I'll tell the world about what you've done.'

Reynard dug the tip of his sword into the table, eliciting a gasp from Sandison. 'You have a point.' He cleared his throat, 'The brave guardsmen and women defeated the servants of evil, including the old witch, Halla Grenfyle and her monstrous get. There, that should do it.' He focused a meaningful glance about six inches behind me. The sword point that had been touching my elbow was withdrawn.

'Sorry,' said the old greenshanks.

'Don't be,' I replied.

Thoasa have something akin to a second brain that controls the body while the other brain, the one I was in charge of, could relax and think about just how I was going to rip the heads off the smug fuck-stockings who had planned my demise.

Soldiers old or new make poor assassins. They tend to lack finesse and in this case, speed. I turned to the greenshanks; his blade missed me and thrust into empty air. I grabbed his hand and crushed his fingers into the hilt of his hunting knife and twisted his wrist until it broke. He cried out, I relaxed my grip, let the blade fall from his useless fingers and caught it with my free hand. Without letting him go, I spun back to face the court and hurled the blade at the greenshanks holding the priest. More through luck than judgement I hit him and not Tobias. The guard staggered back, clutching his ruined eye. Cackling like a madman, Tosspot somehow managed to avoid being stabbed by Reynard, who seemed most perturbed by his antics. I can't say I blamed him.

'Get her out of there!' I shouted at Halla. She didn't need to be told twice. Thanks to the general ineptitude of the greenshanks the cage wasn't locked.

The blacksmith kicked over the table and pulled a knife. The miller fell off her chair in her haste to flee, although gods knew where she was thinking of going. Behind us, the only door was being guarded by the greenshanks with the halberd, and she didn't seem inclined to move, not with half the town outside, hammering to get back in.

'You've made an arse of this, acting Captain,' I said, trying to draw Reynard out. Scarlet with rage, he duly complied and leapt at me while the blacksmith circled round to my right. The greenshanks who'd had hold of the priest had collapsed. The old greenshanks had backed against the wall behind the railing, where he leaned, sweating and clutching his mangled hand. In stories, the hero always manages to fight on after sustaining horrific wounds. In reality, a smashed wrist is more than enough to take the fight out of even the bravest mortal, particularly humans. They break easily and have poor pain tolerance.

I grabbed the knife I'd sheathed in the greenshanks' face in plenty of time to meet Reynard's clumsy attack. Although I prefer to use two blades I'm also quite handy with one. I blocked, and kicked him in the gut. He folded over and kindly offered his neck. How could I refuse? The miller screamed, as did Tobias, who unsurprisingly was bellowing for me to stop. I ignored him, ignored the pain trying to push my eyeballs out of my skull and ducked as the blacksmith leapt at me, waving his knife with all the aplomb of a blacksmith unused to knife fighting. I swayed back and stamped down on his knee. As he dropped I ran him through. He curled around the blade and fell to the floor, mewling as he died.

'That's enough, Breed!' Tobias grabbed my shoulder. I managed to stop the blade an inch from his neck. To his credit he didn't flinch. 'That. Is. Enough,' he said.

Almost killing my master caused an excruciating burst of pain to flare in my skull and I hit the floor.

'Sweet Saint Bart, what have you done...?' he said. The townsfolk were hammering at the door, Clary was sobbing, as was the miller. Someone was choking on their own blood.

'I... just... saved your life, that's what I done—I mean, did. Fuck! This really hurts. I should have just let him stab me,' I said, and I meant it.

'I... er... I...' Sandison mumbled. He hadn't moved a muscle during the scrap. He'd just sat there, rigid, watching his world turn to shit. Now, surrounded by the wreckage of his petty schemes he woke up to the nightmare his greed had created. 'I wasn't going to let them hurt her, Halla,' he bubbled. 'I swear, I just wanted to scare you, I—'

Halla spat at him and hugged her sobbing granddaughter tighter.

I got to my knees. 'I'd shut up if I were you.' I said and, still seeing double, turned to the guard with her back to the door. She shifted her grip on the halberd and braced.

I stood up and weighed the knife in my hand. Stunned or not, I knew I could still take a country greenshanks. 'You might want to step aside, greenshanks.'

'Best do it, Jenna,' the old greenshanks said as he slumped against the wall. He turned to me, his voice shaking. 'I knew your kind was tough, I should have done you quick, without saying anything.'

'Next time, eh?' I answered. I felt anything but tough right then but they didn't know that. I couldn't bring myself to look at the priest.

The miller peered from behind the table; Sandison hunched into his ornate chair. I tried to keep my eyes on them and the guard by the door.

'There is but one way you can redeem yourselves,' said the priest.

'Anything, just name it! Any penance, any recompense I—' Sandison spluttered, his gaze fixed on the still blinking head of Reynard that lay at his feet.

Tobias raised his hand. 'Just shut up and listen. I want you both to go out there and confess your crimes to the people of this town, and then tell them to disperse. You will then take yourselves over to the guard tower and hand yourselves in to whoever is in charge. I'll send word about what has happened to the nearest imperial outpost. Do you understand?'

Sandison and the miller nodded emphatically and stumbled to the door. I had to give it to the priest; despite being as pale as a fish belly, he was remarkably unruffled by what had just happened. Now if only he had a legion behind him to shore up his words. In my experience 'authority' meant nothing without steel reinforcement. I just hoped the yokels didn't know that too.

The greenshanks unbarred the door. There was a sizable crowd waiting outside, some had armed themselves with clubs and other makeshift weapons. When they saw the councillors they backed off a few feet. Sandison raised his hands and patted the air to still their chatter.

'The holy father…' he stammered '… is a demon! Kill him! Kill them all!' he screamed and dived into the crowd. The greenshanks cursed and tried to hold the crowd back, but their blood was up. They'd come for a fight and one greenshanks wasn't going to deter them. The miller cast a glance over her shoulder, hesitated for a breath, before running to join Sandison. I looked around for any other way out.

The few windows were high and small, too small to get everyone out quickly, and even then, the villagers were just about bright enough to run us down before we got very far. I could leg it on my own and leave the others to their fate, but the thought of spending the rest of my short life in blinding agony because of a bond with a dead priest didn't thrill me. The crowd edged forward.

'Step aside,' Tobias ordered. He looked like he was about to puke.

'You can't talk this mob down, let me—'

He grabbed my shirt, sweat stood out like coffin nails on his pale forehead. 'The angles are right, Breed.'

I immediately backed towards Halla and the girl. The old greenshanks caught on that something was about to happen and shoved his comrade out of the doorway and back inside. The crowd surged forward.

Tobias went to meet them.

The air turned sharp and metallic, like a storm was about to break. The priest raised his arms…

It was a strange feeling, being near to but not the target of a huge discharge of raw, magical energy. The first thing that happened, after a heart-stopping moment of utter nothing, was that lightning arced from the priest's hands and leapt to the iron chandelier, showering the room in sparks before lancing a dozen jagged forks into the crowd. The accumulated dust of decades was blasted loose, filling the air with the smell of rust and ancient insect droppings. The second thing was being knocked on my arse by a huge percussive *whump* of hot air.

Lightning leapt from one member of the mob to the next, binding them in dazzling azure chains. They jerked, spasmed and burned as the wreath of fire incinerated their clothes and melted the flesh from their charring bones. The acrid stench of storm clouds combined with the fatty stink of burning human made my eyes water. Mere seconds later, it was over.

Black, fire-trimmed flakes of crispy human floated into the sky before gently drifting back down to earth as the intense heat dissipated. From what I could see through the smoke, none of the mob had escaped, including the two treacherous councillors. All that remained of Sandison was a leg that was strangely untouched by the magical fire. I knew it was his as it was still clad in a white stocking and a bright blue shoe. There was nothing left of the miller. Like the rest of the mob, she'd been reduced to charcoaled dust. A few errant flames idly licked at the doorframe, but on the whole the blast had been extremely focused.

'I see what you mean about those angles,' I said to the priest, but he didn't hear me; he was too busy fainting. I caught him before he kissed the dirt and carried him like a babe in arms, over the cindered remains of our attackers and out into the drizzle. The smell of death hung in the air, mixed with the gloom of late summer rain bleeding from the heavens. I looked up; let the water wash the ash from my face…

Although the sound was buried beneath the planishing hammer of rain, I heard the distinctive *clunk* of a trigger being pulled, but by the time I realised what it was, it was far too late.

My first and, as it turned out, only reaction was to drop the priest. A moment later I was hit in the chest with the concentrated force of a charging urux. The impact punched me off my feet, turned my ribs into jagged splinters that sliced into my chest and shredded my heart and lungs. I vomited a spray of blood.

I knew I'd hit the ground because all I could see was the

sky. I didn't feel the landing. As I bled out, my consciousness retreated from my limbs to a tiny point somewhere in the back of my skull. It felt like I was looking out of the well of myself through the rain-blurred windows of my eyes.

'That was a damned risky shot. You could have hit Tobias,' said someone I couldn't see. Whoever he was, he had a deep, well educated voice not unlike the priest's, save that it was replete with self importance.

'No, it wasn't,' said another man who, by contrast, spoke with a soft, breathy purr that lacked the cultured indolence of the truly noble. 'He was never in any danger. I do this for a living and, even if I say so myself, I am really rather good at it.'

Annoyingly, they remained beyond the scope of my dwindling vision as I was curious to see what my killers looked like.

'What in hell is it?' demanded the first. I assumed he was talking about me.

'Dead is what it is. Why yes, it was a bloody good shot, now you mention it,' the breathy one sniffed.

'I'm paying you, isn't that enough?'

'Not really, no. I, am an artiste. Coin pays the bills, but praise feeds my soul.'

'What rot.' Deep voice laughed.

'You wound me, sir.'

'Don't tempt me, Schiller. Now, if you wouldn't mind, help me bind Tobias.'

'With pleasure.' Breathy tittered. 'We don't want him coming round and turning us into charcoal, now do we?'

Someone nearby groaned. I guessed it was the priest. I knew it wasn't me because—I acknowledged with a surprising lack of rancour—I was already dead.

Chapter Eight

After the initial excitement of dying I learned something interesting: Nothing happened. One minute I was bleeding out beneath a suitably maudlin sky, and the next I was covered in dirt and someone was dragging me from the ground by my ankles.

In between dying and resurrection nothing had happened at all. There hadn't been any flames of hell, no divine rivers of wine, no twelve-cocked thoasan love gods came to greet me, no holy winged vaginas, not even an army of sacred golden newts to show me the way to the source of all life. Just nothing. Part of me was disappointed although, given the life I'd led to this point, I suppose it could have been much worse. Still, death was something of a disappointment.

I tried to struggle free of the iron grip around my ankles but I couldn't move. Panic struck as my nose, mouth, and eyes were full of dirt. Before I choked, I popped out of the ground like a turnip. Harsh daylight forced tears from my eyes, I blinked, it felt good. Whoever had pulled me out of the hole let go of me. To my dismay I found I still couldn't move but my vision was clearing quickly. I spat out a mouthful of dirt, focused on my rescuer and immediately wished I hadn't.

It was a corpse, or more accurately, one of the restless dead.

It wasn't fresh but it was still recognisably male. A noose was hanging around its twisted neck; its shrivelled muscles creaked like hawsers as it grabbed me under the arms and hauled me over to a tree. Its empty eye sockets wept grave dirt and grubs as it propped me against the trunk. And there was me thinking there was nothing worse than being shot. It seemed that like life, death was full of unpleasant little surprises.

The corpse shuffled back, tilted its head to one side and tried to smile with its atrophied facial muscles. *Breeeeed*,' it hissed. I recognised the voice. It was Shallunsard. 'You are without doubt the most amusing creature I have met in centuries.' The demon laughed.

I didn't. Something to do with being shot to death had quite muted my normally robust sense of humour.

'I'm the *only* creature you've met in centuries,' I gasped. Air whistled through my shredded lungs. 'Am I dead?'

The corpse nodded. 'As good as, save that *thing* you term a soul has not yet left your body.'

I never thought I'd miss him, but I really wished the priest was here. 'Sooo… I am or I aren't?'

'You am, but that can change.' The corpse demon plucked a grub from its chest and stroked it with a rat-gnawed finger.

'Ah.' I sensed another deal looming. 'What do you want?'

'That which is mine. You owe me a hammer, remember?'

'How could I forget, and why the corpse?'

'Why not? I could have come to you as a cloud of flies, a flock of ravens, a gaggle of vengeful chickens, but none of those are much good at digging stupid breeds out of graves.'

'If you'd come a day earlier, there wouldn't have been any need to dig.'

The corpse demon squeezed the bug and flicked the remains at me. They hit me in the face. 'I find your priestly friend rather… irritating, and besides, I don't have time to drop everything and rescue your pathetic carcass; I have civilisations to destroy, cities to level, that kind of thing. The damned make perfectly able minions.' He sketched a bow. 'You don't have to pay them, they don't answer back; perfect.'

'I'm still dead, though.'

'Don't sulk, Breed, I can repair the damage… for a price.'

'Now why doesn't that surprise me?'

'Because I'm a demon?'

'Aye, that'll be it. So, other than a holy relic that belonged to one of the greatest heroes of the Schism War—'

He growled at that, and fire blazed in the empty eye sockets. '—*someone regarded by fools*, as one of the greatest heroes of the Schism War.'

'Alright, alright, whatever you say. Other than his hammer, what else do you want from me?'

'Your immortal soul.'

'Really?'

'No, of course not, stupid.' The fire faded. 'Souls are ten a penny, why would I want yours when there are people eager to give them away? There are a lot of needy, bitter people out there, Breed. No, I want you to kill the priest.'

'If I kill the priest before my term of servitude is up, I'll end up dying a slow, painful death. I'm not seeing anything in this deal for me.'

The demon-corpse's eyes glowed pale blue. The cuff around my wrist became cold and rimed with frost. A hairline crack raced across the polished surface. The glow subsided. Just like that, I felt the bond break.

'There. Do we have a deal?'

'Yes, we have a deal, but I need him to get me into the tomb, that's if he's still alive.'

'He's alive; you may slay him when he's no longer useful.'

'Right you are.'

The corpse tried to frown. 'Just like that? Ah, Breed, your lack of scruples is heartening. If all mortals are as craven, the war will be over before the battle has begun.'

'You might as well send your spew maggots home now then because I'm a paragon of loyalty and compassion compared to most.' I had no intentions of killing the priest, at least not at the moment and certainly not at the behest of the demon. Shallunsard's contempt irked me; and for that reason alone I wanted to thwart his will. Mother was the only person who could treat me like an idiot and get away with it.

'Are you ready?' the demon asked.

I grunted.

'Good, because this *will* hurt.'

The light in the corpse's eyeless sockets flared again. It reached a hand towards me. I wasn't a stranger to pain, but what happened next was a singular experience.

My ribs had been blasted into my heart and lungs. Now every tiny splinter of bone was pulled from the substance of my pulverised organs before knitting back into ribs, right before my eyes. Not only could I see the demon's infernal powers at work but I could feel them—acutely. I felt every torn vein slither through my ravaged flesh, every fibre of my shredded vitals grow anew. When my lungs were whole again, I screamed to the limit of my breath.

When it was over, the corpse demon lowered its arm. The light faded from its eyes. I rolled around on the ground, reliving the agony of being shot for about ten more minutes until it finally stopped hurting. My chest was a mass of scarred pink flesh and orange scales.

'Sweet salvation, did it have to hurt so much? My head feels like it's going to burst.'

'You should thank me, Breed—pain is life; only the dead feel nothing. You're too far from your master; the headache will last until you're reunited.'

'What? But you just... I thought you'd sorted that, I thought the bond was broken.'

'It is... more or less. I have ensured that you won't die and that you can function, but a little pain will—I feel—lend a measure of urgency to the performance of your task.'

'You bastard.'

'Demon.' He grinned and the corpse shambled off, its head lolling on its broken neck.

Now that I could move again I saw that I was on the edge of a neglected cemetery, overgrown with ivy and crooked saplings. It looked like something that had belonged to a much more prosperous settlement than Little Lea. Cracked tombstones and bleached wooden plaques poked through thick clumps of whiptail grass and grey billows of granddame's mantle. Although there were no recent burials that I could see, it was probably still used for suicides, murderers, and the occasional warspawn who happened to die in the village.

The corpse stood a moment on the edge of its own grave, staring into the unmarked pit as though contemplating the eternity it would spend rotting in the ground. It turned to me, looked at me with its sightless eyes. Its mouth opened and closed, it reached out to me, silently pleading as it collapsed into the hole.

It took me a few attempts to stand up and gain full control of my leaden limbs, but once the blood started flowing again, I let my nose lead me back to Little Lea. It wasn't a hard trail to follow; the smell of ozone and burnt meat clung to the trees in clotted webs. I'm not one to dwell, not even on my own death, so I didn't.

When I reached the edge of the wood, I climbed a warty old fir and took a look-see at the town. From what I could see from my vantage, a few people were milling uncertainly outside the village hall around the semi-circle of blackened ground. Another group had gathered outside the guard tower. If they were still alive, that was where Clary and Halla would probably be holed up. I wished them luck, but they'd have to fend for themselves, I had to find Tobias. As much as I never wanted to set foot in the miserable dung pit of a village again, I felt invincible now that I knew Shallunsard was looking out for me. I didn't like the idea *as such*, but as I had far more enemies than friends, I was grateful for what I could get. I was alive, and being alive felt really good now that I had something to compare it to. Emboldened, I headed for the village.

The moment one of the pig-eyed plough-boys set eyes on me, he shrieked, alerting his companions. Before I could say 'risen from the dead' they scattered.

I knocked on the guard tower door. 'Let me in, it's me,' I said. There was no answer. I knocked again, louder. The spyhole opened a crack.

'You're dead! I... I buried you.'

'A bit premature, but it's the thought that counts. Now let me in before the yokels grow some spine and come back.'

I could hear muffled conversation before the bolts were thrown and the door opened. I made sure my shirt was tied to cover my unnaturally healed chest before I went inside. The greenshanks called Jenna and the greybeard had their halberds levelled. Halla and her granddaughter were sitting by the stove. Unsurprisingly, everyone was giving me the fish eye.

'Is this it?' I asked. 'Where's Tosspot and the priest?'

'How the fuck are you standing?' Jenna demanded. 'You were dead, I saw you; there was a hole in your chest the size of my fist.'

I sighed. 'You have small fists and you obviously don't

know anything about warspawn. Thoasa can heal just about anything faster and more efficiently than any other race.'

'Oh, aye? So if I run you through you'll be able to heal that, will ya?' She set her weapon.

'You run me through? That's a bit optimistic, don't you think?'

'That's enough, Jen,' said the greybeard. He looked tired and his hand was heavily bandaged.

They all looked tired and confused except Clary. She was sitting by the fire, swinging her legs and gnawing a chunk of bread.

Tosspot ambled in from the other room clutching a brass-buttoned uniform jacket in his grubby paws. 'Can I borrow this?' He asked the greenshanks. 'Only, yer Captain won't be needing it no more.'

'No, you damn well can't. Put it back!' Greybeard snapped. I snatched the jacket from Tosspot and put it on.

'Oi! Get your own, demo—' Tosspot began.

Short on patience due to the whole being shot to death incident, I had him by the throat before I realised. It would have been so easy to snap his scrawny neck but I let him go. At least his drug and booze-addled brain accepted without pause that I was back from the dead, and the sooner I could move everyone away from that awkward topic the better.

'I need some weapons, preferably swords, and I need to know who and where they took the priest.'

Greybeard squared up to me. 'Now, just you wait a minute. Why should—'

'—because you're outnumbered.' I gave both greenshanks my best killer stare. 'And I'm in a very bad mood.' I hoped they understood how sincere I was about that. As useless as human senses were, they both had the wit to realise that I'd end them if they made a move. They relaxed. The woman put up her weapon. 'Now, what happened after I was k— shot?'

It turned out not a lot had happened after I went down. Greybeard kept the girl, her grandmother, and Tosspot inside the village hall until the ambushers had tied Tobias up, thrown him in the back of a wagon and headed off north. The leader of the crew of four sounded very much like the cove who'd attacked Tobias in Appleton, the one Father Benedict called Marius.

When they'd left, the old greenshanks had quite rightly taken me for dead. It was Halla who'd insisted they bury me—in the unconsecrated graveyard, of course. It was a lucky escape; the old man thought thoasa should be burnt, as was their custom.

The only noteworthy information I could garner from the greenshanks' and Halla's accounts was that the four humans, one of whom had a firelance, had headed north on the main road.

'Are you going after them?' Greybeard asked while I tried the two swords he'd brought me. They were well balanced, standard issue short swords. I sheathed them and buckled on the scabbards. It felt good to be armed again, splitting headache aside.

'Aye.'

'Well, good luck to ye, but I think you're going to need more than a couple of blades to deal with that crew.'

'You volunteering?'

He laughed. 'Holy Eye! If I hadn't promised to take Halla and Clary to Middleton I might do just that. I don't like what Reynard had us do, not one bit, but I'm near retiring, see? I need my pension,' he shrugged.

'Next time then, although there is something you can do, as a thank-you for me not killing you.' I grinned.

He frowned. 'What?'

'Keep Tosspot here until after I've gone. I don't need him following me.'

Greybeard nodded. He looked relieved. 'Oh, alright, I'll do that for ye. Anyway, I'll need him to be a witness when I explain this mess to the area commander. Although I've no idea how I'm going to explain how you came back from the dead…'

'I'd brush over that part if I was you.'

He scratched his chin. 'Aye, maybe you're right. So, what are you, really?' As he was smiling I got the feeling he was more curious than fearful.

I shrugged. No matter what I said he'd make up his own mind. 'Just another breed.'

It was dark when I set off north. I ghosted the road, careful to stay in the trees in case any of the denizens of Little Lea still fancied hanging someone. Because the ambushers were humans, I was counting on them resting up somewhere. They might have even dared an inn this far from real civilisation and without any fear of pursuit. About twenty miles from Little Lea I came across such a place. There weren't any carts outside, just a few journeymen and women inside, huddled around their ale.

I asked the innkeeper if he'd seen my 'friends'. Despite the heavier than normal traffic on the road he remembered them. They'd stopped briefly and much to the innkeeper's surprise had headed east, away from the main road to Valen. He'd been glad to see the back of them on account of their sick companion who'd stayed in the cart. The innkeeper suspected he had the plague, or worse given how secretive they were about him and how they wouldn't let anybody near the cart.

I dropped him a couple of coppers from Tobias's purse for his trouble. I'd taken the money from the priest's gear; I'd hidden the books in the old graveyard, in the same hole as my rescuer—give him something to read if he got bored.

My head was pounding, but after a mug of ale and a bowl of something hot, I felt refreshed and eager to track down my killers. I hoped they were enjoying themselves, I hoped they were squeezing every ounce of amusement and delight from every moment because these were the last few hours they'd be spending this side of hell.

The tree cover and scrub became sparser the further east I went. The ground lay in balding folds that rose into humps and hummocks crowned by fangs of sword thorn bushes. The road dwindled to little more than a scratch in the landscape. My headache was now a rhythmic pulse, a regular thud that kept pace with every step.

I stalked the road, following the faint impression of cart tracks. After a couple of hours, the ground took a sharp, upward sweep. The higher ground had been scoured clean of greenery by rain, harsh sunslight and freezing winter frosts. It hadn't always been a wasteland; I could see the ghostly outlines of terraces glittering in the moonlight and the faint traces of walls scarred the barren landscape. Another mile further on, with the road still climbing, I came across a cart. Nearby, a horse stopped chewing a silvery grey shrub long enough to give me an appraising glance before returning to its meal.

I let the shreds of a lazy headwind roll over my tongue. It had a peculiar taste, a cross between acid and fire. It called to something in my blood, something ancient. My hair spines bristled, the demon mark in my palm itched. I crept over to the cart. It was empty but the priest's soapy smell clung to the boards. Five sets of footprints vanished over the brow of the hill about twenty feet away. The horse hadn't just escaped; its harness had been unbuckled. Whatever they were planning it didn't seem to involve coming back this way.

Mindful that I might be close to my quarry, I crawled up to the crest of the ridge. The ruffled breeze shifted, drenching me in the strange smell. It was hard to decide if it was the denatured air or the sight that greeted me that made me gasp.

I was on the lip of a massive crater, level with the rim, the sightless eyes of a huge stone face gazed through me, out to the west. The face was that of a human woman, carved on a massive spire, the pinnacle of which had snapped. But, and this was the particularly striking part; it hadn't fallen. I blinked, unsure if my eyes were playing me false. But they weren't. The tip of the spire had *started* to fall, to separate along a jagged fissure, but some force held it at an impossible angle. For how long I couldn't guess, but there it was, frozen in the gelid air, surrounded by clouds of stone dust that glittered beneath a sky of serried stars.

When I was able to drag my gaze away, I peered into the depth of the crater. The face was one of four on the pinnacle of a massive pyramidal building that looked like the world had risen around it. The crater was huge and littered with other similar, but smaller structures. What civilisation had flourished here was still dying, caught in the moment of its destruction, probably thanks to the Schism War. The base of the stepped pyramid I was looking at was lost in the shadows of the crater but I guessed it went down at least two hundred feet.

A frosty mist filled the crater, made ghosts of ruins, islands of spires. As I looked more closely I could see shattered columns, porticoes, and statuary hanging in the air around the pyramid and just like the face, they weren't falling. The core of the building was shot through with ragged cracks. Chunks of masonry, some as small as a fist, others as big as a horse, hung at odd angles up to a foot from the main structure, as though locked in the first burst of an explosion. Whatever it had been; palace or temple, every square-cut, staggered tier was carved with human figures that danced, fought, and fucked across the walls. Fantastical beasts, the like of which I'd never seen, anchored every corner of every tier of the wedge-shaped edifice.

Whatever force held the building in thrall didn't seem to extend more than a few feet beyond the main structure but it was still unnerving being so close to something that I was convinced was in the process of exploding, albeit extremely slowly. That it was Schism-touched was beyond doubt, but I hadn't a clue why the ambushers would have brought the priest here.

Five sets of footprints ploughed a trail down the ashen slope. Here and there, cascades of rock marked where one of them had slipped. Down below, I spied a flicker of light that might have been a campfire.

'Demon!' someone behind me shouted.

Tosspot had crept up from downwind and, lucky for him, was beyond the range of my blades. A foot closer and I'd have vented him.

He grinned and coughed a rasping laugh as he squinted at my sword tip. To add to my profound joy on seeing him, I saw that he'd brought a friend. Clary gave a shy wave. Cursing, I bundled them both back down the slope, away from the rim of the crater. 'What the fuck are you doing here?' In truth I was more annoyed that he'd managed to sneak up on me than the fact they were here.

Clary stepped forward. 'We've come to help.'

'You can't. Go away, go home.'

She folded her arms. 'No, we're here to help Father Tobias.'

'I'll kill that fucking greenshanks. You,' I glared at Tosspot. '*Take her home.*' I should have known better than to waste my breath. The insane are immune to threats.

'We're here to help the priest, not you.'

I resisted the urge to slap the filthy little gobsnot. 'Listen, the priest needs your help like he needs a second arsehole. Now, go away.' Clary giggled. Tosspot muttered. Neither of them made any attempt to leave.

'You need us, Breed, you can't handle these coves alone. They've killed you once, already,' said Tosspot.

'Wounded. They wounded me,' I said. They both grinned. 'And they caught me by surprise. I can't for one moment imagine what help you think you'd be against a rough crew like these. Now get lost.'

'We can keep watch,' said Clary.

I was running out of time, a faint band of light was already bleaching the horizon. 'Just stay here, then.' I loomed over Tosspot. 'I swear, if you follow me, I'll beat *you* to death with *her*.' The horse let out a massive fart. 'Fuck's sake, even animals are mocking me now.' They both laughed. If I'd had any reputation left worth keeping, I'd have killed them both and buried them in a shallow grave.

The steep slopes of the crater were knee-deep in soft dead earth. When I reached the bottom I avoided touching the unnaturally tilting slabs of stone that were peeling away from the building. I didn't want to wake them from their slumber and remind them that they were supposed to be collapsing. As I edged round the structure, I stepped over a fallen column and roused a cluster of beetles the size of cats. They took to the air and droned away on darkly iridescent wings.

I quietly drew my blades and waited to see if their flight had drawn any unwanted attention. The heavy blanket of silence fell again, marred only by the occasional gust of wind. I continued to make my way round the ruin until I could see the fire I'd spotted from above. There wasn't anyone by it, just a couple of backpacks. I was about to go over and search them when the wind shifted and I caught the faint whiff of something familiar that I couldn't quite place. I pressed myself against the wall and tasted the air. Amid the several strands of fresh scents, one stood out, but it took me a minute to place it. When I did, I almost laughed. The stuff was so prevalent back home that I almost ignored it. What I could smell was calthracite powder and it was coming from somewhere above and to the right. I ducked back behind the corner, sheathed my blades and started to climb. The instant my hands touched the stonework I knew why there wasn't anything growing down here. As well as being freezing it was also vibrating. The intense, low level thrum made my fingers tingle.

I followed the scent trail until I spotted the source. The gunner was sitting cross-legged, overlooking the campsite. He had his back to the building and a sleek-barrelled firelance resting in the crook of his arm. I climbed up to the next tier and carefully inched along until I was directly above him. His shoulder-length black hair was curled into a mass of glossy ringlets, the height of foppish fashion. He smelled of expensive perfume; musky-sweet and spicy, with just a hint of sweet iron. He was wearing a fine black velvet coat with silver buttons and breeches to match. I dug my feet into the stonework and lowered myself down until I could feel the slight wash of body heat rising off his wiry frame. In one swift movement I grabbed the barrel of his gun and a fistful of his silky tresses and yanked him off his arse.

He let out a high-pitched shriek and reached for the hanger sheathed at his hip. I ripped the firelance from his grasp and bashed his head against the wall before throwing him off the building. I should have been more careful— the last thing I wanted to do was alert the other three—but this foppish bastard was probably the one who'd killed me, and I was still a tad annoyed about that.

The gunner lay groaning, face down in the dirt. When nobody came rushing to his aid I jumped down. The footsteps I'd seen led to what must have been a balcony but was now a ground-level entrance into the building.

The gunner rolled over and opened his entirely black and glittering eyes. 'Urgh... Holy Eye, didn't I kill you?'

I kicked him in the gut, hard. 'Clearly, not enough, though it was a damn good try, I'll grant you.'

He rolled over, groaned some more before pushing himself up onto his elbow. 'I aim to please, if you'll pardon the pun. I pray you, would you allow a fellow to take a pinch; I've come over all queer.'

'What?'

'Snuff, would you mind if I took a pinch of m' snuff?'

'Help yourself,' I said, and checked that the lance was primed and loaded.

The gunner sat up and reached inside his coat. A thread of blood dripped from his nose onto his white silk shirt.

'Finger and thumb, or you lose the arm,' I said. I had every intention of killing him as I felt it only fair to return the compliment, but not before he'd answered a few questions about his crew. He dabbed blood from his face with a lace cuff and, with finger and thumb only, tugged a silver snuff box from his coat pocket. 'Tell me about your friends—who hired you?'

He plucked a pinch, and sniffed. His fingers were long, pale, and slender, and hardly looked strong enough to pull the trigger of the lance, let alone lift the thing. 'That's better,' he said when he'd passed the point at which he might sneeze. 'I believe introductions are in order.' He made to rise, I shook my head. He smiled and remained on his arse. 'Schiller, Sebastian Schiller, at your... mercy, it would seem.'

There was a burr to his voice, not quite a buzz, but his entirely black eyes and the cottony body odour lurking beneath the smell of perfume marked him out as something other than merely human. I wasn't sure what so I kept my distance.

'Breed,' I said.

He gave a thin-lipped smile 'Charmed, I'm sure. As to my comrades, we're honest mercenaries, hired to apprehend the patrician priest. That's all I know. Do you mind if I stand?'

'Lose the sword, same drill.'

He carefully unbuckled his sword belt and let the weapon

drop. 'If it's any consolation I only shot you with a third of a load.'

'Er, no, it's not. Who hired you, what's the job?'

'Cassia got me the job; we've worked together before. *Father* Marius hired her and she found Richter in some dive in Valen. As to why he hired us, who knows? Perhaps they're having theological differences.' He shrugged elegantly. 'I'm just doing what I was paid to do—you really need to ask Marius, but you'll need to be quick.'

'What do you mean?'

'They're off to Valen. There's apparently an apportation device inside.'

'They're apporting? Why the hurry to get back to Valen?'

'Marius said something about a synod meeting. Look, I honestly don't pay much attention to the man—he's a terrible bore. Do you mind if I take off my coat? I feel faint.'

'How come you're not apporting with them?'

He took off his coat, folded it neatly and laid it next to his sword. 'I'm not going back to Valen, I have business elsewhere.'

'Had. I don't take kindly to people shooting me.' As much as I was itching to see how he took to being shot, I didn't want to alert the others and so I drew my sword. The gunner smiled.

'Snuff?' he said and threw the box at me. Although I looked away and held my breath as the cloud of spicy dust enveloped me, the distraction worked. With an impressive display of agility the gunner leapt into the air… and stayed there.

Wings. That explained why he wanted to take his bloody coat off.

As fine as silk, they unfurled as he leapt. I dropped my sword and aimed at him. By this time he was thirty feet up, gossamer wings beating furiously. If I shot him I risked alerting the others, if I didn't, he'd get away, and maybe ambush me again. The feather-boned bastard was laughing. He understood my dilemma.

'Don't worry, my scaly friend, I really do have to be elsewhere. I was only contracted until daybreak. But I will want my firelance back at some point, so make sure to oil it regularly.' He flipped a salute and soared up and out of the crater.

That was my introduction to Sebastian Schiller, also known as the Mosquito.

I watched him along the length of the barrel but I didn't pull the trigger. Even though he might very well come back, I had to go after the priest and sharpish because if what Schiller had said was true and they apported, I was going to have a very bad headache for a very long time.

Schiller's sword was a thing of beauty, a master-crafted weapon sharp as a needle, and absolutely no good to me save as a toothpick. I snapped it in lieu of its owner's neck. After a quick search for more calth powder and zanthe crystals I set off to find the others. By the time I'd tucked a few more loads into my belt the stars were fading into the grey gloom of dawn. I hopped over the balcony, sidestepped an eternally falling stone lintel and entered the building.

Daylight would have been cruel to this age-scraped canvas but night's dying shadows painted grand swags of shade across the walls and lent the room an air of poetic grandeur. As I explored further I discovered that the strange ruin was a labyrinth of dark passageways and rooms, a veritable kingdom of darkness and therefore home to me, a noble of the Midnight Court.

I followed the trail of footprints down a broad flight of stairs and was soon rewarded by the echo of voices winding up out of the darkness. I counted a further ten subterranean levels before I found them. One of the kidnappers, a bald cove who I took to be Richter, decided to make my task a little easier by choosing that moment to relieve himself near the stairwell. The first he knew that he was not alone was the last he knew of anything. I let the body lie where it fell.

The doorway at the end of the corridor was flanked either side by slowly crumbling statues. The chips of stone flaking off the granite warriors were, like the building itself, falling over aeons instead of seconds. My skin tingled, the air was alive with magical energy. I stole a quick look inside, ever mindful that the Mosquito might be behind me, waiting for his chance to strike.

To my great relief the first person I saw was Tobias, and he was alive. He was bound and gagged, sitting on the floor with his back to one of the dozens of the dark glassy menhirs that ringed the room. The fangs of stone were veined with gold; no two were alike. Tobias was glaring at the bastard who'd tried to kill him back in Appleton.

A woman who must have been the one Schiller called Cassia was pushing one of the stones. I saw now that they were bedded into metal grooves set in the floor. Some kind of mechanism allowed them to be slid with relative ease around a series of concentric circles.

'Now move the 4th of the 2nd to the meridian of Canuta,' the bearded fuck ordered the woman. He was pacing and reading from a scroll. 'Ah, no, correction, move the 2nd of the 4th to the meridian of Canuta.'

'Are you sure?' she asked.

'Yes, of course I'm sure.'

'Only you said that last time and…'

'I know what I said last time. Just do what I say now, alright? And where's Richter?'

'He went for a shit.'

'What, now? I need him in here.'

'He's got a bad stomach.'

'Just hurry up and move that and then get him in here. Or we're going without him.'

Tobias shook his head; he seemed to be laughing behind the gag, something that did not go unnoticed. It earned him a hard slap across the head from the man.

'I'm glad you think this is funny, brother. I wonder if you'll be laughing when father sees you. Cassia, go find Richter, the circle is almost complete.'

The woman shot Marius a filthy look before leaving the room. 'Move the keystones, Cassia; find Richter, Cassia; shove a broom up your arse and sweep the floor, Cassia…'

She was still grumbling when I hit her in the face with the butt of the firelance. There was an audible crack; her head snapped back and her nose exploded in a burst of crimson. I caught her before she fell and dumped her beside Richter.

I checked that the zanthe crystal was secure in the firing

claw and, just to be on the safe side, poured another charge of calth down the barrel.

'Cassia! Cassia? Where the fuck… There's one more stone to align. Cass—'

Marius didn't finish his sentence, probably because I stuck the barrel of the firelance in his face the second he stepped into the corridor. I backed him into the room and prepared to spray his brains all over the stones. I waved at Tobias and curled my finger around the trigger.

The priest yelled through the gag and vehemently shook his head. I lowered the gun. Marius opened his mouth. Just in case he was a sorcerer I cracked him on the side of the head with the butt of the firelance. He went down but was still conscious and yelling so I hit him again. This time he just lay there, nice and quiet. Tobias frowned and although I couldn't make out exactly what he was saying, he was quite definitely unhappy about something, despite having been rescued. There was just no pleasing some people.

'What?' I said to Tobias, knowing full well he couldn't answer. 'I didn't want him to do to me what you did to those villagers, now did I?' I went over to where he was sitting in the innermost ring of stones. The air was different here. It stank of blood and steel and felt like a storm was about to break. I untied the priest. He had a black eye but seemed no worse for his ordeal. Now that I'd found him, my headache vanished.

He scowled at me. 'Marius said they'd killed you.' He got up and went over to Marius.

'You're welcome. No, please, don't mention it. Oh, you didn't.'

'He said they shot and killed you, and yet here you are, like nothing happened.' He rolled Marius over. The side of his face was swollen but he was alive and moaning, more's the pity.

'They lied to you. So, why are they after you, priest?' I said in a bid to change the subject.

'Nothing, just a misunderstanding. Who the hell are you, Breed?'

We stood there for a long time, weighing the lies we were

telling each other against the truths we were keeping to ourselves.

'I met the gunner, Schiller. He said he used a light load so that he didn't catch you in the blast and so that he could get extra range. He shot me alright, just not enough,' I tried very hard to blot all thought of the restless dead from my mind. Satisfied my story was convincing, I leaned on the firelance and waited for him to cough.

'Marius is a priest of the Order of the Sanguine Shadow and a fellow member of the Synod. Our respective orders had a theological dispute.'

I waited some more.

The priest flipped Marius onto his front and bound his hands and, with a deal of relish, gagged the semi-conscious man. 'There's a prophecy that says the demons will return. This much was accepted by all, and indeed seems to be happening as predicted. Some factions within the Synod are using the prophecy to push for all non-humans to be removed from the Empire. It's a populist tactic, designed to win votes.'

I shrugged. 'It's not the first time. The 'Send Them to Shen' campaign reached Appleton. Bunch of cracked pots, nobody paid them any heed.'

'This is worse, much worse.

'Tell me later; we better get going. I don't know if Schiller's still hanging around.' I made to leave but Tobias grabbed my arm.

'No, we're going back through the angle gate.' He gestured to the stones. I didn't see any gate, just four concentric rings of six-foot-tall slices of stone set in steel and marked by symbols.

'Ah, yes, this is the apportation device,' I said as though I knew what I was talking about.

'Oh, you're familiar with the concept? The magic is pre-Schism. Saint Bartholomew understood the…'

'I'm sure he did. But do you have to use it? I've heard Schism magic isn't safe.'

'I do, yes. I need to get back and deal with the trouble Marius and his faction are trying to foment. There's no time to waste.'

'How many can go through?' I asked, hoping the answer was two.

'As many as can fit within the inner ring, a dozen or so. Why?'

'Just wait here, I've got to go pick a few things up.'

An hour later, just as the suns were rising, I returned with Tosspot and Clary.

'What are they doing here?' Tobias asked. Marius and the woman were conscious, bound and gagged and propped against the wall by the door. They glared venomously at me. I smiled.

'Because some aching-heart holy man thought he could make the world a better place by adopting any waif and stray that crossed his path, without any thought to what might happen to them in the future. Do you want me to turn them loose? I can dump 'em back on the highway for the wolves, if you like.'

Tosspot reached out to touch one of the stones, Clary slapped his hand away. 'We had to hide from the Dandyman,' she said in that matter-of-fact way children speak. 'He killed the horse and sucked its blood, but I'm good at hiding, aren't I, Rubin?'

'Yes, Clary, very good,' said Tosspot.

Tobias looked like he'd just received a blessing from the angel of guilt. 'We can't leave them. I just have to make sure I get the angles right with this thing.'

I'd already decided they were coming with us, but I let him think the decision was his. 'As you wish. So, where will this thing take us? Only, I'd rather not appear in the middle of Valen's high street.'

Tobias grinned. 'Don't worry, Breed that won't happen.'

Chapter Nine

I've never been able to apport. Mother is a master of that particular sorcerous art, but all I can do is boil water, make light, and deepen shadows. It's the thoasa in me; warspawn can't use magic. That I can cast any spells at all is an aberration, and testament to what excellent tuition and sound, regular beatings can achieve.

This was something different to what Mother did. This was an apportation *device*; a sorcerous machine from the time of the Schism. Looking at the gleaming slices of calthracite crystal it was hard to imagine a world where these things were common and my sire's ancestors didn't exist. For all that their palaces were grand, their civilisation mighty, and their magic powerful; it must have been a dull world with only humans around, which might explain why some of them started worshipping demons.

There was no sign of Schiller, but I kept a weather eye out for him just in case and set Tosspot to keep watch over Marius and Cassia. We'd had to truss them up because, apparently, it would be barbaric to slit their throats. Tobias set to work adjusting the stones, taking copious notes, and doing a lot of muttering and head-scratching. Clary seemed happy to sit and watch what was going on.

'Is it nearly ready?' I asked. I was bored and more than a little disturbed by being in a building that was collapsing around us really slowly. Dust particles caught by our turbulence drifted across the room like ribbons of smoke. 'I said, is it—'

The priest hurled his notebook across the room.

'I'll take that as a no then.'

'I just… if I've miscalculated I could send us miles, even continents, off course, or worse; send us somewhere that no longer exists.'

'Don't worry; you're good at all these… angle things. It'll be fine.' I said, quite certain he was worrying unnecessarily. Right then I was feeling supremely confident of my ability to survive anything having escaped death's mean grasp once. I was also eager to be in Valen and one step closer to the Hammer of the North's tomb.

'That's easy for you to say, but if I get an equation wrong…'

'Your head will explode. Yes, I know all about the paradox of power, or whatever you've decided to call it. You'll be fine.'

He stopped what he was doing, the look on his face hardened. 'Marius and the others were adamant that they'd killed you. How did you survive, Breed?'

I sighed. 'Not this again.'

'How?'

'Why does it matter, *sorcerer*? Just be glad that I did.'

Marius and the mercenary exchanged knowing looks.

'Don't you understand? They don't want to hurt *me*, Breed. It's you and your kind they want to destroy.'

'Yes, I got that when they shot me, but—and correct me if I'm wrong—didn't he have a knife to your throat the first time I saw you? This cove just has a taste for killing.'

'Marius and his faction want to be rid of people like you and Clary—all warspawn, all Schism-touched. The demons' return was prophesied and he and his cronies are seeking to make capital from it.'

'That's ridiculous,' I laughed half-heartedly.

'Which part, Breed? Do you dispute that demonic forces are at work? Is that even possible after what you've seen?' He folded his arms, gave me a measured look.

The urge to slap him was once again upon me. Given his abilities, I refrained. 'Yes, I do, I think it's a steaming pile of urux shit.'

'I have proof that it isn't,' he said, and cast a triumphant glance at Marius, who was shouting through his gag and kicking his heels like an angry child. The mercenary elbowed him in the ribs.

'Go on,' I said, dreading what Tobias was going to say. My palm itched.

'The prophecy,' he said.

I breathed a quiet sigh of relief.

'The one I found while researching the life of Saint Bartholomew.'

'You need to get out more.'

He poked me in the chest with his stump. 'This is serious, Breed. You know what you saw in Appleton. It *is* happening; the demons have returned.'

'A few big maggots don't prove anything.'

'The prophecy I found was written by the Red Witch herself.'

I pretended to stifle a yawn.

He gave me a look laced with venom. 'It speaks of a time when the demons will return and...' He paused, looked pointedly at me. '... it infers that the warspawn will aid them.'

'Might I remind you of my earlier comment with regards to urux shit? Warspawn were made to fight *against* demons, not *with* them.' I ignored the nagging little voice that suggested my association with Shallunsard could be construed as aiding demons. That the Red Witch might have scried my malefaction, might have seen *me*, sent a shiver down my spine.

'Indeed they were, but the wording of the prophecy is ambiguous and has been used by some within the Synod to make political capital.'

'By 'some' you mean this cocksnot?' I pointed the lance at Marius, who tried to hide behind a disgruntled-looking mercenary.

'Lower the weapon, Breed,' said Tobias. 'Marius is a greedy halfwit, but the blame for this mess lies with me.' He scratched his close-cropped pate. 'At first, I only discovered part of the prophecy. I shouldn't have told the Synod anything until I'd found the whole of it. I should have known it would be used for base, political gain.' He sighed and tucked his stump into his sleeve. 'I was just so excited; so few texts survive from the time of the Schism and it was written and signed by the Red Witch.'

'I understand, I do.' I tried not too sound too pleased that he'd failed to connect me with the infernal disaster that had befallen Appleton. 'Why, only last month a colleague and I were lamenting the lack of good books.' The conversation I'd had with Wulf had gone more along the lines of what was better to wipe one's arse upon. We decided that thin-leafed books of poetic whimsy and fanciful tales were much nicer than dry old texts, but weighty tomes stuffed with history, philosophy and other fantasies were much more absorbent, it seemed that a lot of old shit soaked up a lot of shit.

'I have been terribly naïve, to the detriment of all,' said Tobias. Marius sniggered. 'If you don't shut up, I'll let Breed shoot you,' said the priest.

'Come, Breed, walk with me.'

It rankled that I had to pretend that I was still bound to the soapy cull, but I had to tickle this fish carefully. I still needed him, *and* he could turn me to cinders without breaking a sweat, so I followed him from the chamber.

'I knew the manuscript was incomplete, but the Synod immediately debated what I'd found, as though that was the whole of it, despite my protestations.'

'Well, that's all very unfortunate, but why are you telling me? Why aren't you back in Valen arguing with the Synod or, you know, turning them into a smoking pile of charcoal?'

He scowled. 'I'm going to pretend you didn't say that. I couldn't go back until I'd found the missing part and I did, in our chapter house in Appleton, just before I met you. I sent word back to Valen to try to halt the Synod vote until I got back. That was my second mistake.' He leaned against the wall, his gaze drifting to the cooling carcass of Richter. 'Seems everything I do turns sour. Maybe father's right, maybe I am cursed.'

'Sorry?'

'Never mind. Suffice it to say, I told someone I thought I could trust and he told his son.'

'What does the second part say?'

'That we will be *saved* by a warspawn.'

'Well, that's wonderful. You should go back and tell the arch mumblers in the Synod.'

'I'll most likely be arrested before I get to the Synod. I was accused of theft of the original document, a total fabrication.'

'You're a Vulsones; who'd dare swear falsely against you? Who'd dare swear against you at all, come to that?'

'My father.'

'Why would… ? Ah. He's the one you told, the one who betrayed you.'

'Aye, to Marius and his faction.'

'Marius isn't just a 'brother'; he's your real brother.'

'Yes.'

I had to laugh. These so-called nobles were no better than us sewer-dwellers when it came down to it. They just smelled sweeter. 'Do you want me to kill him? I'm an only child and it's never done me any harm.'

'No, absolutely not. I forbid it.'

'He was fixing to kill you back in Appleton, or have you forgotten?'

'No, he wasn't, he was just threatening me. He wanted the part of the prophecy that I'd tracked down to our monastery in Appleton.'

'Did he get it?'

'No.'

'Well, that's a relief.'

'I sent it to our father for safe keeping before my brother arrived.'

'Oh. Back to the urux shit.'

'Quite. Father sent Marius to keep me out of the way until after the Synod votes.'

'Why not sit on you out here?'

'Because Marius wanted to get back for the Synod meeting. The leader of his order, the Sanguine Shadow, is going to stand for Eklesiasti. If she wins, she'll make sure that warspawn are banished from the Empire.'

'Oh.'

'Is that all you have to say?'

I shrugged. 'Oh, shit?'

It took another hour of scribbling, handwringing and pushing stones back and forth before myself, Clary and Tosspot were invited to join Tobias on the central platform within the rings of stones.

'Remember, Breed; just shoot the stone. Do not shoot my brother.'

After a long and tiresome debate, the priest had agreed that I could shoot one of the stones to stop Marius following us when he eventually got free. I played along to keep him sweet. Death and the demon had freed me from servitude to the priest, and now I needed the priest's help to free me from the demon.

'You two sure you want to come?' I asked. I wasn't overly bothered what they decided. They'd do alright there. A big city like Valen had rich enough pickings to keep a couple of coves like those two alive. Clary nodded.

'Got to see the city, demon, got to see the city one last time,' said Tosspot. He looked in worse shape than the restless dead Shallunsard had possessed. His skin was sallow and drawn tight as rawhide over the fleshless planes of his face. I wasn't surprised he was keen to go to Valen, it had been days since he'd had any pel or drink.

'Is everyone ready?' the priest asked. I nodded. He gave me one of his sad-and-disappointed smiles and raised his hands. 'Remember what I said, Breed.'

'Trust me,' I said, and pretended to aim at one of the stones. As soon as the priest turned his attention to casting the spell, I aimed up on Marius.

Luckily for him, the shock of apportation caused me to miss. It felt like I was being dragged backwards into the teeth of a calthracite grinder. Through the ghostly sandstorm of a disintegrating world, I saw the flash blaze from the muzzle and a million, shining points of light erupt in another place and time. The light seemed to twist and stretch before finally falling into the ice-rimed well of eternity.

By the time the roaring echo of the shot died, we were somewhere else. The scintillating air turned black and jarringly solid. For a moment it felt like I'd just stepped into my skin and it didn't quite fit. I decided that apportation by device was the most unpleasant thing I'd experienced other than being killed.

I was about to step forward when I sensed something in front of me, something inanimate. I tucked the lance under my arm and cast a light spell. The pale globe grew into a ball of diffuse light which revealed a jumble of stones that had partially fallen and jammed against each other to form a low roof of jagged angles. This room, unlike the one we'd just left, had not been warped by Schism magic and had fallen wholly into time's withering grasp. The rings of stones had survived but crumbling masonry crowded around them like a pack of hungry dogs. It was pure luck that we hadn't apported into rubble. I took a breath, tasted fresh air.

'Dark in here, innit?' Tosspot giggled.

Tobias leaned heavily on one of the stones.

'Sit before you fall.' I said.

Tobias sat. 'Where did the light come from?'

'Me. I think I see a way out.' I ducked past the jutting blocks and set off towards a paler patch of darkness that I could see in the distance. 'Stay here, and keep quiet while I take a look.'

The taste of fresh air grew stronger; the kiss of a breeze brushed my skin and stirred cobwebs that draped the shadowed exit. Cracked and at a rakish angle, a carved bloodstone door lintel still held, but the rich veins of scarlet had bled from the stone and streaked the canted uprights with rusty tears. I loaded the firelance. Priming the pan and ramming a charge home was easy, though it took a few attempts to lock the zanthe crystal into the tiny claw. The weapon wasn't designed with hands like mine in mind.

A locked iron grille sliced daylight into rust-framed rectangles. We weren't in a city; we were in a cemetery and an old one at that. I smashed the lock off with the butt of the firelance and took a look-see outside. The cemetery had been built on a steep-sided valley. Ancient tombs jostled for space and climbed in tiers one upon another. Some had been destroyed, robbed of bloodstone and gold-veined marble; others were rigged with frayed ropes and rotting blocks, ready for dismantling. A cart had been so overloaded with lintels that the axle had cracked and it had been abandoned and left to rot.

It was a typical human cemetery. Mausoleums thrust spires to the sky, oversized porticos sheltered flattering statues of the wealthy dead. Warspawn don't go in for this kind of thing. Seems we weren't bred to think over much about how we'd look or what people would think of us when we were dead, which is handy as most warspawn in the Empire are shit-poor.

The ghostly outline of a disused road snaked out of the valley, not a hoof or footprint marred its rain skinned surface. The spires of the necropolis walled the world from view but I guessed we must have been near a big city, given the size of this place and the smell of sewage and wood smoke carried on the breeze that swooped down the valley.

'The cemetery was built on the site of old Valen, part of it anyway,' said Tobias when he got his wind back. 'I thought we'd come out near the Halls of State, but of course they weren't built until after the War.'

'How far is it to the new city?' I asked.

He half smiled. 'That sounds so odd. Er, a little under an hour on foot, I'd say. I must confess, I've never walked here.' The priest leaned against a wall, as pale as pastry that had been rolled too thin.

'The suns are setting. We should stay here the night,' I suggested. 'Decide what we'll do on the morrow.'

'Yes, good idea,' said Tobias as he slowly slid down the wall. 'In the old days they had six dedicated technicians to control translocation.' He smiled. 'I can see why. That quite took it out of me.'

I sent Clary and Tosspot to collect wood while I found us a nice tomb to camp in. The one I chose was old and grand. More importantly its bronze door still hung from one hinge, with enough of a gap for us to get inside. According to the name engraved above the door the occupant was one Amari Geran. His massive bloodstone sarcophagus had a neat hole cut in the side. I had a look; his coffin had been smashed open and his earthly remains plundered for what gold and gems his family had decided to donate to the grave-robbers. The bronze door intended to protect his resting place was far too heavy to steal but someone had given it a damn good go.

I half carried, half dragged the priest inside and propped him against Amari's sarcophagus.

'So, Breed, tell me about the demon,' he asked when he came round.

'Which one would that be? I've known a few in my time.'

'I think you know,' he smiled. 'Listen, Breed, there comes a time in everyone's life when they have to make a choice. For some few, the choice they make can affect hundreds, sometimes thousands of people.'

I picked dirt from under my claws with one of the greenshanks' blades. '*They* might not give a shit, have you considered that? *They* might think, 'Fuck everyone else, as they have fucked me over the years.' They might be so used to being shat on that they cannot ever imagine a circumstance where they would give a flock of flying-monkey arseholes about anyone, other than perhaps a tiny handful of people, and then, not enough to stir their conscience above not actually stabbing those rare few to death for a piece of bread.'

'I can only imagine the life you've had and how difficult it's been.' He propped himself up on his elbow. His breath smelled of peaches. 'Listen to me, Breed; you have a choice. I've read the prophecy, I've seen the mark on your hand.'

'What mark, what are you talking abou—'

He lowered his voice, drew close. 'That night in Appleton, when you saved me, that's when I saw it. I knew then that you and I were meant to meet. It took me a while to find the right official to bribe, but eventually I had you released into my care.'

I had to laugh. '*Released into your care?* Funny, I thought you had me bound to you as a slave.'

'The bond works both ways.'

'No, it doesn't.'

'Well, alright, it doesn't, not quite, but it was the only way I could get you out. I had to pay a lot of money; there were other interested parties who wanted you to go to the mines and die there.'

'Well, I've quite literally died for you since then, so I think that more than makes up for your misguided attempt to 'help' me. And for your information, I wouldn't have spent above a month in the mines.'

The priest coughed, leaned back against the sarcophagus. 'No, probably not. Not with the bounty on your head—don't worry, I paid that too.'

This was the first I'd heard of a bounty, although I should have guessed. 'How much was it?' I had to know, my professional pride was at stake.

'Five hundred crowns, plus one hundred for the inconvenience and hurt caused.'

I laughed; five hundred was a good price, that wouldn't do my reputation any harm at all. '"Inconvenience and hurt." Pork Chop has a sense of humour, I'll give him that.'

'It wasn't Jing, it was someone called Mother Blake? She's the head of another den of thieving murderers. I dread to think what you must have done to gain her enmity, but it's not too late to change, Breed.'

Right at that moment I found a whorl of sandy grit on the floor to be the most interesting thing in the world. I ignored the priest's prattle in favour of studying how the tiny peak curved with the sharp precision of a knife blade, forged by no other force than the breeze that sneaked inside the tomb. It was quite remarkable.

'Five hundred's a good price,' I said, and meant it. 'I know a fistful of coves who'd do me for free.'

'Tell me about the demon,' said Tobias.

After his latest revelation I was more than happy to tell him about the demon, anything to change the subject. 'It's called Shallunsard, it tricked me into freeing it, and for my trouble I got a mark in my palm to dog me the rest of my days. That's it; the simple, embarrassing truth of it. There, are you happy now?' I knew my patter was sweet; I could lie like a whore when I needed to.

The priest thought about it before nodding slowly. He looked disappointed. We sat in silence, listening to the wind sigh until he eventually broke the silence. 'Let me tell you about the prophecy.'

'Actually, it's six hundred, which is a *really* good price. She must really give a damn to put that much up.' The more I thought about what Mother had done the less bad it seemed. 'Sorry, yes, the prophecy. Please, tell me a story.'

'You can be very irritating sometimes.'

'It's been mentioned. Do go on.'

'The manuscript I discovered spoke of a time when the demons and their infernal minions will return. I believe this is happening now. Some of my colleagues in the Synod have interpreted the wording of the Red Witch's prophecy to mean that warspawn are among the ranks of the infernal. Particularly one paragraph that says warspawn will aid the demons. I think it refers to one warspawn, not all warspawn.'

He paused as though waiting for me to confirm what we were both thinking. I didn't, I kept my mouth shut.

He shook his head. 'I think that part refers to you.'

'Now wait a minute, I didn't plan on freeing the demon. It tricked me.'

'I believe you,' he said which surprised me. 'Gods help me, but with regard to this, I believe you.' He waved his stump at me. 'Do not think I extend that faith to everything that falls out of your mouth.'

I laughed. 'Fair enough. Now, supposing Shallunsard and his cronies *are* planning on laying waste to civilisation again. Surely having warspawn fighting for the humans makes more sense than kicking them out of the Empire.'

'Those who own calthracite mines disagree, for obvious reasons. People like my father. He's backing the imbecilic racial purists out of greed. It's sickening, and he is not alone.'

'Well, nothing we can do then, is there?' I was still thinking about the bounty Mother had put on my head, trying to angle the cold deed in a light that showed she cared about me, in her own twisted way. It wasn't easy. As for the prophecy stuff Tobias was talking about, I gave not one shit for what a bunch of robe wearing, knife-tongued coves in the Synod were plotting. I wanted nothing to do with the schemes of princes.

'Is that all you have to say?' He looked shocked.

'What do you want me to say? I'm not the official representative of all warspawn, you know. I speak for one, me. So it'll go badly for the warspawn, nothing new in that is there? Some will live, some will die, life will go on.'

'I don't understand you, Breed.'

'That much is obvious.'

'Listen,' He leaned close. 'The second part of the prophecy—the part I found in Appleton—said that a warspawn will lead the fight *against* the infernal forces... one who is cursed by demons and blessed by gods.' He looked at me expectantly.

'I'm only half what you're after. Sorry, priest, but I've not been blessed by any gods.'

He shook his head. 'I prayed, Breed. I sought the guidance of Saint Bartholomew. When I was in Appleton I prayed for a sign, and you came.'

Now I felt sorry for him. 'It's just coincidence. I'm not who you're looking for.'

'It also says that 'Only the one who has been blessed and cursed shall wield the hammer of the North'. We can find out if you're the one and at the same time silence the malcontents in the Synod.'

I was instantly converted. 'Sorry... the who can do what with the what?'

'According to the parchment I found in our library in Appleton, only one blessed by the gods can wield the hammer. You must have heard of the Hammer of the North?'

'Of course I have, I don't live under a rock.'

'Good. Now listen. I have a plan, it's very simple, but if it works, it will prove that the prophecy is genuine and not even my father would dare gainsay the gods. We can stop this travesty before it goes any further.'

'Let me guess; we find the hammer, I wield it and we show the Synod, thus verifying the prophecy?'

'I told you it was simple.'

'What's in it for me?'

'You get to be a hero, demon!' Tosspot cackled as he crawled through the gap under the door.

'Aren't you dead yet?' I snarled.

'Ha! No. Not yet.' Tosspot's red-rimmed eyes shone like

beetle backs in the narrow slice of sunlight. 'Got to see the city one more time, see the Hall o' Heroes.'

Dawn of the next day the priest went alone to the city to make contact with his order. I climbed one of the tombs to keep watch on the road and wait for his return. Tosspot and Clary busied themselves hunting rock rats for the pot. Nailed above the rusting cemetery gates was a makeshift sign promising harsh penalties for anyone other than those entering with rightful business. The sign was as ancient as the bones that lay scattered about, scavenged by dogs and rats from the plundered tombs of the ancient great and good.

It occurred to me that I spent a lot of time in cemeteries these days. I wasn't sure if it was a step up or down from sewers. What *was* a step up was owning a firelance. Tobias 'I-don't-like-weapons-but-I'll-turn-you-to-ashes-if-you-displease-me' Vulsones, hadn't anything about it, save to offer a few disapproving grunts.

From my vantage point, crouched between the turrets of one of the larger mausoleums, I could see the walls of Valen to the east. Slick and shining grey against an iron sky, they were imposing even from a distance. A highway skirted the cemetery, but further west I could see the faint outlines of other, long-abandoned roads leading from nowhere to nowhere, stretching across the scrubby fields that were studded with the rubble of old Valen.

It started to rain again, but I was as mindful as a tyrant's wet-nurse about the care of the firelance and made sure to keep the barrel and the pan covered with an oiled cloth Schiller had thoughtfully left with his gear. Until recently, I'd thought there was some skill in using one of these beasts, but truth was, any fool could do it, as I had so ably proved. An army equipped with firelances would be devastating. And whoever supplied the calth powder and zanthe crystals to that army would be rich indeed. All you needed was a nice, bloody war, and now, thanks to me, that looked likely.

I also realised that, as villains went, Mother was an amateur compared to the powerbrokers in the Synod and the Senate. I looked to the south where storm clouds were gathered and thought of Shallunsard. I was sure that I could hear the distant growl of thunder or perhaps it was the sound of an army of demonspawn baying for blood and vengeance.

It was late in the afternoon when Tobias wandered into view. He was leading a jakanta. Like urux, the scaly beasts of burden were slow and dependable but about half the size, and far more tractable. The beast plodded on, saddlebags bouncing. I sighted him down the barrel, just for practice and waited until I was sure he hadn't been followed before roof-hopping back to our temporary home. We were not alone in the ruins; wild dogs, human flotsam, and plump rock rats eyed us suspiciously from the shadows but wisely kept their distance.

'Ah, Breed there you are,' said Tobias when I got back. He tossed me a brown robe much like the one he was wearing and those that Tosspot and Clary were examining.

The two of them were laughing at the garments. They'd formed an inexplicable friendship in the short time they'd known each other, Tosspot entertained Clary by making up nonsense songs and she made sure he ate and drank. So long as it kept them out of my spines, I didn't care what they got up to.

'It might be a little tight across the shoulders but it should be long enough,' the priest said to me as I eyed the garment.

'You've seen your people then?' I said, and put the robe on. It didn't quite cover my feet. 'Do you have any thoasa acolytes? Only my feet are a dead giveaway that I'm not human.'

'And they stink,' Tosspot added. Clary laughed.

'You could wear a necklace of urux arseholes and not smell any worse for it, you old turd-mangler.' I said. All three of them sniggered. 'I'm glad I amuse you all. So what's your plan, priest?'

'We take Clary and Rubin to the mission house and I'll speak with the order, after which I imagine you and I will be able to go to the Hall of Heroes and the tomb of the Hammer.'

'That's it? They're just going to let us in, let us open the tomb, nick his hammer, and walk out again? If you don't mind me saying, it sounds a little optimistic.'

'Why wouldn't they let us in? The hall is open to all citizens of the Empire,' he grinned.

'What, that really is your plan? I was joking. It won't work.'

'Have a little faith, Breed.'

'Fuck faith. No amount of praying ever sprung a lock.'

'Just trust me, the matter is in hand but first things first; we need to get into the city.' He scowled, stepped back, and rubbed his chin with his stump.

'What is it?' I inspected myself, keen to discover why he looked like he was trying to shit a porcupine. What's wrong? Is it the colour? Doesn't brown go with orange? What is it?'

'Although I'm sure there aren't any restrictions, I've never met any warspawn in the order and, well, you're right, your feet *are* very distinctive. Your hair we can hide beneath the cowl, your hands are human enough to pass in gloves, but your feet… can you wear shoes?'

'Aye, if someone made me a pair.'

The priest sighed. 'We need to think of something else.'

And so it came to pass that the three of them travelled to the city dressed as members of the Order of Saint Bartholomew and I got to lead the jakanta, dressed in my own worn breeches and shirt, silver cuff on display to show that I was bond servant to a parcel of fools. My beautiful firelance, swords and stolen jacket were strapped to the jak, wrapped in the robe that didn't fit me.

'It smells bad,' said Clary as we approached the towering gates of Valen. They were flanked by two carved reliefs of gods with the bodies of lions and eagle wings fifty feet wide, spread across the implacable walls.

The gods, one male, one female, gazed at each other across the copper-clad gates that outshone the suns when the clouds fleetingly parted. Towers as big as castles anchored the hundred-foot-high walls which were patrolled by entire companies of spear-wielding knights. Before we reached the gates we passed through a tented encampment that must have been as big as Appleton. Clary was right, it smelled, but no worse than any city on a summer's day. As a born thief, I knew that where there was shit, there was gold, and by the smell of it there was a lot of wealth in Valen. The gates were slowly pulled open by two teams of four urux. The All Seeing Eye etched into the gates gazed down on us and a hundred other travellers queuing up to enter.

I wasn't convinced that the main gate was the best way to enter the city, given that the priest's enemies were looking for him, but he assured me it was safer than trying to sneak in through the sewers or over the walls that he said were heavily guarded and warded by sorcery. Once we got through the outer gates, we were funnelled along a walled road that was also heavily patrolled. At the end of the road there was a second set of gates, plainly decorated, but equally sturdy, and two ramps leading into a city the like of which I'd never seen.

One ramp rose fifty feet above the ground and widened into squares and avenues. It was supported by massive towers and arching columns that stretched above and below the walkways. The other ramp sloped gently down into the shady, stone and steel underground of the city. Iron grilles spanned the spaces between the higher roads and frilled the edges of the raised plazas. The grilles allowed light and air to filter down and no doubt stopped careless citizens and heavy debris falling into the busy undercity. It was the most incredible thing I'd ever seen. Sure, it lacked the beauty of pre-Schism architecture, but the ingenuity and scale was impressive.

When Tobias and the others shuffled past the guard at the ramps the priest offered a benediction. She nodded, indifferent, but polite, until she saw me. As I passed, she eyeballed the cuff. Her expression hardened but she waved me through after the others.

'Durstan the Third was afraid that if his feet ever touched the ground he'd turn to stone, so he had those areas of the city he frequented raised up,' said the priest, anticipating my question.

It struck me as odd how madness and power seemed to go hand in hand in all levels of society. 'Makes you wonder how there ever came to be a Durstan the Fourth.'

'He killed his father,' said Tobias.

'Now why doesn't that surprise me? I take it the poor folk live down below?'

Tobias gave me a *look*. 'No, we kill all the poor folk and use their bodies for fuel.'

'I hear patricians burn better, all that fat.'

He laughed. 'Some of the less well-off live down there, aye, but it's also where the markets are. We have to stable the jak here; they're not allowed on the high ways.'

'What about our gear?' I asked.

Tobias smiled and took the jakanta to a stable that was just beside the gate, where he exchanged it for a token. I then became the pack animal, like a dozen other poor culls waiting by the gate, only they were getting paid for their labour. When I was loaded with our belongings we took the high ramp into the city. As we walked I looked down through the grille to see a whole other city stretched out beneath us. The stink rising up from the depths was intense, not just of filth but animals, spices, and smoke from a hundred ovens. My nose started to run, beset as it was by so many new smells.

The highways linked open plazas and elegant courtyards and were thronged with culls and coves of every stripe. The only animals that were allowed were defanged uxatzi. The docile giants made slow progress around the city, pulling huge covered wagons. Due to a lack of animal traffic and what I took to be signs for public latrines, the streets were amazingly clean. There were even culls with carts whose sole purpose seemed to be shovelling up the uxatzi dung and trundling it away. When a wagon slowly rolled past us, I could hear music and laughter coming from inside. Sweet-smelling smoke curled from a copper chimney poking through the wagon's rear wall. The six-legged uxatzi pulling it was brightly painted; its capped horns were garlanded with silk and hung with silver bells.

'What the hell are they?' I asked as we followed the beast into a massive plaza studded with squat towers.

'They're stair towers. They're for access as well as support.'

No, I mean the wagons. What's in them?'

He smiled, clearly amused by my ignorance. 'Taverns, chai houses, gambling dens, and brothels that cater to every taste. It's best to avoid those with black silk tied to the uxatzi's horns, unless you like pain.'

I laughed. 'Pain's more an occupational hazard than a pleasure.'

I'd just about stopped sneezing by the time we were halfway across the plaza as my nose became more used to the host of new and exciting odours. The eastern section of the city was dominated by the palace of the Empirifex rising above Valen like a stepped and gilded mountain. Tame dagori glided in lazy circles around the highest levels of the palace, their gossamer wings shimmering crimson and azure, their ululating song ringing out across the city.

Tobias led us north; as we travelled further, I realised the city wasn't just on two levels but here and there the ramps dipped into wide basins and open marketplaces, and where the city feathered out at the edges, neat streets of modest dwellings brushed up against the city walls.

Upper and lower city came together in split-level markets and gardens. Tall, skinny trees speared out of brick-walled valleys, eager to reach sunslight. Their upward sweeping limbs were hung with lanterns and signs proclaiming the type of goods and their prices being sold below. From what I could tell, the different markets specialised in one type of merchandise, from silks to spices, meat to livestock. One of the ramps we took dipped into a flower market where vendors sold their wares from houses on stilts that lined the road. Polished mirrors reflected light onto terraced gardens crammed with potted plants and small, shallow pools.

I was drunk on the smells, blinded by the profusion of colours and shapes of what seemed like every flower that had ever bloomed. Intoxicated, I floated along on an ocean of perfumes too numerous to unpick one from another.

It seemed that all of life existed in Valen; every shade of cull and cove strutted like kings and queens, knowing they lived in the greatest city in the world. I felt like a shadow, lost amid the sheer bullish exuberance. I was convinced the dips must swank about with gilded fingers from the sheer bump and crush of wealth brisking along the ramps and streets awash with the riches of the Empire.

A hobbling cove scurried along beneath the gaze of ordinary citizens. She tipped me a nod and made the sign of downturned horns with the fingers of her right hand. I hid the same gesture in a casual brush of road dust from my leg, also using my right hand, thus ensuring it was a friendly gesture both ways. There was no crime in a cove passing through another gang's manor; the crime was working it without permission or without giving the local chief their due. I had bigger fish to fry than dipping silks and, to be honest, I was a little irked that I'd been taken for a common bung-nipper. I'd mastered the art of picking pockets and moved up the slippery pole of criminality almost before I was weaned.

It was suns' set when the priest led us down a quiet side ramp. Until then I'd have thought it was a major thoroughfare, but in Valen the clean-swept avenue lined with slender trees, was little more than a back alley. A dark arch wrapped itself around the end of the road, where I could see robed figures coming and going. We passed beneath it and into a gated courtyard, in the centre of which was a fountain topped by a slime-covered statue of Saint Bartholomew. On the far side of the courtyard was a mansion house that I guessed must be the order's headquarters. A skinny priestess with a nose like a ship's prow paced the steps of the building. Tobias waved to her. She smiled and beckoned us over, all the while casting nervous glances behind us.

'So, these are your friends,' she said as she hugged Tobias. She gave me, Clary and Tosspot the sly-eye once-over and said 'friends' like she was talking about arse lice. 'I'm so very pleased to meet you all. Toby has told me all about you.'

'Never mind, eh?' I said. It was a joke but she looked at me like I'd just threatened to strangle her.

'Ignore Breed, Sister Kyra. That's what passes for a sense of humour in Appleton.'

'Oh, I see.' She laughed nervously and brushed a swag of light brown hair away from her face. I don't know how humans put up with the stuff. If I had hair like that I'd shave my head. Sister Kyra was obviously very fond of her tresses and her appearance in general. Rather than rough homespun, her robes were silk and her hair had been carefully tonsured. Expensive but subtle gold and diamond studs winked in her earlobes. The yardstick pendent around her neck was also gold. It seemed the Order of Saint Bartholomew attracted a better class of cull than your average cult.

'Can I pee in there too?' said Clary. 'I'm bursting.'

Everyone looked round to see Tosspot pissing in the fountain.

Sister Kyra gave Tobias a look that was composed of equal measures of horror and bewilderment.

'Best hold your water for a bit, Clary,' I said.

When Tosspot was finished we went inside and a ruddy-faced housekeeper appeared and took Clary off with the promise of somewhere to pee and a slice of fruit pie. Tosspot wandered off on his own, trailed by a nervous-looking acolyte.

Tobias and I were led into a large office so elegantly appointed as to look decidedly plain. The building itself was the grandest I'd ever been in, either by invite or to rob, although drab compared to many we'd passed to get here. A huge silk rug had been placed on the floor, right where everyone could walk on it, and indeed bald patches marred the scrolling leaf design in several places.

The vast desk was oak, and carved with such skill that it must have taken years. The walls were panelled, the sideboard dressed in silver ewers and goblets of plain but solid manufacture. The silver statue of Saint Bart standing on a plinth in the corner had sapphire eyes and I'd bet my arse the yardstick in his hand was made of gold. I tried not to drool.

Kyra politely elbow-guided Tobias towards one of the windows that looked onto the courtyard. They bowed their heads together in whispered conversation. I could hear every word, but feigned indifference.

'Are you sure, Tobias? Are you sure this is the one? So much is at stake, it… it doesn't look… Well, it's not what I expected.'

'I'm as sure as I can be, Kyra. The question is, are you sure you want to get involved?'

There was the nervous laughter again. 'Of course, I support you Tobias, but it's just, if Augustra finds out about what we're planning she'll stop it and that will be the end of us, possibly the whole order. The Empirifex favours the Sanguine

Shadow. He apparently admires their devotion, and red is his current favourite colour.'

'He admires them today, who knows what the morrow will bring?'

Until I met Tobias I'd never heard of the Order of the Sanguine Shadow, or the Scienticians of Saint Bartholomew come to that. There were so many religious cults and sects, so many gods and saints in the Pantheon it was hard to keep up, even if you tried, which I didn't. Every Empirifex since before the Schism had elevated friends and favourites to the status of saint or demi-god; it was a time-honoured reward for arse-kissing. I believed in the All-Seeing Eye of the Universe; uncaring, unblinking, just watching and keeping its own counsel, and that was as far as my beliefs stretched.

'If Breed is able to use the Hammer, we will have irrefutable proof that the prophecy is true and Augustra's support will evaporate. Not even the Empirifex himself could deny such evidence. There are those in the Senate who'll stand with us.

'Hmm, that's true. Augustra has made some powerful enemies, just a pity your father isn't one of them.'

'I blame Marius for that, but I'll deal with them when the time comes.'

'As you say. At least finding the hammer isn't going to be a problem.' Sister Kyra turned and looked at me, probably to make sure I hadn't taken a shit on the carpet. I smiled brightly. She blanched, forced a thin-lipped smile of her own and looked away. 'Are you sure you want to do this by stealth, Toby? Perhaps we should speak to our friends in the Synod and do this openly and with permission?'

'No. The Sanguines are too strong at the moment. They'd vote down any legitimate attempt and then we'd never get near the tomb. Once we have it, it'll be too late for anyone to argue.'

Oh, but their schemes were dull. They were mice trying to run with dog rats. I had the strong gut feeling that it would end badly for them, not least because as soon as I had my claws on the hammer, I was gone.

'Breed?' the priest called. I didn't need to feign surprise; I'd stopped listening to their prattle and was instead planning on how I was going to get out of Valen once I had the weapon. My plan involved robbing them blind in order to pay a sellspell to break what was left of the geas binding us. I was already taking an audit of the goods I'd liberate to fund my escape. For once, everything was going my way. I went over and bowed to the woman. She smiled, but couldn't quite stop herself taking a half step back and wrinkling her nose.

'I'm pleased to meet you... Breed. May Saint Bartholomew bless you and keep you in the right angle of his wisdom.'

'Thank ye kindly, Holy Mother. I hope I'm worthy of his grace.'

Tobias narrowed his eyes; perhaps the bow was a step too far. 'This is serious, Breed. The fate of all warspawn may depend on you succeeding in this task.'

'Alright, what do you want me to do?'

They looked at each other, their faces knitted into patterns of worry as they worked up the courage to ask me to do that which I already intended to do.

'As we've already discussed, we want you to steal the Hammer of the North's Hammer,' said Tobias.

I nodded with, I hoped, just the right level of anxiety painted on my face. It was all I could do not to piss myself laughing. 'Well, priest, you know I don't go in for all this prophecy stuff, it's...' I was tempted to say 'too clever for me' but I knew that wouldn't wash with him anymore. 'Suffice it to say, there comes a time in everyone's life when they have to make a choice. Count me in.'

That was it, I'd cracked him. The lock on his trust sprang open like the arms of all heaven's whores. Tobias beamed from ear to ear; there might even have been a tear in the soapy cull's eye. He thought he'd saved me, and so he had—just not in the way he thought.

Sister Kyra was obviously not one to be left out and ran over to the statue of Saint Bart and flung herself on her knees. 'Saint Bartholomew has shown us the way! We will prevail, we will not bow down before tyrants. We will stand against both men *and* demons in His Holy name. No matter the obstacles, no matter the dark road we must travel, we stand in the right angle of his love. Praise be to Saint Bartholomew!'

After an hour or so of Sister Kyra explaining at me in laborious detail, why it was going to be necessary to break into the Hall of Heroes instead of gaining permission to rob the tomb of one of the Empire's most revered heroes, she and Tobias excused themselves. I was shown to another well appointed chamber where a bath, a bed, and a table of food were waiting for me.

As soon as the acolyte left, I set off to find where Tobias and Sister Pain-in-the-arse had gone. It was dark now; the windows were shuttered, the corridors dimly lit and mostly empty as good prayer-mongers were early-to-bed types.

Tobias and Kyra didn't look like they were going to bed when they left. They had the look of sneaking coves about them. Deep recessed doorways and alcoves full of maudlin statues of Saint Bart were perfect shady nooks for me to duck into as I followed the silken thread of Tobias's scent. The ghostly skein led me down to a chapel that was buried in the bowels of the mission house. I say 'chapel', it looked more like a workshop with pews. A knot of brown-clad figures, Tobias and Kyra amongst them, were gathered at the far end of the room. Before each pew was a work bench. While they talked, the priests measured and sawed, hammered and welded metal, wood and leather components for sculptures that spun with flywheels and turned with cogs. Interlocking plates of copper, brass, wood and steel wove abstract angles that vexed my eye as I tried to follow their intricate movements.

Sister Kyra's work bench erupted with light. I ducked, unsure of what was happening; a chorus of *'praise be to Saint Bartholomew'* followed. The light died and Kyra stepped forward and bowed before the semi-circle of workbenches. Another of the priests' machines emitted a low droning hum; more praise was offered. Tobias's machine vented tiny jets of flame, and lightning chased across the surface of a polished steel ball suspended at the apex of his pyramidal creation. After they'd all done their party piece I concluded that Tobias's show, and mastery was the best.

I wasn't sure, but I think they were praying and honing their magical skills while strengthening their resistance to the paradox of power. After watching a repeat of the elaborate and somewhat ridiculous ritual I slipped out of the chapel workshop, no wiser than when I'd entered.

Back in my room I stripped off my filthy and threadbare clothing, snagged a chunk of meat and climbed into the bath. I lay in the pleasantly cool water until my scales softened and I was able to clean a month's-worth of grime from under my claws and out of the roots of my hair spines. The room smelled of camphor and cedar, redolent of temple incense. A mournful chorus of religious singing echoed along the hallway.

I felt a twinge of guilt, knowing that I was going to double-cross Tobias at the earliest opportunity. A plaster Saint Bart gazed sadly at me from a cobweb-draped shelf as though it knew what I was planning. Time passed, and I dozed off. I was woken by a knock at the door. Tobias entered. I got out and dried myself with the robe that was too short.

He froze by the doorway, looked anywhere but at me. 'Oh. I... er.' He quickly closed the door. 'Kyra and I have just spoken with the senior members of the order. We have their blessing to go ahead.'

'That's wonderful.' I stretched, tired but relaxed. The bed looked torturously soft but the deep pile carpet felt just right for a quick nap.

'Are you sure you want to go ahead with this, Breed? I realise you only have my word that any of this is true.'

'I trust you, priest,' I smiled. 'And you can trust *me* when I say this is as important to me as it is to you.'

He smiled, looked up, blushed, and looked down again. 'I'm certain that the Empirifex will not look unkindly on anyone who brings him one of the greatest weapons from the Age of Heroes.'

'Why hasn't anyone dug it up before now? The Hall of Heroes must be stuffed with magical weapons.'

'Dear gods. You're talking about the greatest heroes of the Empire. You can't just plunder their graves for treasure.'

'You've lost me, isn't that exactly what we're planning to do?'

'No… Well, yes, in a way, but it's not the same as theft. It's complicated.'

'You're telling me, because from where I'm standing it looks like theft, or is it only stealing when someone like me does it?'

He rubbed his head. 'No, of course not, but there are circumstances when such actions are necessary.'

'Feeding your family is necessary, but poor culls still swing for it.'

'Look, will you do it, or not?'

'I said I would, didn't I? When do you and your friends want me to do it?'

'Tonight. The Synod is meeting in two days. I want us to be there to tell them about the prophecy and to present you with the Hammer's hammer.'

Highly unlikely. I smiled. 'As you wish.'

I can't say that I expected much but 'the plan' was less than reassuring. It involved Sister Kyra using some trusted contact to bribe a couple of guards to look the other way while we sneaked into the hall. Tobias assured me that there was nothing to worry about which, naturally, made me worry. Apparently there was no need to break in and absolutely no need to kill anyone. We were going to be let in through a side door and, more importantly, the tomb itself would be left unlocked for us.

I wasn't convinced by 'the plan', but I kept my own counsel and went along with it. I was a sharp cove, well able to improvise should the job go topsy. So long as I got within strike of the hammer I'd work out the rest on the fly. As a kindness, I'd tell the demon that I'd done for the priest when I handed over the drubber. I figured once he had what he was after, he'd be too busy to hunt down either me or the priest. In truth I didn't care, I just wanted to loose that mark and go to ground.

The Hall of Heroes was south from the order's mission house. I didn't see Clary or Tosspot before we left but I knew they'd fare well as they were both savvier than the sop-souled preachifiers I'd left them with. The priest and I set out alone and headed along a road that snaked away from the spectacular heart of the city out to a wide spoon-shaped valley. This time I was wearing a robe that covered my feet. Although older, the buildings we passed were even more lavishly decorated than those I'd already seen, lavish but tasteless. Many were lit up by great flaming torches that burned the night to amber and sheened the sandy facades in shades of bronze. Tobias explained in hushed tones that this was the administrative district and that most of the offices of state were located here, amid parks and temples dedicated to some of the more prominent gods of the Pantheon.

Night seemed hardly less busy than day in Valen, so cowls up and heads down, we hurried on until we reached a square on the other side of which stood the Hall of Heroes. Beyond it, the lip of the valley swept up to a grand parade of buttressed mansions, their shuttered windows picked out by faint rectangles of rosy gold. The Hall itself was laid out like a gigantic seven spoked wheel. A great rotunda with a copper-tiled dome formed the hub. If I hadn't had such a pressing need to get inside and rob it, I might have spent a minute or two being awed. The size alone was intimidating, made a body feel small, insignificant. That humans lavished such wealth on the dead while beggars huddled in doorways said more about their contrary nature than anything, no poem, song or tale could better sum them up than follies such as this.

'Each of the seven spokes is a chapel dedicated to one of the heroes of the Schism War.' Tobias informed me as we skirted the square. 'Their tombs are in their chapels, except the Red Witch. No one knows where she was buried.'

'Or cares, I'll wager,' I said under my breath.

'What?'

'Nothing. Lead on.'

We passed the main entrance as we made our way around the building. Standing triumphantly on the necks of fallen demons, a pair of giant basalt heroes flanked the bronze doors. The plaza outside of the hall was deserted. One of the knights standing guard tapped out her pipe on a dead demon's horn, the other leaned against the sandaled foot of a giant warrior queen. Tongues of torch light licked at the smooth contours of giant shoulders and gilded the manes of heroically flowing hair.

'This way,' the priest whispered.

'You don't need to come with me,' I offered hopefully. 'Just tell me where the tomb is and I'll be in and out before anyone knows.'

The priest shook his head and hurried off along a side street dripping with vines. 'The guard we bribed knows to expect two of us. One alone would arouse suspicion.'

I suspected that the real reason he was coming was that he and his friends didn't trust me. I wasn't offended, they were right.

'Over here, hurry,' he said unnecessarily, I was sticking to him like a louse on a cock-sack until I had that hammer.

I adjusted the shoulder strap of the firelance. The long barrel lay comfortably snug between my shoulders under the robe. Tobias had tried to insist that I didn't bring it, but there was no way I was going to leave it with the priests. Truth be told, I was looking forward to using it again. He wouldn't understand that, he had power at his finger tips, or maybe he did and realised that, for coves like me barking irons levelled the field.

The vine-draped street tapered out behind the Hall of Heroes. Surprisingly, there were no high walls or spearpoint railings, just a cobbled path leading through a grove of lemon trees to the rear of the hall. The nearest chapel, one of the seven spokes, rose fifty feet above the street. Just below the roof, soft light embellished a narrow strip of stained glass that ran the length of both sides of the chapel. The walls were covered in flamboyant carvings in basalt and marble. Its scale was impressive but it was an ugly building, a brash shout amongst the raucous visual noise of the city.

I think Tobias was trying to sneak, but the soft cull couldn't lift his feet clear of the ground for more than two steps. His scuffing gait was erratic, the way his shoulder brushed the wall irritating. He was not the person I would have chosen as a lamplight comrade and that was certain. A small side door was nestled into the wall of the chapel, just before where the spoke met the hub of the atrium building. A city guard loitering nearby stepped forward when she saw us.

'Who goes there?' she asked.

'The night watch,' Tobias replied.

Without saying another word, she shouldered her spear and marched off around the building. Tobias tried the door. As promised, it was unlocked.

The atrium was lit by a huge fire bowl held aloft in the middle of the chamber by a quartet of angelic beings thirty feet tall. Its radiance reflected off the painted dome and spread fingers of gold into the surrounding chapels. Rather than illuminate, the wavering firelight merely served to add variance to the depth of shade that wrapped the hall.

This chapel, if the frescos painted on the walls were anything to go by, was dedicated to a flaxen-haired sorceress. She was shooting ice spears from her fingertips, cutting down swathes of demonic hoards that looked more than a little like me. As far as I could see, the only non-humans represented in the sprawling frescos that covered the walls were the hordes of demonspawn. The side of *good* was entirely human.

'Magnificent, isn't it?' Tobias whispered.

'Words fail me.'

Hugging the walls, we crept into the atrium.

'There are no guards within the hall and all the priests and visitors have left by now. The guard won't return for an hour,' Tobias whispered.

The Hammer's chapel was directly opposite the entrance to the hall. I walked on the balls of my feet, but every now and then Tobias scuffed the marble. It sounded loud to me, but Tobias didn't seem to notice. His shoulders were hunched, his head was down. He was cowed by this place, overawed by its significance. I could smell his doubt, his fear.

An openwork iron screen separated the chapel from the atrium. Inside, the walls were painted with the heroic deeds of a hammer-wielding man-god. Swathed in furs, the golden-haired, square-jawed hero was smiting vicious demons with his overly large hammer. He looked familiar, probably because he looked like every picture of every hero I'd ever seen. All that was brave and noble was lovingly reproduced in the image of the giant. It meant nothing to me, but Tobias bowed his head and mumbled a quick prayer as we passed.

The entrance to the crypt was at the far end of the chapel. Beneath the murals were rows of verdigrised plaques bearing the names of fallen warriors who I assume our hero had led to their glorious deaths. The tomb door was set in the plinth of another giant, black basalt statue. It portrayed the Hammer smiting a horned and scaly demon with his stupidly large weapon. I waited for Tobias to open it, while I kept an eye out. Minutes passed without a key being turned.

'What's wrong?' I hissed.

'I can't do it,' he replied.

I went over. 'What do you mean you can't?'

'I thought this was the right thing to do, but I… I'm not sure it is. What if…' He looked at me, eyes brimful of accusation.

'What if what? Come on, priest, spit it out.'

'I can't trust you, Breed. What if you betray us?'

'You incinerate me with your holy fucking calculation of smiting!' I didn't want to hurt him, genuinely didn't want to, but I wasn't going to let him stop me, not now I was so close. I folded my arms, mostly to stop myself strangling him prematurely. 'Now listen to me, patrician. We either get on and do this, or you work out how you're going to explain to your friends why you let them and everyone else down.'

'This is sacrilege.'

'Only if you decide it is.' I don't know why I said it; it didn't mean anything, I was just trying to push him to act before I had to knock him out. For some reason the empty words struck a chord with him and he opened the door. The sound reverberated through the chapel. I took off the robe, unslung the firelance, and shoved the hesitant priest inside before quickly and quietly closing the door behind us.

It wasn't as dark as I'd expected it would be inside the tomb. Glow stones the size of my fist had been embedded in the walls and bathed the flight of stairs in an eerie, grey-blue light. We descended cautiously with me in the lead. The air was cold and tasted of dust but again it wasn't as stale as I'd imagined it would be. There were also the faint ghosts of other smells down here and the steps were swept clean.

'People have been down here recently,' I said.

'Yes, the tomb is maintained by priests of the Order of the Hammer.'

'Ah, of course. I should have guessed there'd be a sacred order of tomb sweepers.'

'Just shut up, Breed. Now is not the time for levity.'

'Who said I was joking?'

The stairs came out in a chamber lined either side with statues of the Hammer in a variety of heroic poses. In the middle of the floor was a massive catafalque atop which was an effigy of the hammer. I shouldered the lance, grabbed the lid and started to push. Tobias gasped.

'Breed, for gods' sake, wait!'

I ignored him. This wasn't the first tomb I'd robbed and although the lids were heavy, if you were strong enough, or had enough leverage to lift the male lid out of the female box they slid easily. I lifted and turned the lid. It growled, stone ground against stone. Behind me I could hear the priest praying. When I turned it almost entirely at a right angle I stopped pushing. Dust tickled my nostrils. I looked inside, expecting to see the legend: the Hammer of the North. Other than a rusted suit of armour, the sarcophagus was empty.

'He's not here.' Surprise turned to dread as I searched amid the armour and rotting furs for the hammer. 'The hammer's not here, either.' I couldn't believe it. I searched again, in case I'd somehow failed to spot a body and a dirty great hammer.

Nothing.

The priest grabbed my arm. I shrugged him off. 'It's not fucking here. I slumped against the edge of the tomb.

'It's not your fault, Breed. I should have guessed this might happen.' He muttered something under his breath and a ball of golden light bloomed in his palm.

'I might as well climb in and just close the fucking lid,' I said. As well as still being indebted to Shallunsard, a small part of me was disappointed that the hammer wasn't there.

I admit it, I was curious about the prophecy. I'd not paid much heed to the priest's insane ideas, but for a brief spell, I'd let myself believe that I might have been part of something important.

'Come on, let's get out of here,' I said.

After he'd had a good rummage, I put the lid back on the tomb. To say I was disconsolate was an understatement of epic proportions. I still had time left before the demon came after me, but no blasted idea where I might find the damned hammer.

'I wonder if he's ever been here,' said the priest as we made to leave the tomb.

'Does it matter?'

'No… I suppose it doesn't, not anymore.'

We retraced our footsteps through the hall to the side door. I let the priest go ahead of me, while I considered my next move. As he reached for the door handle I caught a whiff of body odour and heard shuffling from outside. It was more than one person. I reached for Tobias, tried to pull him back as I unslung the firelance. Both mistakes; I should have just run.

The door was blown off its hinges and the hall lit up like it was day. The priest staggered, I shoved him out of my way and levelled the firelance at the door a heartbeat before a blast of magical energy hurled us across the chapel.

I hit the wall like a wet rag. Tobias hadn't been in the direct line of the blast but I heard him wheeze like a broken bellows when he landed. Dozens of armoured knights swarmed through the door, their shouts reverberated around the chapel, the clamour of their armour bounced off the walls. I'd managed to keep hold of the firelance and once I'd stopped seeing stars I got to my knees and took aim at the first knight I laid eyes on.

'Drop the lance, demonspawn, or I'll blow you back to hell,' said a woman standing in the doorway.

I switched targets to her. 'Then you'll be coming with me, cunt.'

The knights put themselves between us.

'No, Breed!' Tobias shouted. 'It's over, drop it.'

I looked at Tobias. Saw a broken man.

'Don't give her an excuse,' he pleaded. 'Please, surrender, live to fight another day.'

I don't know why, but I did as he asked and dropped the lance even though I was sure that he was being a mite optimistic about the whole 'living' thing. My assumption appeared to be correct as, when I dropped the lance, the knights piled me. In the process of binding my hands behind my back I was kicked with rib-breaking gusto. The woman, who until now had been little more than a silhouette, came forward into the light. She was wearing blood red robes that perfectly matched her hair and the stripe of colour painted across her eyes. It was not her appearance that gained my rapt, if watery-eyed attention but the dirty great hammer she was carrying slung over her shoulder.

'Looking for this?' she said, and tapped the dusty shaft with henna-reddened fingers. 'Well, Tobias, you *are* in a spot, aren't you? Having heard rumour of your villainous plan to steal this holy artefact, I gained permission of the Senate, your father included, to take it into safe keeping and help the knight captain here apprehend you, should the rumour prove true.' She walked over to the priest who was being held at spear point by the nervous knights. 'Surely as a Vulsones you have enough personal wealth that you don't need to steal our nation's treasures to pay your order's debts?'

'You know damn well that's a lie. I know Marius told you about the prophecy.'

'Now, which prophecy would that be, Toby? There are so many, I lose track. Your father is going to be very disappointed.'

'Please, Augusta there's more at stake here than winning the approval of the Senate. Hundreds, perhaps thousands of lives are at stake.'

'Oh, please, Tobias, enough prattle I pray you. All this, being right and saving the day has given me a terrible headache. You'll have chance to say your piece when you go before the Synod. I'm sure they can't wait to hear why you desecrated our holiest shrine. Until then, the captain here'— she indicated one of the knights with slightly more gold embroidery on his cloak than his fellows—'will escort you to the temple of the Sanguine Shadow.' She leaned close to the priest. 'And unlike your soft-headed brother who came crawling back this morning, *I'll* make damn sure you don't escape.' She turned to the knight-captain. 'Gag him and bind him with the chains I brought and be careful, he may look like a half-wit but he is not entirely without power.'

'There's no need for that, Augusta. I give you my word as a Vulsones that I won't try to escape.'

She laughed too hard. 'I don't trust the rest of your family, so why the hell would I trust you? Bind him, and in the name of all that is holy, don't forget the gag. I can't bear to listen to his whining for another minute, let alone the next few days.'

'Yes, Holy Mother.' The knight saluted. 'What shall we do with this?' He head tossed in my direction. There was no actual malice in the look he gave me, just bored contempt. The woman however gave me a look brimming with hate.

'Throw it in the dungeons.'

Chapter Ten

Tobias was bound in warded chains and gagged before being carted off by the red-clad cunt who had my fucking hammer. Shortly thereafter I was dragged from the hall and thrown in the back of a prison wagon. I didn't resist, I was grateful for the chance to lie down as every breath I drew elicited a stabbing pain in my side that told me all was not as it should be in my giblet sack.

The journey to the lock-up gave me time to consider just how deep I was in the arse-pickle. I concluded that I was up to my eyes in the nasty stuff. And thus began the recriminations, the wishful thinking, the torture of examining paths not taken and the indignant self-pity of a life-long recidivist. Time flies when you're feeling sorry for yourself and before long the wagon stopped. The knights were nothing if not consistent and I was dragged from the wagon with the same casual brutality as I was thrown in it.

Disappointingly, the prison's dramatically theatrical façade belied its joyless interior. Whilst being promised all manner of unpleasantness, I was hauled past the nice airy cells where wealthy coves could languish in comfort, and taken down to the dungeon. Even with my hands bound I know how to protect my vulnerables from casual jibs and culps, but no amount of acrobatics can shield a body from a concerted effort to give it a damn good kicking.

The tepid contents of a slop bucket brought me round after I so rudely fell unconscious before the knights had finished trying to kick the tar out of me. The poor fellows quite wore themselves out giving me the beating of my life, not to mention the hours it was going to take some poor cull to clean all that blood off their nice shiny armour. I don't remember losing consciousness again, I just remember thinking I was going to die and how, on balance, that didn't seem like such a bad thing.

As it turns out, I didn't die. I only wished I had. I woke up sometime later in a cell. There was no light to give me a clue as to the time of day, but the blood on my face had dried to a tight crust, so I guessed some hours had passed since the beating. My head felt lumpy and swollen. I managed to prise my right eye open but the left remained resolutely closed.

There was enough chain between the manacles that I was able to bring my swollen hands from behind my back to in front of me. After feeling my way through this latest collection of cuts and bruises, I surveyed my domain. The cell was no more than eight feet long by five feet wide and about five feet high. Knights occasionally peered through the slit in the door to assure me that I wouldn't be in here long. They were very pleased to inform me that the pyre was already being built on which they would burn my partially strangled body after my guts had been torn out. That they were going to such efforts for a humble cove like me was really rather flattering and given how rough I felt, almost welcome.

As well as my ribs, my right hand was particularly painful due to being stamped on, but it just about worked. I once again thanked the Holy Eye for my strong, thoasan bones. The knights had done more than enough to maim or even kill a human, but thoasa—even half thoasa—are made of tougher stuff. Even so, every time I moved a couple of ribs grated against each other.

As I sat there in the darkness, contemplating my gloomy fate, a fly buzzed unpleasantly close to my ear. I swatted at it and shook my head. The cell spun wildly, I threw up.

'Keep it down! You fucking animal,' one of the knights snarled, and banged on the door. 'I'll flay your fucking hide if I've got to come in there.'

Tempted though I was to offer him an invitation to do just that, I refrained. I'd had my fill of pain for the day and quietly fell into an exhausted and dreamless sleep.

I awoke to the sound of the fly buzzing near my face. I prised open my eye to see that the end wall of the cell was covered in flies, thousands of them. How they'd got in here was a mystery as there wasn't a window and the peephole in the door was closed. Perplexing though that was, what was really strange was their odd behaviour. The only one making a noise was the one buzzing around my head. The rest were hardly moving at all, as though they were deliberately being quiet. Confused, I watched the glittering black mass crawl across the wall. I coughed up a lump of something slimy that I hoped wasn't lung. I don't know who was the bigger idiot, Tobias for trusting Kyra or me for trusting him. I should have known better. There was only one person I'd ever been able to trust and that was me, and even then I quite often let myself down.

As if I wasn't sore enough, my palm began to itch. As I watched the flies an idea slowly wormed its way into my brain. I dismissed it; it was stupid, desperate and stupid. The itching grew more intense. I tore off my glove and had a good scratch. I could just make out the dark outline of the demon's sigil embedded in my flesh. I looked at the flies on the wall. I looked at my palm. I laughed.

The flies had formed the same pattern as the sigil.

I crawled over to the wall. 'Shallunsard... is that you?' I whispered. Of course the flies being flies, didn't respond. 'What the fuck am I doing? I'm talking to flies.' I punched the wall, crushing a cluster of the bloated corpse-pillagers into the brick. The rest didn't move, didn't take to the air in an angry fizzing cloud of black like normal insects should. The wall was stained with blood and mashed bodies, broken wings glittered like diamonds in my hand. The idea, half formed and utterly insane, wriggled deeper into my brain. I crushed all of the flies forming Shallunsard's sigil and waited... and waited.

After half an hour of staring at the bloody mess nothing had happened. In desperation, I concentrated on the pattern of smashed bodies and poured what little sorcerous energy I possessed into the bloody sigil.

Nothing. Disgusted at my foolishness, I rolled away from the wall. At least there was nobody around to see my descent into madness. I rolled over in a bid to find some way to lie that didn't hurt and as I did, I saw it.

The sigil was still on the wall, but the wall wasn't where or what it should have been. It had opened like a door, but one that could only be seen from a sidelong angle. It was so thin and so perfectly matched to its background that in the dark the break was all but invisible from where I was lying.

'The angle's right.' I chuckled until I coughed and then crawled through the gap.

I don't know who decided where I'd end up. Perhaps it was me, perhaps it was the demon or perhaps it was just chance. I didn't care. I fell out of the cell into familiar territory. The perfume of the sewer filled my nostrils as I sank up to my elbows in the thick sediment of a sewage channel. I scrabbled back and managed to stop myself falling face first into the flow. I was on a tiled walkway, a *glazed* tiled walkway at that. I guessed that I must be in Valen's sewers. I looked at the wall that I'd just fallen through. It didn't look any different to any other section of wall. I touched it, just to make sure it was as solid as it looked. I didn't want to be followed by the guards because I certainly couldn't run or fight. I coughed and tasted iron, felt a rib dig in to my giblets.

'That isn't good,' I gasped and lay back to try and ease the pain. As if that wasn't bad enough something in the darkness growled, low and threatening. Whatever it was sounded big. I tried to get up, but that simple act was now beyond me. Falling through the wall had pushed the broken rib deeper into my vitals and I was feeling it acutely.

Fuck it, I thought. I was tired. I decided to lie there and wait for whatever it was to try its luck. I could probably still give whatever it was a nasty bite if it came close enough.

The growling turned to snuffling and was soon accompanied by the click-skitter of claws on tiles. As it came closer I got a noseful of its scent: the unmistakable aroma of wet dog rat. I'd escaped hanging, drawing and burning, only to be eaten alive by rodents.

Something sniffed my hair. I opened my eye and saw twitching whiskers, a wet brown nose and a pair of huge yellow fangs swam into view. This was it, I thought, and then a familiar face loomed into view behind it.

'Breed!' said Clary.

Content that I was among friends, I relinquished my grip on consciousness.

I wasn't sure if I was dead or dreaming, or both. After my previous experience I was reasonably sure that the dead didn't dream, but then there are probably as many ways of being dead as there are of being alive. I felt like I was floating on a river of velvet, drifting through underground grottos lit by exotic, spongiform blooms of fungi. Something was dragging me, guiding me through miles of passageways and tunnels. Warm brown eyes stared down at me; a soft, wet nose sniffed me.

'Breed, wake up!' said Clary, too brightly, too loud.

I coughed blood into my mouth, tried to sit up, failed.

'Stay, stay!' Clary ordered. I was in no position to argue with an eleven-year-old. I stayed.

'Clary's right. Don't try to get up. I've sent for a healer. Rowan will fix you up, or kill you. Hopefully it won't be the latter, but I make no promises on her behalf.'

That little nugget of information didn't perturb me overmuch, I'd grown inured to death threats. I did find the flash lad who'd spoken intriguing, even in my battered state. I say 'lad'. It was hard to tell if it was a boy who looked like a rat, or a rat that looked like a boy.

Whatever he was, he wasn't your average Schism-touched cull. Hovering behind Clary the boy rat was wearing fine breeches, silk stockings; silver-buckled patent shoes, a white linen shirt and an embroidered silk waistcoat. That I felt so wretched and yet made note of all his finery was a testament to the skill of his tailor. His fur was sleek and dark, his tail as thick as my arm, and restlessly active. His front teeth were long, but nowhere near as long as those of the biggest dog rat I'd ever seen that was sitting at his feet and eyeing me like I was the main course of a Gods' Day dinner.

'Where...?' I managed to say in between gasping breaths.

The boy rat came over, the dog rat padding at his heel like a faithful hound. 'You're in my home in Nightside. I am Leopold, the Duke of East Point.'

'Clary... priest, Rubin...?'

'Rubin, is it now, eh, demon?' Tosspot cackled.

I hadn't noticed him until he spoke. The mangy old sot was sitting on a watermarked silk divan, stroking a fat, white rat that was asleep on his knee.

'Bet you're wondering how we got here, eh? How you got here,' he said and took a pull on his pel pipe.

I nodded.

'Not sure I should tell you.' He chuckled again. The rat on his knee stirred and draped the tip of its tail over its nose.

Drawing breath and trying to talk was like trying to suck an egg through a penny whistle. I lay back and focused on breathing.

'You're no fun today, Breed,' Tosspot said, sulkily. 'When you and priesty boy went off gallivanting, me and Clary were in the kitchen of the big house, weren't we, Clary?'

'Yes, Rubin, we were. We were told to help with the washing up. Which I thought unfair and so I curdled their milk, a whole churn.' She laughed, and Leo laughed with her.

Tosspot's eyes lit up. 'You'd been gone a spell when we heard a right ruckus. Knights kicked the doors in; the demon-dodgers were all yelling and crying.' He grew animated, the rat on his knee woke up and started preening. 'Me and Clary sneaked out the back and into the sewers.

'Into my domain.' Leopold bowed.

'Heard you got arrested for trying to steal something, and was all set to be hanged,' said Tosspot. 'How did you get out of that?'

'Apported.' It wasn't *exactly* a lie. 'How long since me and Tobias set off?' I gasped. I had no idea how much time had passed since our ill-starred venture.

'Two nights ago,' said Clary. I noticed she was making eyes at rat boy and that he was giving her coy come-hithers in return. 'We came down here and Leo found us and took us in.'

'It was the least I could do,' said the Duke of wherever.

'The Synod must have met,' I said. Tobias had failed and if I wasn't much mistaken, I was dying, *again*.

The next hour or so I spent fighting to breathe as the right side of my chest swelled like a dead pig's belly. I discovered that if I lay perfectly still, it only hurt a lot instead of too much, which was a relief because I hate crying like a babe in front of strangers. At least the couch on which I was expiring was comfortable. The room was windowless as was only to be expected, but had surprisingly good ventilation and was brightly lit by dozens of fine beeswax candles. Unlike Mother's lair, Duke Leo's audience chamber was elegantly appointed; no expense was being spared for my death watch, but I can't say I was grateful.

I must have dozed off again but woke in the sure knowledge that Rowan had arrived. The air in the room had turned crisp and smelled of frost-rimed loam, flint, and ghostberries. I opened my eye and tried to balance what one sense told me against the evidence of another and I couldn't. It smelled like an autumn morning in the mountains and yet I was most definitely in the sewers of Valen, looking at a myth made real.

I'd seen some strange things in my time but nothing like Rowan. It wasn't that her appearance was outlandish; compared to coves like Ludo she was positively ordinary. It was more that Rowan appeared to be made of the unreal fabric from which dreams are woven. Her presence served to highlight how tawdry the world was, how lacking. Tall and thin, she had a pair of violet eyes, virtually transparent skin, and hair like fine strands of spun glass that absorbed and reflected the colours in the room. She was wearing a long coat over breeches and a fine linen shirt and vest. The first thing she did was tip Leo a polite nod. The second was look at me like most people looked at me.

'Demon,' Rowan hissed and crossed the room faster than a thought. She grabbed my hand and tore off my glove. The world around us receded into shadow. If she was going to kill me, there wasn't a damn thing I could do to stop her. Rowan was an Annurashi. Just as the humans had made warspawn, the Annurashi had made them.

She grabbed my face and stared into my eyes. Up close, I saw that hers were flecked with gold and silver and her pupils were purple and not quite round. Her breath was as fresh and sweet as snow dusted apples.

'Did you choose this?' she asked. Her voice was many layered; it reminded me of Ludo and was utterly compelling.

I knew my continued existence depended not only on giving the right answer, but an honest one, two things that didn't often go together in my world.

'No,' I croaked. 'Tricked.'

She didn't take her eyes off mine while I talked. My jaw throbbed where she had it clamped in her bony, four-jointed fingers, but I didn't have the breath or guts to complain. I heard the distinct sound of a blade being sheathed as she let me go.

The most disconcerting thing that happened next wasn't having an Annurashi tending to my wounds, nor was it the way she mixed sorcery with actual doctoring; that was just confusing. It was when she stuck a long, hollow needle into my swollen chest and the air whistled out. The pain in my lung lessened immediately. It didn't vanish altogether, but I could breathe much easier. She hovered her hand over my chest. Her eyes shone with a cold, blue light and the offending rib wriggled out of my lung and realigned itself. It was disconcertingly similar to the way Shallunsard had brought me back from the dead and just like then, it hurt like hell.

Without another word or second glance, the Annurashi packed up her things and went over to talk to Leo, who'd been loitering near Clary while the Annurashi worked. His faithful giant rat was cowering in the corner of the room. I had to give it to the Duke; he showed remarkable composure when dealing with Rowan. After a brief conversation, he clicked his heels and bowed. She acknowledged it with the slightest of nods.

'Keep your head down, Leo; trouble is coming. I'm going to go and speak to the rest of the Council. They, *you* need to prepare.' The Annurashi flicked a blade sharp glance in my direction.

'Yes, I know. Take care, Rowan, and thank you,' Leopold said to the closing door.

I felt better than I had done in hours, if somewhat drained. My eyelids started to close… and then my palm began to burn as though I'd stuck my hand in a fire. It hurt so much that I fell off the couch. The giant dog rat yapped, a dozen of its kin bounded into the room. I thought of Wulf.

The Duke calmed them with a wave of his hand. Clary and Tosspot actually looked concerned. I looked at my hand. Overlaying the demon mark was another sigil. Unlike Shallunsard's which was as black as squid ink, this one was pale grey. The two did not sit well together and as I looked, actually seemed to be writhing under the skin like eyefly larvae, fighting for dominance.

'I am so sick of hurting,' I said through gritted teeth and repeatedly slammed my open hand against the floor, trying to beat the pain away.

Tosspot came over. His pipe was hanging out of the corner of his mouth. As usual, he was scratching his nethers. 'Best stop all this mucking about, demon and get some shut eye if you're going to go rescue priesty boy.'

'Who said I was going to rescue him?'

'I did!' said Clary. She was cuddling the fat white rat. 'I asked Leo to save you, so you could save Father Tobias because he saved me. That's fair, isn't it?'

'I think so,' said Leo. He smiled indulgently at Clary.

I didn't need to ask what was in it for Duke Rat Boy. The soppy way Clary was looking at him said it all. I crawled back onto the couch, and buried my face in a cushion. As I said, I hate strangers seeing me cry.

Clary told me it was morning when she woke me with a bowl of stew and reasonably fresh bread. I ate the lot and asked for more, I was starving. While she went to see what she could find, Duke Leo turned up. He was reading a letter. He smiled.

'She's too young for tumbling,' I said without thinking.

The Duke's smile faded. His tail twitched. 'What do you take me for? Some foppish cull who'd tup a bud like Clary?'

'I don't know anything about you. All I'm saying is she's a nipper.' I got up, stretched my legs. The dog rat growled.

'All you need to know is that I'm the nib of this manor, and a gentleman,' said Leo, polite and threatening in the same breath.

Those big dark rat eyes were unreadable, but that twitching tail and tone of voice told me I was on dangerous ground. I put my attack of concern down to the lingering effects of the geas and wondered how anyone with integrity ever survived long enough to go grey. Maybe they didn't. Maybe all old folk were selfish bastards and, as the saying goes, the good all die young. I tipped him a nod— his due as a prince of the Midnight Court.

'Point taken, Duke.'

He inclined his head. His tail curled around the missive and tucked it into his waistcoat. The giant dog rat set about grooming, so I fancied his master wasn't planning to do me a mischief, not now at least

'Tell me, Breed, how old are you?'

Seemed a mite personal as questions go, but this was his manor. 'I'm not yet a quarter of a century... I think.'

He nodded. 'The oldest thoasa I ever met was thirty five.'

I chuckled. 'I'll be happy if I live that long.'

'And not a little surprised, I'll wager.' He smiled. 'Joking aside, doesn't it bother you that your species is so short-lived?'

'Thoasa aren't much given to introspection and anyway, I'm only half thoasa.' I shrugged. 'I might stick around a bit longer, if I go live in the wilderness.'

I was all too aware of the short lifespan of thoasa. It was the price they paid for their incredible strength, speed and stamina. Thirty-five was actually five years older than any thoasa I'd ever met, or indeed had heard of.

'So how is it you know an Annurashi?' I asked, intent on steering the questions away from my mortality.

'Rowan? It is more that Rowan knows me, knows everyone with pretentions in Nightside Valen, and a fair number in Dayside too.'

'I didn't think they bothered with mortals.'

'I don't think they do as a rule.' He snorted. 'Nor can I blame them. My guess is that Rowan is an ambassador for her kind. The Annurashi's eyes and ears in the Empire: keeping an eye out in case anyone starts another Schism War, or releases a demon, that kind of thing.' He gave me a *look*.

I laughed.

Clary came back with a full pot of stew and I ate until my stomach felt like it was going to burst. She'd changed out of her filthy homespun and was now wearing a peach gown embroidered with pearls. Her hair, such as it was, had been expertly curled and tied with a bow. She seemed more than pleased with her transformation from country peasant to fashionable young lady and took every chance to flounce and swish her skirts. I found my gloves under the couch. I was tempted to beg a clean shirt, but there didn't seem much point. I was about to get all unnecessary with the base culls who'd taken Tobias and my hammer.

Duke Leo excused himself on an urgent matter of business and Tosspot had wandered off somewhere, probably on the hunt for more drugs. This left me and Clary kicking our heels. After listening to the girl prattle breathlessly about how wonderful Leopold was and how marvellous his domain, I asked her to show me around, something she was only too happy to do. I cared not one whit about how pretty everything was, I needed to know how to get out of here quickly should the need arise.

I thought I knew sewers, until I found myself wandering the halls of Nightside Valen. The place was enormous, labyrinthine. Built on many subterranean levels over centuries, from what I could tell, each previous buried incarnation of the city became part of the fabric of Nightside. The whole history of imperial civilisation was here, layered in a dozen slices, hundreds of years thick.

Barrel vaulted halls were lit by antique glowstone chandeliers and waterfalls cascaded beneath suspended bridges. Nature as well as magic and ingenuity had also been harnessed, and glowing fungi clung to the inside of coloured glass domes, lighting side streets and alleyways. Other, wilder varieties clambered unfettered up the walls, their luminous polyps hanging like fat lanterns above the denizens of Nightside as they went about their daily lives in much the same way as those above ground. It was a whole other city beneath the dayside streets of Valen. The two had to interact;

nothing this big could go unnoticed and I guessed a lot of money flowed between greasy palms at both ends of the pipe.

'I need some cutlery, Clary.'

'Knifes and forks? What do you want them for?'

'Ah, I forget you don't know what most kinchin coves ought.'

'Come again?'

'You weren't born in the shadow of the nevergreen tree.' She looked at me blankly. 'You're not a cove like me, leastways, you weren't.'

She chuckled and skipped across one of the swinging bridges that spanned a foaming underground river. 'You'd be surprised. I've done a bit o'sharp and shady work in my time.'

'Oh, aye? And what nefarious deeds should we credit your slate with?'

'Hexes mostly, only on them what wronged me, mind. My ma taught me manners and some fine dark tricks before the fever got her.'

Despite the gloom hanging over me about the priest, the demon, and everything else, Clary's confession was the funniest thing I'd heard in weeks.

'So all that cunning work they were accusing you of in Little Lea…?'

'I done it.' She dipped a curtsey. 'Anyone who messed with my gran, I fixed. I killed their cattle, poisoned their wells and…' she beamed, '… curdled their milk. They deserved it though; they'd been after Gran's land for years, ever since she found calth in the stream.'

'So why did you come with us? Why not stay to look after your gran?'

'Father Tobias solved all our problems, didn't he? Burnt 'em all up in a nice, tidy pile. Gran said I needed to broaden my horizons, so here I am and a good thing too, eh? Saved your life.'

It was a good job my ribs had been mended because I just about broke another laughing. Culls passing by looked at me like I was moon-touched, but their censuring stares only served to make me laugh more. I eventually stopped before I did myself another injury.

After scouting out a few boltholes and rat runs, I returned to Leopold's mansion which was located in the heart of his domain. Compared to this Darkling Court, Mother was a peasant, a country squire at best, and I had thought her queen of the world. My ignorance scared me; I therefore judged it was best to pretend I knew everything until proven otherwise.

When we got back, Leopold was waiting for us in what I now knew wasn't his audience chamber but was in fact a modest side room. The Duke was deep in conversation with an arch rogue if ever I saw one. The cove looked and smelled human; he was tall for their kind, broad in the back, narrow in the waist and wearing dark clothing. His soft-soled boots were made for climbing or sneaking rather than marching, giving a hint to the type of trade he practised, as did the hooded cloak he was wearing. It was traditional attire, favoured by many a bladesman and woman who fancied themselves a night-blessed bravo. This one certainly did. When he turned around I saw that he was wearing a brace of knives bandoliered across his chest and a matched longsword and dagger sheathed at his hip. The only thing missing was a sign around his neck saying 'I am a rogue'. Going on what he looked like he was either very good at his job or very bad.

'So, this is Breed.' He was well spoken, but there was a hint of an accent under the judgemental sneer. He gave me a cursory once over. His cold grey peepers were nailed deep into a hard, lean face. He folded his arms. 'I don't know, Leo...'

'Please, Cyrus. I wouldn't ask, but the priest is dear to someone who is dear to me.' He was pleading, but the Duke's tail swished lazily. Despite his words the lad was confident of the outcome making me think this was a show for my benefit.

The hooded man rubbed his bristle-sprinkled chin. 'The monastery will be heavily guarded, and even if we get in, this Tobias is most likely dead already.'

'Nevertheless, I would like you to try, Cyrus.'

'I wouldn't,' I said, as now seemed to be the time to offer opinions. 'No offence. But I work alone.'

They both looked like a turd had just recited poetry and then carried on their conversation too quietly for me to hear.

'I'm going to look for Rubin. I'll see you later, Breed,' said Clary. She cupped her hand to her mouth and whispered, 'Leo's only trying to help; he doesn't want you getting caught by the imperials again.' She smiled as though that little bit of wisdom would make me feel better and went off, only stopping to bow coyly to the Duke. The fat white rat followed after her. The big dog rat remained at its master's heel, smoothing the hair on its tail. It glared at me, which was actually quite heartening. At least something was taking me seriously, even if it was only an overgrown rodent.

'Then it's settled. Cyrus will help you find the priest. Are we all agreed?' Leopold looked at me. 'Breed?'

'It's not like I have a choice, is it?'

'No, *Breed,* you don't,' said Cyrus.

I was impressed. The cove managed to pack a lot of contempt into a few short words. If he didn't seem so matey with rat boy I'd have guessed he didn't like warspawn or the touched. Given the way they bantered while discussing how *we* were going to rescue Tobias, I surmised it was just me he didn't like.

Duke Leopold stepped in and smoothed the ruffled air before things got all unnecessary. 'You don't know the city, Breed. I think it would be best if Cyrus went with you. I assure you, nobody knows Valen better.'

The only thing I was assured of was that Cyrus wasn't coming along to help me or the priest. He was coming to either quietly kill me or, at best, to keep an eye on me. Quite understandably, the Duke didn't trust me running around his manor without an escort. I wouldn't have been surprised if he'd paid Cyrus to vent me somewhere nice and quiet where Clary would never find out about it. I know I'd want someone like me out of the way if I was in charge of a fief and had a reputation to maintain. I was trouble in tooth and claw.

'Could I borrow a couple of blades? Only, I lost mine,' I asked.

Cyrus snorted. 'You won't need them.'

I ignored the human. The duke's tail swished thoughtfully. He smelled of rosewater and just a hint of mousy sweat, but it was only a hint; the lad was a cool one.

'Certainly, Breed. And perhaps a change of clothes? Those are rather... distinctive. If you have to go abroad in Dayside it's best not to give the clanks a reason to stop you, especially now.'

I guessed *clank* was slang for imperial knight. 'I take it the Sanguines won the vote in the Synod?'

Cyrus and the duke exchanged knowing looks. It was obvious that they had a stake in this business. That they seemed surprised I did was just another indication of how stupid they thought I was. I decided not to attempt to disavow them. I'd play the idiot and see if I could work their underestimation to my advantage.

'Aye, they did, in the main. They verified the legitimacy of a rather awkward piece of prophecy, which in turn has led the Senate to consider drafting new laws.' Leopold's tail flicked angrily from side to side, belying the placid expression on his face and the calmness in those dark eyes. 'They have yet to be voted on, but there seems little doubt they'll be passed. How do... what do you know about the Synod and the Order of the Sanguine Shadow?'

I shrugged. 'Just what the priest used to babble on about. In truth, I didn't pay much heed. He talked too much for my liking.'

I was given a couple of cheap old knives and a pair of breeches and a shirt. The clothes were dark grey and made of soft leather. They were also the finest clothes I'd ever worn. For the first time in weeks I actually felt good, which was due in no small part to the Annurashi's healing. I was still weak, but I could see out of both eyes, my various aches had diminished and my lung felt almost as good as new. I didn't know what significance the new mark in my palm had, or how kindly Shallunsard would take to being usurped, but I could tell him what I told her, with the same confidence: I didn't ask for what she did to me.

Chapter Eleven

Leo and Clary bade me a lacklustre farewell before scampering off somewhere, leaving me alone with Cyrus. I wasn't sure what to make of this garlanded wolf. He looked too much the bravo for me to take him seriously. What I couldn't dispute was the map he owned detailing the main routes through Nightside and the sneaky sewer entrances and exits up to Dayside Valen.

From snatches of conversation I'd pieced together, and a few casual questions here and there, I'd found out that Nightside was divided into four quarters, each ruled by a duke. Like above ground, the dukes sat in council and made citywide decisions together.

'Are you paying attention?' Cyrus snapped. It was a fair call. I hadn't been paying much heed while he droned on about patrols and rock falls, and all the usual, petty inconveniences that seemed to worry humans.

'Of course I am,' I replied.

He grunted. 'Good, because I won't be going over this again.'

'Pity. You have such a lovely speaking voice.' I have to say, he was quick for a human. To be fair to myself, I was still recovering from my injuries, but credit where it's due, he was on me like a fly on shit as soon as the words left my lips. Without giving the slightest indication that he was going to move, he did, and I was pinned to the table with a blade across my throat before I could say: 'Fuck, you're quick.'

'I am.' He assured me. 'And while we're about the truth saying, let me tell you this: I do not like you.' He spoke very calmly and clearly. The knife pressed a fraction harder against my throat. 'You traffic with demons, and like the cold-blooded fucking lizard you are, you don't give a damn about anyone but yourself, and worst of all, you have brought trouble to my friend's house.' The pressure increased ever so slightly. He held the blade there for an uncomfortably long time before letting me up. 'Now don't speak unless spoken to because I find your voice irritating, and if you so much as look at me askance I will end you. Is that clear?'

I might be a touch impetuous, but contrary to common opinion, I'm not a complete lackwit. I nodded. I also promised myself that I'd close this shit-stain's account before the game was done.

According to Cyrus, the plan was to avoid the sewers by going up through a storm drain that fed into the underground river which ran through Nightside. Apparently, the main sewer routes in and out of Nightside were being more heavily patrolled by the clanks since the attempted robbery at the Hall of Heroes. This was said with emphasis, as if I might have forgotten I was the idiot who'd made a turnip out of that little nut of a job.

He told me that the storm drains had an inlet near the Sanguine Shadow's monastery but that it was difficult to get through. Again, I kept my mouth shut and didn't express my doubts as to the veracity of his claim, or its lack of importance to any except a soft human pus-sack like him.

Once inside the monastery, I was informed that we'd still have to locate Tobias, if he was there and alive. How I'd managed to survive all these years without Cyrus there to point out the blindingly obvious was a mystery. One useful piece of information he offered was about the woman who'd stolen the hammer and thrown me and the priest across the Hall of Heroes. Her name was Augustra Octarius the leader of the Sanguine Shadow and as of three days ago, she was also the favourite to become the next Eklesiastis of the Pantheon. As much as I needed the damn hammer, I wasn't looking forward to dancing with her again.

After finishing the threat peppered briefing, Cyrus led me into the bowels of Leopold's sprawling holding. The more I saw of Nightside the more I was convinced that it could only exist with the knowledge and approval of those above ground. There was no doubt the cement that bound the two was gold, which made me wonder whose side the royalty of Nightside would stand on should war come to the city, particularly as Leopold was touched. It made me curious about his fellow council members. I caught myself. I was starting to think like a schemer and that never went well from what I'd seen.

The gutterhaunt led us to some smugglers' tunnels. The rough-hewn passageways smelled of urine and seeping water but were dimly lit by a few cracked and covered glowstones. The floor was smooth and heavily compacted from the passing of many feet over many years. In dingier side tunnels I glimpsed the ghostly outline of barrels and sacks, and lurking amongst them the bright beady eyes of dog rats and the occasional splatter of luminous fungus. Cyrus moved confidently and quietly. I was fairly confident that I could beat him in a fist fight but blade to blade might be interesting.

He didn't talk much, save to point out holes, low ceilings, or how noisy I was, which was bollocks. For the most part we walked in near silence. I still had a headache but felt better to be up and moving, even if it was with someone who might try to kill me at any moment. In fact, it was that aspect of our otherwise dull trip that kept me awake. The question was, did I wait until he made his move, or pre-empt him?

The cove was carrying enough blades to open a shop and looked like he knew how to use them. He even smelled mean, his scent being comprised mainly of meat, hard liquor and blade oil. I felt better than I had, but I wasn't at my best by any means, and my head was a constant aching reminder that I needed to find Tobias. I'd have to give killing him some thought and in the meantime keep my guard up. About an hour into our little excursion, I heard the unmistakable sound of rushing water.

'Almost there,' he said and lengthened his stride.

A little further on, the tunnel widened to a crescent-shaped ledge. The ground had been worn away by the water pouring from a drain above us and into the underground river that flowed below. Cyrus stood on the edge, hands on his hips, watching me with measured disdain from beneath his hood.

'Over here, Breed,' he said, like I might decide to go somewhere else. Dutifully I went and stood beside him.

'I take it we're climbing up there?'

He sniffed. 'Aye,' he said, and pointed to the outlet of the drain some twenty feet above us. 'We need t—'

Without over-thinking the deed, I straight-armed him off the ledge. I got the impression he turned his head, but the hooded cloak cut down his peripheral vision so that he didn't see me move until it was too late. He grappled with air ropes as he plunged into the muscular torrent and vanished.

'Threaten me, will you?' I demanded of the raging water. It didn't answer.

Had I been inclined to feel a crumb of guilt over settling Cyrus's account, the climb up the wet wall and into the drain would have rid me of it. A few feet beyond the opening, the tunnel was sealed by a grille and had been for about a century if the rust was anything to go by. I checked for cunning levers or false locks, even had a quick feel with magic to see if there was a glamour cast upon it, but no. Unless you were very thin or made of water, it was a dead end, and would have been *my* dead end, had I not beaten that cunny-bucket to the kill.

Relieved, annoyed and soaked, I climbed down and sat on the ledge. I had to go back, but I couldn't return to Duke Leo, given he was the one who'd probably paid the late and unlamented Cyrus to scratch me. As I pondered my next move, I heard soft footsteps in the tunnel behind me. I leapt to my feet, blades in hand. Of all those I imagined it might have been, Tosspot wasn't one of them.

Even though he'd bathed and was wearing clean linen, he still looked grubby, the grime accumulated over years tattooed into his pel-poisoned flesh.

'Got yourself lost, eh, Breed?' He grinned his brown-toothed grin.

'Have you been following me?'

'I was following *both* of you. You lost your friend as well as your way, eh? Very careless.'

'Just fuck off, Tosspot. I'm not in the mood.'

'Don't weep, demon. I know the way out.' He skipped on the spot. '—know the way t'the Shadow house. That's where you're after, ain't it? Need t' find the good father, eh?'

His appearance and offer of help was a little too timely. I tasted the air; just to make sure it really was him and not some sharp cove cloaked by a spell. It was Tosspot alright. No mere demon could replicate the frowsty stink of self abuse that clung to the dirty old cull.

That he was here did not sit well with me, and neither did his claim to have followed me and Cyrus without either of us spotting him. Unfortunately, time was prancing on like a homebound urux and I needed to find the priest.

'Alright, show me, and be warned: I'm in a killing mood, so cross me at your peril.'

He laughed and skipped along the tunnel. Again, I got the distinct impression that I wasn't being taken seriously.

We doubled back to the last branching tunnel. It turned out that Cyrus hadn't led us far wrong. Perhaps he'd intended to do for me then go find the priest himself. Tosspot turned off the main path and led me through a side tunnel to where a fissure had cracked the roof in some much earlier collapse.

'So how did you know this was here?' I asked, nosy as a lurcher. Tosspot smiled, got out his pel pipe and licked the sticky residue from the bowl.

'I bin exploring, having a look-see while you were playing with fairies.'

'Eh? You mean the Annurashi? I'd love to hear you call her that to her face.'

Tosspot capered like a drunken puppeteer was yanking his dangle. 'You're moving up in the world, Breed. Up! Up you go.' He flapped his spindly arms. 'I'm going to find Clary, get her to cadge me some pel from her mousy dimber damber.'

'Aye, you do that. Oh, and Rubin.' He stopped, spun on his heel and eyed me suspiciously. 'Don't tell anyone you've seen me, alright?'

He just laughed and skipped out of the tunnel.

I chimneyed up the fissure and along a narrow crawl space that had been hacked out of the rock. The old lunatic hadn't played me false; the tunnel came out on the other side of the grilled storm drain. From there on it was only a matter of wading through relatively clean runoff water that flowed ankle-deep along the outlet. I say relatively clean; I still had to dodge the occasional floating island of fatty and decaying agglomeration, but I felt more at home here than I did wandering around Nightside or Dayside Valen.

It was dark when I crawled out of the drain. As Cyrus promised, it came out beside the monastery, which was surrounded by a culvert overflowing with trailing vines of blood red viper's tongue. I could hear singing coming from the building. It was the usual loud, pompous dirge favoured by religious culls although the singing was nowhere near as pompous as the temple itself which was a gilt edged nightmare.

The whole edifice had been painted a lurid shade of red. It was so screamingly bright, even at night that it hurt my eyes just to look at it. But that wasn't the worst thing about it. Oh, my no. Some demented genius had decided to imbed spells into the walls, which wasn't unheard of except these spells weren't wards. The monumental waste of money had been spent on a purely decorative effect and I use the term 'decorative' loosely. I watched as every few seconds, deep red shadows rippled around the building. It was horribly literal.

Like a good glazier, I quickly spotted an open casement. Satisfied that I was unobserved, I scaled the wall and took a look-see inside. As befitted an order dedicated to a shadow, the prayer room was dark and joy of joys, it was also empty. I hopped inside as another ripple of shadow crossed the building.

Getting inside was always going to be the easiest part of this venture. Finding the hammer was the tricksy bit. It might take all night to search the place room by room so I resolved to lay hands upon one of the sanctimonious little arse-weevils and persuade them to tell me where it was being kept. I was about to go hunting when I heard footsteps coming towards the door. I dived behind the altar as the door opened and a couple of gospellers bumbled in.

'That went really well, didn't it?' one of them said, it sounded like they were carrying something.

'You think so? I thought the choir was off tonight and Prenam's sermon was the same one he gave last week.'

'Was it?'

'Aye. Don't you remember? He quoted Chankuk the Venerable's speech to the masses at the slaughter of Riven Eye Gorge.'

'I don't think he did.'

'He did, I'm telling you.'

'Well, I liked it. Yay, I say unto thee that rivers shall choke on the corpses of our enemies and we shall know glory—'

'You missed a line.'

'No I didn't.'

'You did. After the rivers shall choke on the corpses there's a bit about flowing with blood.'

'Not in Prenam's version.'

I'd heard enough.

They'd brought a lamp with them but it was small and cast more shadows than light and so I risked a peek from behind the altar to check where they were before I made my move. There were two of them stacking books on a shelf. I leapt from my hiding place, grabbed one by the neck and bashed his head against a wall. The other I punched in the mouth before he had a chance to shout. The one I was holding went limp, but the other was staggering about, moaning and clutching his face. I let go of the unconscious one, drew a knife and slapped the moaner on the pate.

'Shut your yap or I'll vent you,' I hissed.

That got his attention and very wisely he did just that. I slid the door bolt and gestured for him to sit.

'Right, you, where's that cunt Augusta stashed my fucking hammer?'

'I… I don't—'

I slapped him on the head again, a little harder this time. 'Don't tell me you don't know, or I'll clip those shells from either side of your head as they are apparently a waste of skin and I hate waste. Course, I'll have to cut out your tongue first, just to keep the noise down.'

'Shekeepsthehammerinherstudy,' he blurted. Tears smeared his red eye make-up and ran down either side of his snot-bubbling nose.

'Slow down.' I tapped him again.

'Her study. It's… it's on the third floor, big door at the end of the hallway, you can't miss it.'

'Good lad. Best close your eyes, eh?'

Blubbering, he closed his eyes and fell to his knees. 'Plu... please... don't k—'

I laid him out with a punch and stripped his robe before divesting the other cull of his garb. I put on the one that fit me closest and tore the other into strips. I bound the pair of them and shoved them behind the altar.

As usual my feet stuck out of the bottom of the robe but it was blessedly dark in the hallway and I managed to reach the stairwell without bumping into anyone else. All the noise seemed to be coming from the lower levels. The air in here was thick with the smell of incense laced with pel and the underlying odour of unwashed human.

I crept up the stairs, beneath the painted arrogance of gilt-framed hierarchs. My feet sank into a deep pile carpet, so luxurious it felt like I was walking on clouds. The walls were draped in a fortune of red silk. If the intention had been to make the place look imposing it had failed. It looked more like a high-class brothel than a temple. Of course, I didn't know much about the order of the Sanguine Shadow. It might very well have been one of those kinds of orders where to fuck is to pray, in which case it had struck a reasonable balance. The Pantheon had hundreds of cults, all competing for patronage and membership. Each had their own unique twist, but the sex and drug cults were always the most popular.

A splinter of light squeezed from under an imposing door at the end of the hallway. I drew my blades and hoped Augustra wasn't in. Alas, I was out of luck. A woman's throaty laughter rang out.

I listened at the door. There was no way I was going to rush her. Like Tobias she was a sorcerer, and like him, she could flay me down to the nub before I got within a yard of her. I sheathed my blades and crouched at the keyhole to see what I could see.

Standing against the glare of a crackling fire was Augustra. She was wearing an open, loose red robe and had a dildo strapped around her nethers. More importantly, above her on the mantelpiece was the Hammer's hammer.

'Just sign the confession and I'll stop... Unless you don't want me to?' She smiled at someone I couldn't quite see.

I angled myself and saw that the poor cull she was talking to was bent over a table. His brown, homespun robe was pulled up around his waist and his drawers were bunched around his ankles. I heard chains rattle and gagged shouting.

My headache vanished in an instant. It was Tobias. I'd forgotten all about the poor cull.

She adjusted her borrowed member. 'Still won't? Then you leave me no choice.'

There was more muffled shouting.

'Don't blame me. Your father said he'd kill me if you have so much as a bruise when I hand you over, but I must have that confession—you see my problem?'

He shouted almost intelligible curses. I could see he was shaking, straining against his bonds.

Augustra laughed. 'And you a priest. What would Saint Bartholomew think? Now, where were we?' She walked over and squared her hips behind him.

It was an ornate door, heavy, highly decorated, inlaid with shell and polished bone. Funny the things you notice. It was also unlocked. It took me just three quiet strides to reach her. I didn't bother to announce my presence; I just snapped her neck.

I stepped over the body and pulled the priest's robe down. He was chained across a table. A sheet of parchment was crumpled beneath his stump and a quill lay beside it. Ink was splattered all over his hand and sleeve and had soaked into the table top, clouding the bright inlay. The chains might have been marked with a ward against sorcery but they weren't proof against me smashing the lock off with a hammer that happened to be lying close at hand. I say *a* hammer because as soon as I picked it up I knew it wasn't *the* hammer.

Free, the priest tore the gag from his mouth and coughed, steadied himself against the table. His gaze fell on the body of Augustra.

'Oh, Breed.'

I girded myself for the inevitable admonishment, but it didn't come.

'Is she dead?' he said at last.

'Oh yes.'

He shook his head. 'You're too late. The Synod voted. The Senate will follow—'

'Not now,' I said. He was wide eyed and trembling, what little colour he possessed had bled from his face. 'We need to get out of here.'

'They told me you were dead,' he said, still staring at the body.

'What, again? You really need to stop listening to them.' I tossed the hammer.

'What are you doing?'

'It isn't the hammer.'

'It's clearly the hammer,' the priest insisted.

'It's clearly *a* hammer, but it's not *the* hammer.'

'Of course it's the fucking hammer. I've had to listen to Augustra telling me about how she opened the tomb and took it. It has to be the hammer!' He was furious but not because of the hammer.

'My guess is that the Hammer and his hammer were never in that tomb.'

His mouth twisted in an ugly sneer. 'And you're an expert now, are you?' His fist was clenched, the air charged.

'You've been hurt, you're itching for a fight, I understand, but you're looking in the wrong place. The hurt will pass.'

'You seem to know an awful lot all of a sudden. Has your demon been educating you?'

'A demon, aye, but not the one you think. Mother Blake trades in flesh as much as any other commodity. They come in all shapes, ages, and sizes, bound for the brothels... many are unwilling. I've met a lot of people like Augustra.'

'I knew you were despicable, but—'

'That's enough.' I was trying to be all understanding, but he was pushing it. 'I stayed away from that part of the business. Mother said it was a weakness of character, but then, she always did talk shit.'

'But you knew it was happening.'

He seemed determined to pick a fight, to vent all that pent-up rage. I didn't blame him. I just didn't want it to be with me. 'Listen, so does anyone with eyes in their head. We all live in the same fucking world... just about.'

He ran his hand over his stubbly head. He was struggling to make eye contact like he was embarrassed or ashamed. I didn't think it would do any good to tell him that there was no need to be. We both knew he hadn't done anything wrong, but that didn't matter right now, so I held my tongue.

'So, so how do you know this isn't the real hammer?' he asked.

'I don't know. I just know it isn't.'

'*How*? Where does this insight come from? How do *you* know?' Pain was fuelling his anger, never a good thing for a sorcerer, or those around them.

'I don't have the answer, Tobias, I'm sorry.'

'It isn't fair.'

I shrugged. 'No. It isn't fair and there's no justice, I know, and now so do you. Come on, let's get out of here.'

Tobias said a prayer over Augusta. I opened the door a crack just in time to see a handful of red-robed figures coming up the stairs. Closing it quickly I signalled to Tobias. He looked at me but didn't seem to be taking anything in.

'We can't go that way.' I braced a chair behind the door. 'We'll have to go out the window.'

'Allow me.' Tobias raised his hands; the air crackled.

'You sure the angles are right?' I asked.

'Fuck the angles,' he said, and before I had a chance to try and calm him down, or duck, he blew the wall out.

I'll give him this, he didn't believe in half measures. As he crumpled, I scooped him up and slung him over my shoulder. A light drizzle misted the air, damping down the clouds of dust rising off the rubble. I scrambled out of the gaping hole and climbed down what was left of the outside of the building. When my feet hit the cobbles I ran like a dragon was chasing me.

'Sweet salvation, I didn't expect that to happen,' said the priest when he finally came to.

I'd legged it as far from the Sanguines' temple as I could while avoiding the main roads. Eventually I broke into a derelict house that was tucked at the end of a quiet, residential street and hid in the cellar with my unconscious charge. It would do for now, but we couldn't stay here long, given what we'd just done.

'You killed Augustra.' Happily, there was no hint of recrimination in his voice; he was just coming round, and trying to recall what had happened. Being slightly fuddled wasn't a bad thing for him right now. Being raped was hard to bear so perhaps it was best that his memory was hazy.

'I did, and you blew a dirty great hole in their temple.'

'Oh. Yes. I did, didn't I? They will not forgive either act. We're in trouble, Breed.'

I laughed. 'For a change. I think a trip abroad might be in order, somewhere like Shen.'

'None of this would have happened if they hadn't been so damn greedy. So bloody…' he put his head in his hands.

I decided that I wasn't going to abandon him just yet. No matter what my next move would be, I was going to need coin and Tobias was my best chance of getting it. Given my somewhat strained relationship with a lord of the local Midnight Court it was probably best to avoid robbery as all fences were bound to be affiliated. Though I hated to admit it, I was running out of room to manoeuvre and gaining enemies with every stride. The only useful ally I had was the demon, but I'd be damned if I asked him for help.

'You should get a message to your friends in the order.'

He shook his head. 'No, absolutely not.'

'Unless you're planning on swimming to Shen, we're going to need coin.'

'I haven't decided what I'm going to do yet, but I cannot go to the order. They're in enough trouble because of me. I won't endanger them further.'

This wasn't what I wanted to hear. 'They'll probably do much better now that Augustra isn't on their backs. You said yourself, your brother's a halfwit. And Sister Kyra will be desperate to know what's happened to you.' I thought that sounded rather good as persuasive arguments went. The priest shook his head again. There was just no pleasing some people.

'I… I don't know if I can trust her. Someone told Augustra of our plans, it could have been her, and why do you care?'

'I won't dignify that with an answer.' I couldn't, I didn't care. I just needed money.

'I'm sorry, Breed. I'm sorry about everything. I'll get word to Kyra, somehow.'

'Somehow' involved me swapping clothes with Tobias and sending him off to find a bakery.

I waited anxiously for him to return while wearing his scratchy, too-small robe. He was a thin-shouldered cull and no mistake. He returned with a loaf of fresh bread.

'Did you do what I said?' I asked.

'Yes, yes.'

'Nobody saw you? Nobody asked any questions or saw what you did?'

'Gods, Breed. Paying a baker's boy to deliver a loaf of bread is not beyond me. Do you want your clothes back?'

'Yes, I bloody do. You put the note inside the bread, right?'

'I'm not even going to answer that.' We exchanged clothes. As before, he didn't know where to look while we dressed. I didn't give a shit; a body's a body clothed or naked but humans, like arrachids, have some strange ideas when it comes to modesty.

We waited out the day in the temporary sanctuary of the cellar. It was raining outside and if a search was being mounted they hadn't made it this far yet. The street was quiet save for the usual sounds of children shouting and wailing and neighbours passing the time of day. While we shared the bread I told him about what had happened after we were caught. I didn't tell him about the flies and the demon sigil, instead of that I told him that I'd escaped into the sewers after overcoming one of the clanks. I did tell him about the Annurashi which was a mistake.

'How stupid can you be, Breed?'

The shock of his ordeal seemed to be wearing off as he sounded more like his whiny, judgemental self, although I could smell anger lurking just beneath the surface. He pored over the mark in my palm, turning my hand this way and that while muttering to himself.

'Hold my hand much longer and we'll be betrothed,' I said at last.

He let go. 'This could be very bad. The Annurashi don't do anything by chance.'

I held up my hands. 'Nothing to do with me your priestship. I had nothing to do with it. Blame Clary, in fact, blame yourself. Clary had her boyfriend save me because she wanted me to save you, not that I wouldn't have anyway.' I smiled.

'Oh, I believe you. After all, it's not like you have a choice.'

I was an unlucky cove, I'll grant you, but right then I was thankful that I was me and not him.

Chapter Twelve

As we made our way to the singular dump where Tobias had arranged to meet Kyra, I broke some rules of the Court and dipped a few pockets. I also lifted a couple of cloaks. With a basic disguise and a handful of coin, the priest and I settled into a corner of the designated backstreet cellar-dive with a couple of mugs of the vilest ale I'd ever drunk. Tobias paid a yawning link boy a copper penny to keep an eye out while we got down to the serious business of cradling our flat beer and waiting.

The cellar was in marked contrast to the sumptuous palaces and guild houses I had lately frequented. It was much more my kind of place. I wondered if we were still in Duke Leo's domain or if we'd crossed onto the turf of another Duke or Duchess. This place felt like one of those gaffs that no one ever claims, somewhere that's fallen through the cracks. It was places like this where poor culls with nowhere left to go fetched up; flotsam's end, which was appropriate given our situation or rather *my* situation. Tobias would be alright, he had friends who'd look after him but I had no idea where to look for the real damned hammer.

I supped my ale. It tasted like the dregs of a pool of stagnant piss that someone with a bag of hops had once walked past.

'This is more like it,' I said to the priest. He grunted and curled his stump around his mug, but didn't touch a drop.

'My father knew where I was, but he left me there. Nicus Lutius, Mattarax Vulsones, Hero of the Battle of Gutomer, soldier, senator, Advisor to the Empirifex. What a cunt,' he sighed.

'I'll drink to that,' I said. He looked different; a little sadder, a little wiser perhaps, but that was no bad thing, even if how he got there was. Like I said, I'd seen it before. 'Look on the bright side; at least your father didn't put a bounty on your head. He just wanted you out of the way until this is sorted in Senate and Synod, and he becomes even wealthier than he already is. It's going to make for a fine inheritance. Think how many brown robes you'll be able to buy.'

'I foreswore wealth when I joined the order; this is the only robe I own.'

I almost choked on my ale. 'You're a very strange human.'

He straightened, curled his stump against himself defensively. 'What do you mean by that?'

And then it hit me.

I drew a sly breath, tasted the air to confirm what I'd known all along, but had been too stupid to understand. Soft as a feather, there it was, that subtle, peachy taint edging his human sweat smell. I glanced at his stump. His cheeks flushed.

'Nothing, it was just a joke.' I said. He looked away. The conversation died.

After a couple of hours sitting in silence, listening to the old sots fighting over slops from the penny barrel, a robed figure heaved his bulk down the stairs. Wrapped in a heavy cloak that was glittering with raindrops he slowly made his way over to us. There was no sign of Kyra but Tobias obviously knew this panting fellow and beckoned him over.

The newcomer was old. His wine-soaked face had collapsed in on itself like a soggy pudding. He gave me a slight nod of acknowledgement before sitting down beside Tobias.

'I'm so sorry, Toby,' he whispered. 'The guard at the hall betrayed us. Kyra is devastated.'

Tobias clasped the old man's hand. 'Never mind that now. What's going on, Jared?'

The older man shuddered like a speared brachuri. 'The Synod's in uproar. Soon after your escape, Marius convened an emergency session where he called for the order to be excommunicated.' His rheumy eyes glittered, his lip quivered. 'He's understandably furious about Augustra's death and is trying to blame the order. Dear gods, Toby, you didn't kill her, did you?' Tobias looked like the arse had just fallen out of his world. He stared at the table.

'No.'

Jared shook his head. 'Of course you didn't, forgive me. He won't get his way. None of the Synod would want that precedent to be set and then, well, your father has been in talks.'

'What do you mean 'talks'?' He narrowed his eyes. 'What's happening, Jared?'

'Your father was summoned to the Senate. I—that is, we have agreed that you will be spared, and the order will be given a substantial donation.' Jared put his hand on Tobias's arm. '*Substantial*, Toby, but only if we support the Sanguine Shadow in the Synod and agree to put this whole episode down to interference from… undesirable elements.' His gaze flicked to me.

'What? You mean Breed?' Tobias sounded surprised. I wasn't. 'No, that isn't right. And this is more important than a new statue, Jared.'

'More like an entirely new monastery to put the statue in, Toby.' He licked his lips. 'Would you have us cast out just to prove a point?'

Tobias slammed his stump on the table. 'The demons are returning, the fate of the world is at stake.'

Jared looked around nervously to see if anyone was paying attention. They weren't. 'There's nothing we can do. Kyra thinks it's best that we stick together. A united front against the chaos. It's too complex, Toby, we don't know…' He glanced at me again. 'We don't know who's who, but we know who *we* are. Sweet Salvation, the fate of the order is in your hands; I'm begging you, Toby.'

Tobias looked at me as if I had the answer. I felt colder than when the dragon breathed on me. Numbed to the core, I shook my head as the stitch-up was laid out right in front of me. Jared gave a sly smile and pressed his point.

'You need to leave Valen, my boy. The Empire in fact.' He cast another wary glance over his shoulder and oozed a bit closer to Tobias. 'I've taken the liberty of booking passage for you on a ship leaving for Shen. For your own safety, I urge you to take it.'

Tobias gestured to me. 'What about Breed?'

I knew where this was going. I could tell by the way the cull had been giving me the shark eyes. I leaned in close. 'Aye, what about me?' I asked, more out of sport than anything else. I knew I was being offered up as the lamb for this job.

'I... we. That is...' He couldn't look me in the eye. 'Kyra and the order thought it best that you find your own way.'

I waggled my wrist. The silver cuff gleamed. 'I can't be separated from Brother Tobias. I'm bound to him.'

The old pissbag fumbled under his cloak, wafting the vinegary stench of his unwashed flesh into the air as he flapped the sodden wool aside and produced a bulging pouch. He slid it across the table to me. I flicked the lacing open. The unmistakeable sound of gold hitting the table got the attention of the locals. I snarled and they went back to their own business.

'That should be enough to pay a sell-spell to break the enchantment before you suffer too ill an effect from separation, with coin to spare,' said Jared.

I nodded. 'But what about finding the hammer? The one Augustra had is a fake.'

'Is it?' He looked to Tobias for confirmation. Tobias looked at me. I said nothing; thought I'd let him make his own mind up.

'Aye, it is,' he said at last. 'I'm not convinced we shouldn't try to find the real one, as we initially planned.'

Jared blanched, licked his lips. 'Kyra doesn't think that's the best course, and I have to say I agree. We have a chance to smooth things over with the Senate; to save the order. This matter can be looked at in the future, but for now everyone has agreed it should be put aside.'

Gloom doused the conversation. The barkeep sluiced the floor. I watched old rushes sail furiously on the sudden tide while I contemplated the coin-induced change of heart of the order of Saint Bart and, more importantly, how it would affect me. The straws foundered against table legs as the beery tide drained away. This was what I'd wanted... wasn't it?

I snagged the pouch, tucked it into my shirt. 'That it then?' I expected nothing from Tobias, he looked beaten, spent. I however had to find the bastard hammer.

Tobias didn't look at me. An ocean of awkward silence

washed away the sandy knot of commitment we'd briefly shared.

'We'd better get going, Toby,' cooed Jared. 'I've arranged a place for you to stay until we can get you out of the city. It should only be for a few days.'

'Wait, no. I can't, I won't abandon Breed.'

The older man frowned. 'You're not abandoning *Breed*, Tobias. Think, man; the two of you are known, a one-handed human and a… well, you're hard to miss.'

'He's right.' I patted Tobias's arm, like we were friends. 'Together we stand out like cocks in a henhouse.' That I'd had every intention of leaving him and had even been charged with killing him was not the point. At this moment it looked like I was doing the decent thing and I liked that picture. It wasn't one that I saw often.

'You didn't abandon me.'

'You better go,' I said, enjoying the brief and utterly false sensation that I'd made a noble sacrifice. 'I'll be off now. You should wait a while before heading out.' I grinned. 'Take care, priest.'

Jared sagged like an overcooked soufflé, visibly relieved that I wasn't going to be difficult. Tobias always looked like a whey-faced pup, so it was hard to tell what he was thinking.

The Order of Saint Bartholomew had sold me out in *the* most polite way I've ever been sold out in my life. It made me smile. I pulled up the hood of my stolen cloak and left. I didn't look back. I didn't know where the hell I was headed, but I guessed that was the general direction whichever path I took.

The inn was on the lower level of the city. Overhead, rain-washed walkways wrapped around stairwell towers like constrictors, and grey daylight filtered through the filigree ironwork, to pool in the rutted mud. All the storehouses that framed this lonely ginnel were shuttered against the bucketing rain. The central drain ran thick and swift. I had no allies in this city that I could go to. I was hunted by the law, the Sanguine Shadow, and probably Duke Leo and his courtiers. And then there was Shallunsard.

I didn't know the demon well, but from our few encounters, I guessed that he wasn't going to be pleased when he found out that I hadn't killed the priest or found the bloody hammer.

I was about to work myself up into a fine lather of self pity when I caught the familiar scent of calthracite and dried blood wefting through the warp of the rain.

'How forgetful of me,' I said, and drew my blades.

Sebastian Schiller stepped into the lane about thirty feet away. About the same distance downwind, an ogren plodded into the middle of the road. I put my back to the wall so I could keep an eye on both.

'Ah, there you are, *Breed*. That is what they call you, isn't it? Most amusing.' Schiller whipped a rapier from its scabbard. Against the rain it was nothing more than a fish-scale flash of silver, a thing made of light and menace. 'I would say you're hard to find, but you're not.' He smiled revealing his fangs. 'Mistake the first was not killing me; very sloppy for a Guild Blade. Mistake the second was leaving Marius and Cassia alive.'

'Only two? I'm just not trying hard enough.'

'You struck me as an underachiever.' He shook his head. 'I see you've lost my firelance. This is a pity, for both of us. For my part, I think I shall carve my displeasure in your hide.' He gave the rapier a casual flick to loosen his wrist. 'Too much? I'm never sure with threats. It's so tricky trying to find the balance between menacing and ridiculous.'

'I don't suppose you'd take a promissory note in lieu of the lance?'

He rested the rapier on his shoulder, put his hand on his hip and smiled like we were old friends talking about the weather. 'Oh, I would, but given that there's a tidy bounty on your head, I don't reckon you're a good investment.'

'Oh? I thought the bounty had been paid.'

'Last I knew the bounty offered by one Pork Chop Jing was very much alive.' He whipped the rapier through the air. 'You've managed to upset a lot of people. I'm genuinely impressed by what a troublesome cove you are.' He smiled and tossed a coil of dark ringlets over his shoulder. His companion chuckled, spat on her hand, and hefted a double-headed axe.

'It was pure luck that I had business in Appleton,' said Schiller as he made a practice lunge. 'Lots of contracts up for grabs there right now, some sort of turf war. I do love a good turf war, don't you? But yes, had I not been there I might never have found out who the sneaky bastard was who stole my lance.'

'Would that be the same firelance you shot me with? Only, I think you're way ahead of me in the sneaky bastard stakes.'

'Let's not quibble over details...' he paused tilted his head, sniffed. 'Ah, you brought a friend too. The priest didn't mention you had a crew.'

I had no idea what he was talking about, though I was keen to find out if Tobias had betrayed me. 'And which priest would this be?'

Schiller shrugged. 'I don't suppose it matters. Brother Jared is such an odd hybrid: a viper's heart wrapped in the body of a pig. He sold you cheaply, Breed.'

'I think you'll find that—' I didn't get chance to finish as, with a roar, the ogren rushed me.

I say *rushed*, but oh, she was a slow cove.

I waited for her to come on. When she swung, I swayed away from the blade. Using the lumbering bravo's arm as a step, I hopped over her shoulder and drew my blade around her neck. Hot blood sheeted the ground. Her axe spun from her grip and smashed into the wall. She dropped to her knees. It was a deep cut and the weight of her massive noggin ripped the bud from the stem, as it were. Stunned and blinking, the ogren's head rolled away from its twitching body.

Schiller sighed. 'Well, that was a waste of five crowns.'

I flicked the blood from my blades. 'That's the least of your worries.'

'I'm not the worrying kind,' he said and darted towards me.

Not only was he tougher than he looked, but he was extremely fast. I fended off his first flurry of blows purely by reflex.

He paused, stepped back and cracked the bones in his

scrawny neck with a side-to-side head toss. 'You have some skill. It's almost a shame that I have to take you in.'

I set my guard. 'Less talk, more fight.'

You know those times when you regret saying something, but can't take it back? It was like fighting air. The muddy spray flew as we danced, every attack was met with a riposte and so it went, along the length of the street and back again. He only slipped up once and lunged clumsily, leaving the slightest opening. I pressed my attack, realising too late that it was a superb feint. His blade slid into my right bicep. I swung with my left to keep him at bay as the blade in my right hand slipped from nerveless fingers.

Schiller smiled, sniffed the blood on his blade. 'Sweeter than I'd imagined, with floral undertones and a subtle hint of halfwit if I'm not mistaken.'

'Do you ever get bored of the sound of your own voice?'

'Not so far, and I'm older than I look. Urgh, these stockings are ruined. Pure arrachid silk, you know; cost a fortune.' He rushed me again. His wings were a droning blur, his blade a flicker of light.

I just about managed to hold my own against him. My arm hurt but it wasn't as badly injured as I first thought. Truth be told, I was enjoying myself until I caught another familiar scent on the breeze which quite soured my mood. It was akin to old leather boots that had been soaked in lemon juice and earthworms. I dared a glance over my shoulder, just to confirm it was who I thought it was.

'Mistake the third,' said Schiller as his blade slid under my guard and skewered me between the ribs.

The wicked splinter burned a breath-stealing path right through me. I fumbled my remaining blade, would have cursed had I been able to draw breath, instead I settled for gasping.

Schiller withdrew his blade and flicked my blood from his weapon. The desire to sit in the mud quite overcame me and I folded like a freshly laundered sheet.

'Easier than I thought.' He took a silk kerchief from his sleeve and dabbed his blade. 'Jing wants you alive. Apparently, he's going to make an example of you, more's the pity.' With a glittering flourish the tip of his blade tickled my chin. 'I find heads so much easier to transport than whole persons.'

Before I had chance to tell him what I thought of his plan the scent of arrachid bloomed strongly in the air, drawing both our attention. I looked up to see a familiar outline crest a rooftop. As I'd guessed, it was the one I'd tussled with in Appleton.

'This scum is mine,' she said. Her foreclaws twitched beneath her green silk haori.

'I don't suppose that you'd believe me if I told you that I wasn't trying to kill your father?' I gasped.

'What you say is irrelevant, vomit-sack. You broke into our home and shamed our house.' She turned to Schiller and gave him a hard four eyed stare. 'You will leave now.'

The Mosquito dabbed the corner of his mouth with his bloody kerchief. 'Now, just a minute, milady, the contract is open; any cove can collect.'

She reared. 'I am the daughter of Shu Lo Jing. You will yield to me or my father will put a bounty on *your* head.'

'And just how will he know to do that?' I asked, keen to foment discord between them.

'Breed has a point, milady.'

The arrachid smiled and dropped to the ground. 'Is this where I'm supposed to say, 'because I'll tell him', so that you can say, 'not if I kill you first,'?' She unholstered a pearl-inlaid hand cannon.

Schiller smiled. 'I wouldn't dream… Oh, all right, perhaps I was. What can I say? I'm inclined to the dramatic. Now get thee gone, fustiluggs afore I'm forced to school you like I did young Breed here.'

The arrachid levelled the cannon at Schiller and fired. He was already moving, up. The shot missed as he leapt into the air. She cursed and drew a heavy Shen blade that was sheathed across her back and advanced. Schiller grinned and came back down to earth. I lay quite still and tried to stay conscious, just in case I got the chance to scarper while they were giving each other a basting.

While I gathered my energies, Jared and Tobias emerged from the cellar. It was at least satisfying to see the look of horror on Tobias's face when he saw what was happening. Jared ushered him away sharpish, half dragging him down the street. I watched him go. He kept glancing back as he let himself be led away. The hard, heavy rain stung my face.

The arrachid and the Mosquito circled each other. They were evenly matched, if very different fighters. She had a blade and a cannon, Schiller was quick and precise. By the time I had the strength to make my move both had drawn blood.

While they were busy making confetti out of each other, I seized my chance and attempted a slow and rather painful escape. I didn't have a hope in hell of outrunning either of them, but I did catch wind of something that might help me hide from them should they notice I was gone and give chase. I let my nose lead me to it. Not too far away, I stumbled gratefully into the fish market.

The cobbles were slick with blood and speckled with scales. The air was wonderfully pungent. Schiller and the arrachid wouldn't be able to track my scent through here with a pack of hounds. If I could just make it out the other side I might be able to lose whichever one survived to pursue me. Unfortunately my strength was fading quicker than that slight hope. You'd think a body would get used to this kind of thing, become inured to the discomfort.

Trust me, you don't.

I was leaking like the proverbial when half way across the market square, my legs buckled beneath me. As I fell I flailed and managed to tip a whole bucket of brachuri fry all over myself. This spectacular, possibly final act of self-sabotage elicited gales of laughter from the crowd and curses from the stallholder. To gild the lily of my misery, a couple of clanks strolled around the corner just as I was being berated by the brachuri dealer. I tried to get up, but my strength had fled so I sat there like an unstrung puppet all too aware of my fate.

'Well, well, well, what do we have here?' said one of the clanks.

I was by now resigned to an untimely and painful death. If they didn't kill me, someone else would. 'What the fuck does it look like, you rusty-haired, tin-arsed self-abuser?' A baby brachuri squirmed out of my shirt, looked up at me with its huge, bulbous eyes before it wriggled off to join its brothers and sisters who were escaping down the drain. The clank turned as red as his hair, he and his sniggering companion drew their blades. The world began to darken at the edges.

'Breed!' Tobias shouted, just before someone snuffed out the candles.

I drifted back to consciousness after the strangest and most exhausting dream involving pickle barrels, prostitutes and fireworks. Wherever I was, I was comfortable. It was cool and dry and the air tasted of dust, wood smoke and familiarity. A breeze stirred, but didn't trouble the air to blow harder than a caress.

I opened my eyes. I knew this place. Above me, the painted life of Amari Geran stretched in fading panels across the ceiling of his tomb. I remembered the fleshy wife, the laughing children, and the favourite hound from my last visit. Their idealised images flaked from the stucco while the man himself mouldered in the robbed-out tomb beneath me.

With consciousness came awareness and, as was usual these days, almost everything ached. I sat up. My side burned but had been neatly bandaged, as had my arm. I was naked save for a cloak thrown over me and I smelled of vinegar.

'Why do I smell of vinegar?' I said to no one in particular.

Tobias was sitting by a fire. He had a black eye and instead of his customary brown robe, he was wearing a pair of voluminous Guldistani slops, black bucket boots, and a turquoise kurta. He smiled. Tosspot and Clary wandered in from an adjoining chamber, Clary had a brace of rock rats in her hand and was wearing an oversized and dented knight's helm, which would have been worthy of comment had Tosspot not been dressed in a rather fetching floral gown. They also looked a little crisp around the edges, soot streaked and slightly singed.

'It's from when you was in the barrel,' said Clary.

I wasn't quite sure if I'd fully woken up, and looked to Tobias for clarification.

'The barrel,' he reiterated. 'Don't worry; you weren't in it for long.' If I wasn't mistaken, he had a twinkle in his eye, which was most unlike him and more than a little disconcerting. 'And at least it helped clean the bear grease off.' He looked at Clary and Tosspot who both nodded. 'The fire got quite close to where the lovely ladies and gentlemen of the Blossom House had hidden us and I didn't want you going up in flames when we had to get out of there.'

Tosspot and Clary sniggered at that.

'How are you feeling?' Tobias asked.

'Confused. How long have I been out? And where did those two come from? What happened to Schiller and the arrachid and Brother bastard?'

Tobias blushed. 'Ah, yes, Jared. I can only apologise. His holy abilities run towards calculating the very best way to put across his point.'

'Eh?'

'He's incredibly persuasive. It took me a while to throw off his influence, but if it's any consolation he did help us to get out of the city.'

'No, it isn't. How long have I been out?' I swung my legs off the tomb. 'And where are my fucking clothes?'

'The spider and the fly scarpered when all the clanks showed up.' Clary beamed from under the helm. 'You've been out for two nights and today. Lady Greenstone said you'd be out for that long and she was right. Your clothes got a bit burned. But we got you some more.'

'Burned? Who the fuck is Lady Greenstone?' I stood up, felt as weak as a newborn. 'What the fuck have you three been up to and… can I smell fire?'

The three of them exchanged guilty looks. They were behaving like a novice crew who'd just pulled off their first rum job and were feeling like kings of the manor.

I gave up. 'Just give me the fucking clothes.'

Tosspot produced a fan and gave himself an angry wafting. 'Well, there's gratitude!'

They spent the next few hours giggling, and talking in the code of a shared experience, one which I wasn't privy to. I did not like that they'd been up to things and I'd been there, but only in the flesh.

What I did manage to glean, other than they'd rescued me from the clanks, was that they had negotiated with a Nightsider to fix me up and then, while that was happening, Tobias had found and beaten the damnation out of his brother. Though I'd rather rip my tongue out than tell them, I was quietly proud of their achievements.

Evening settled over the cemetery and we sat down for a meal of roasted rock rat and stale bread. My side was sore but had healed surprisingly well due, I was told, to the ministration of the mysterious Lady Greenstone. From what I gathered from their chatter she was a brachuri. What one of those fearsome crustaceans was doing as a madame was beyond me. I'd always thought they were strictly monogamous and rather prudish when it came to sex.

I kneaded my right arm, it felt heavy, but at least it was working. Being a thoughtful crew, they'd remembered to filch me a couple of hunting knives along with a pair of black breeches, a linen shirt and a rather fetching if slightly too small, brocade waistcoat. I gave myself a dust bath before dressing which dampened the higher notes of the vinegar smell but didn't get rid of it entirely.

'So how did you get us out of the city?' I asked the priest, who was looking very unlike himself, sitting there, all prinked up in his rum-duds, gnawing on a rat leg like it was peacock.

'Jared lacks confidence in his skills and so it didn't take long for me to come to my senses. I ran back to where I last saw you and followed the arrachid and Schiller. While they had words with the knights, Jared and I dragged you out of there.' He grinned. 'And after we'd rescued you, I had words with Jared. He confessed that he'd sold you out to Schiller and begged me to forgive him.'

'Which you did?'

'Naturally. He was eager to atone so I made him hand over his ill-gotten gold. As I was in a conversational mood I left you in the safe house with Jared and went to find Marius.'

'Not sure that was wise. I'd have preferred it if you'd vented the snakish cull.'

'I'm sure you would but he and Kyra thought they were doing the only thing they could do. There's no excuse for Marius; he's a prick of the highest order and so I gave him as you would say, a basting that he won't forget in a hurry.'

'That's when we found him.' Clary piped up. 'You should have seen him take those Sanguines to task, Breed. He done ever so good.'

Tobias blushed. 'Really it was nothing, the Sanguines are not Scienticians.'

'So why did you bring me back out here?'

'Safe innit, demon?' said Tosspot, still fanning himself, still dressed like a gutter-run slamkin.

I stood up. 'What the fuck have you two been up to?' The world tilted, my stomach pitched like a ship in a gale. 'Because I'm getting bored with being stabbed, beaten and shot.'

''S none of your bizzy, demon,' said Tosspot indignantly.

'None of your bizzy,' Clary echoed.

I eyeballed Clary. 'You're learning too many bad habits from him. And as for dear Duke Leo; that little sly-boots paid Cyrus to scratch me from the ledger.' I stretched, it hurt. Everything hurt. Everything always hurt.

'It wasn't Leo!' Clary got up, planted her fists on her hips, which was quite the most ridiculous sight as she was still wearing the helmet. 'It was his brother. Leopold was very angry with him.'

'His brother? I never even met his bloody brother... did I?'

She frowned. 'Of course you did. It was his brother who was with me when we found you in the sewers. Took a dislike to you, he did.'

'It was that great ugly dog rat that fou... Oh. The dog rat is Leopold's brother.'

She nodded.

'I wonder what I did to upset him? Anyway, never mind. I'm still not happy about being in this pot of arse-pickle. Not happy at all.'

Tobias sighed. 'I know, I'm sorry, Breed, and I intend to make it up to you. Leopold has arranged safe passage for us on a ship bound for Shen. We'll go there for a few months, work out our next move. This isn't over.'

'What, you mean the prophecy? What about the Synod and the Senate?'

'Fuck them.' He laughed. 'I never thought I'd hear myself say that.'

'Me neither. I didn't think you had the stones.'

'I mean it. The Empirifex is half mad and lives in the clouds and the Senate and the Synod will never learn. They're all too caught up furthering their own petty ambitions to see the danger that awaits them, to see further than their next banquet. Nothing changes, nothing ever changes.' He got up, paced to the door. 'That's why this place is a cemetery.'

I leaned against Amari's tomb. 'I did not know that.' Or where this speech was leading. It occurred to me that he might have lost his wits to the paradox of power; either that or he was being poetical.

'This valley and the surrounding area was where the original city of Valen stood—until the demons levelled it. After the war, the citizens buried their dead here near the ruins and rebuilt where Valen is now. Even then, when the demons came the first time, the Synod and the Senate were too busy vying with each other for power that they didn't see the danger until it was too late. That's where the warspawn came in.' He leaned on the broken door, gazed into the gloom of evening. 'I've had enough of them and their games. I'm sick of… Oh. Shit.' He backed from the door and kicked dirt over the fire.

I went to see what was wrong.

'I was sure we weren't followed,' Tobias insisted.

'Uh-uh,' I said as the clanks crested the far edge of the valley, their menacing silhouettes hard against the milky light of the dying day. With them were a dozen or so guardsmen and women. The lightly armoured greenshanks were clambering amongst the tombs, searching, trying to flush us out.

I looked at Tobias.

'Well, I didn't *think* we'd been followed.' He rubbed his head with his stump. That was the old Tobias. I could see his confidence shrinking. 'I'm not sure I can deal with—sweet salvation, there must be fifty of them.'

'If not more.' My side was healing, but the bright spot of blood on the bandage told me that, just for a change, I wasn't quite fighting fit.

'If I must make another calculation, if the angles are wrong and I lose control…'

I laughed. 'We'll take a lot of arseholes with us to hell. C'mon, it'll be fun… briefly.'

I turned to Clary and Tosspot. 'You two keep quiet, and stay away from the door. Tobias and I are going to draw them away.' I looked at Tobias. He nodded.

'Why don't you just go down?' Clary asked.

'Down where?' I asked.

'Down into the depths, down, down, and out to the city that was, stupid demon,' Tosspot rasped; he looked terrible. 'Down to where the rock rats live among the roots and bones.'

Tobias and I looked at each other. The greenshanks were getting closer. The knights weren't far behind. It wouldn't be long before they found us. 'Lead on,' I said.

Clary straightened her helmet and ran off to the back of the tomb with Tosspot in tow. Tobias and I followed.

She led us into a second chamber that held three more ransacked sarcophagi. One of them had tipped into a hole in the floor. By the looks of it, grave robbers had tossed the lid off the bloodstone coffin and the weighty object had smashed through into another chamber buried below. They'd clearly not wasted the opportunity and several more tunnels led off from the lower chamber that was scattered with bones and rock rat nests. Clary slid down the lid and the rest of us followed. Rats hissed and ran for cover. The main passage branched off into other tombs, but gradually angled upwards. Clary and Tosspot had found a tomb-robber's highway.

Chapter Thirteen

From where we emerged I could see the walls of Valen looming dark against the bleeding edge of the horizon. The sense of urgency was much diminished now that we'd put some distance between us and the clanks. I guessed the tunnel came out roughly a mile from the cemetery. At first, I thought we'd come out near a ruined farm as tumbled rocks lay scattered across a hummock of ground too rough to till. On closer inspection I saw that the stones were dressed and carved and that the ghostly outlines of buildings stretched across neighbouring fields, punctuated here and there by fangs of broken columns and remnants of wall too stubborn to yield entirely to decay.

From where we were, the ground sloped down into a shallow valley. In the middle was another hummock, stripped to the bare earth, save for scabs of crusty rubble and half a dozen standing stones each about six feet tall. A large flat slab lay blackened and cracked near the mound.

'This is where the demon hordes were finally vanquished,' said Tosspot with uncharacteristic clarity. He kicked a piece of tile.

'I can't say I've ever been here before,' said Tobias.

'And you call yourself a scholar,' I said and went down to the mound in the valley. From what I could tell, it was a natural rise. 'Any idea what this was?' I asked Tobias who was already heading away from the city.

'That? No. Anyway, come on, we need to get going, they can't be far behind.'

I started to follow; pleased that the priest's confidence was returning but there was something else nagging at me. I stopped. Clary skipped after Tobias. Tosspot was busy taking off the dress. Soiled lace fluttering in the breeze. I returned to the mound.

The slender stones were unmarked and unremarkable save that they were standing and mostly intact. I touched one and immediately withdrew my hand. It was vibrating.

'Breed... Breed!' Tobias was backing away. 'We have to go.' He pointed to the tunnel.

'I hear them. You go on, I'll catch up.' The clattering din of armour echoed through the tunnel. It was accompanied by shouts from above ground. I knew that I should go but something kept me here. Tosspot was standing to one side, watching me. I touched the stone again, put both hands on it and twisted.

It turned.

I wasn't surprised. I'd expected it to move.

'What the hell...?' Tobias made to come over but Clary held him and tried to drag him away.

When I felt I'd turned it enough, I moved on to the next. Nothing happened. I touched a third. Again, nothing. Formless panic prickled my gut. I moved on to a forth and was rewarded by a skin-tingling vibration running through the stone. I glanced at Tobias.

'Do you know what you're doing, Breed?' he asked.

'No fucking idea,' I said and turned the fourth stone. This time I knew I'd turned it enough because a space that wasn't there, an impossible angle, a dark, cold tear in the world, began to open before me. I stumbled back. The tear opened into a narrow slit, a black slash cut in the air.

So this was what fear felt like. I wasn't keen.

Behind me, knights charged out of the tunnel. Clary squealed but didn't run. She took the helmet off and stood her ground beside Tobias.

'In the name of the Empirifex, I order you to surrender!' The lead clank shouted. His troops spread out, a dozen firelances were levelled at Tobias. 'Do. Not. *Fucking* move!'

'Alright, Captain, that's enough.'

I recognised Marius's voice.

'You should have let me shoot him,' I called to Tobias as his brother limped out of the tunnel. He was dressed in the scarlet robes of his order and, like his brother, he had a black eye.

'Next time, ignore me,' said Tobias.

'I can hear you, you know,' said Marius. He stayed near the tunnel.

'How are the angles?' I asked Tobias. He shushed me with a frown.

'I see your friends are all here too. That'll make things easier.'

'Make what easier? Is this it? Do you think you can just shoot us down?'

'If only. No, you, dear brother are coming back to Valen, where you will damn well stand trial for murder, theft, and arson. Father was less than amused by your actions, unlike the Senate. You've done the one thing he will not forgive, Toby. You've made him look stupid.'

'I exposed his and your greed,' said Tobias.

'You fucking killed Augustra!' spittle flew from Marius's lips. 'Did you really think you could get away with that? You killed her, Toby.'

'You don't know what she did to me.' Tobias's words fell like stones.

'Oh, for gods' sake what? What did she do that made you take her life? What could be so terrible…' he paused as realisation dawned. 'What did she do?'

Tobias looked down at his feet. The air turned hot and heavy. A storm was brewing.

Marius looked shocked. 'I… I didn't know.'

A couple of the clanks sniggered. Tobias shrank into himself. The confident cove who'd recently begun to blossom wilted beneath the pitying gaze of his brother and the mocking eyes of the knights. 'I wasn't exactly going to shout it from the rooftops, was I? And the last time we met you were more intent on trying to kill my friends than talking.'

'Nevertheless, you should have told me. Captain.' Marius turned away.

The captain stood forward, pulled an official-looking document from his boot. 'I am charged by the Imperial Senate to arrest and detain Tobias Lucius Vulsones who is hereby charged with the crimes of murder, treason and arson.'

Clary began to cry, a low keening wail.

'Shut that fucking monster up, Toby, or I will,' Marius spat, more like his old, detestable self.

Tobias pulled Clary to him. 'She's just a child, Marius.'

Tosspot backed towards me.

'*It* is an abomination. Step away from it, Toby, and give yourself up. I promise you'll get a fair trial.'

'What are you going to do with my friends?'

I looked at the smirking clanks, lovingly hugging their firelances like they were family. It seemed pretty fucking obvious what they intended to do to us.

Marius thrust his hands into the sleeves of his robe, whistled a deep, sighing breath. 'Toby, Toby, Toby.'

It was a signal. Behind Tobias a pale shade with skin the colour of sand and eyes as white as bleached bone rose from the ground. Dirt dripped like water from her wispy hair and cobweb gown. The ground rippled beneath her and flowed towards Tobias in a gentle, undulating wave. A dozen small dust devils sprang up around him, blinding him. I saw him gasp as the swirling winds stole the breath from his lungs. Clary's wailing cry turned to choked coughing as they were both driven to their knees by the fury of the sorcerous winds.

'You didn't think I'd come unprepared, did you, Tobias? I know what you're capable of,' Marius shouted over the howling gale. Before he had chance to pat himself on the back, a big rat sprang from the rocks and fastened its claw around the neck of one of the clanks. Taken by surprise, the guard discharged her lance into the air as the rat bit her face through her open visor. She staggered back, yelling as more rats poured from the tunnel and began attacking the imperials.

'See, what did I tell you! Shoot them!' Marius shouted in panic. 'Shoot them all!'

I drew my blades, intent on throwing myself at the sorcerer attacking Tobias and Clary. Rats aside, we were grossly outnumbered and, without Tobias's power, as good as dead. Before I could take a step Tosspot shoved me into the space between the stones and followed me through.

The narrow angle opened onto a vast, grey plain gouged with black blasted pits and mounded with the frozen corpses of every stripe of creature that had ever walked, crawled, slithered or flown.

We were on a battlefield, one that had been lost to time, standing by a mound that was the twin of the one we'd just left. On this mound there was a huge slab of darkly glittering starstone which was supported by half a dozen standing stones. I took a step towards it. Beneath my feet ice-rimed bones shattered like glass. My nervous breath came out in short clipped curls. I took a step back and bumped into Tosspot.

'What the fuck is this place?' I said.

'It's the last battle. The high mages locked it in here. Too much Schism magic, too much poison, so they froze it and locked it away forever... almost,' said Tosspot. He sounded different. Above us the sky was black and cloudless and as still as death. The stars didn't twinkle, their light shone cold and indifferent.

'How do you know?'

'Because I was there.'

There it was again, that fear thing. I really didn't like it, it made me twitchy. Before I'd even thought about it, my sword was resting on Tosspot's razor thin collarbone. He didn't flinch.

'Best start talking,' I said.

He chinned towards the mound. 'Best look over there, then you'll understand better than I can explain.'

'You so much as scratch your nut-sack and I'll gut you.'

'No doubt.' He grinned.

I sheathed my blades and climbed the mound. The stone pillars were the twins of those I'd turned to open this space up. I didn't want to touch them, but something more than Tosspot was driving me to look and so I hauled myself onto the slab.

And then I understood.

Lying there, untouched by the vicissitudes of time or death, was the Hammer of the North. The *real* Hammer of the North. I could tell it was him by the hammer he was holding.

He was a good half a foot taller than me and wrapped in a ragged fur-trimmed cloak. A bloodless gash ran diagonally across his face, marring the pattern of orange scales. His claws, like his cloak and his long, pierced hair spines, glittered with frost. Aside from a set of nondescript and battered leather armour, his clothes were patched and worn. His clawed feet were bare.

I don't know how long I stood there, looking at the truth while remembering the lies. It could have been minutes or hours. Eventually, I did what I knew I was meant to do and took hold of the Hammer's hammer.

The moment I touched it, I felt its power. This is what had drawn me to the mound. This was what had called to me across time.

It slipped easily from his frozen hands as though he was ready to give it up. I hefted the weapon, it had weight but it wasn't heavy. The metal was dull grey, the head of the hammer was as graceful as a bludgeoning weapon probably could be, tapering to the middle either side of a sigil-intagliated shaft.

I didn't examine it closely because I couldn't stop looking at the Hammer of the North. I half expected him to crumble to dust or vanish, for time to finally set him free, but nothing about the greatest hero the world had ever known changed. Despite the gash across his face, he looked at peace. Something around his neck caught my eye, something gleaming amid the thick fur cloak. I took a closer look. It was a polished blue bead, not a sapphire or a diamond, just an ordinary, glazed bead hanging from a plain silver chain.

What can I say? Old habits die hard. I unclasped the chain, not just because I was a thieving bastard, but also because it felt like the right thing to do. Truth be told, I didn't know what I was doing. I was adrift in uncharted waters. The only thing I could do was go with the current and see where it took me. I fastened the chain around my neck.

'He looks different in the paintings,' I said to Tosspot, anger and sadness spiking my gut.

Tosspot, unlike the Hammer, looked like hell.

'No. I know,' he said. 'Not least of the indignities he had to suffer. That popinjay in the paintings, the ones in the Hall of Heroes?'

I nodded.

'He was the worst of the lot, if you ask me. He was supposed to be his friend, but instead he helped them erase the real hero from the pages of history.'

'What a cunt.'

'Aye, a complete and utter tosspot.' He bowed.

And now I knew why the golden-haired god looked so familiar. 'No. You?'

'Don't sound so surprised, I've been alive for over six hundred years, and that's after following him onto a dozen Schism battlefields. All that magic takes its toll on a body. Never mind the curse.'

'That talking thing we were discussing earlier? You'd better get to it, sharpish.'

'My name is Rubin, squire of the Hammer of the North.' His eyes shone with tears. 'I would have died for him, we all would, many did. But after the war it was decided, that it was best to...' He paused, took a breath. 'The warspawn were deemed too dangerous to have such a legend to look up to, to aspire to. The truth is that the Mage Lords were afraid that their creations would become their masters. After the war many feared that you...' He laughed. 'Sorry, *they* might get ideas above their station.' He laughed till he coughed. Bloody spit flecked his dry lips. 'I'm sorry, Breed.'

I shrugged. 'S' alright, it happened a long time ago and means nothing to me, but you went along with it?'

He winced. 'I did. We pretended that the fabled hero was a human, swore those of his companions who'd survived to secrecy.' He coughed again. 'Those were hard times, civilisation teetered on the brink of destruction. We thought it was for the best. We were wrong.'

I swung the hammer. It was far more elegant than the monstrosity painted on the walls of the Hall of Heroes. This weapon shone like stars had been folded into the dull metal and it weighed exactly enough to feel comfortable in my hands.

'Why didn't you tell me?'

'I couldn't. By sworn to secrecy, I mean bound by a geas so powerful that I couldn't tell you or anyone.'

'But you found me, you led me here.'

'No, I just followed the road that was laid out for you. The Annurashi knew, fate knew, I just tried to be there.'

'So who cursed you? Someone wasn't in on the stitch-up.'

He scratched his chin through his tangled beard. 'Sweet salvation, she was angry. I got off lightly compared to some. She damn near started another war when she found out.'

'The Red Witch?'

He nodded. 'Her curse has kept me alive all this time, but only just. Nobody can curse like her. Why, I remember—'

'Oh, fuck. Tobias! Tell me all about it later. We need to go back, now.'

Tosspot—Rubin shook his head. 'You do, but this is the end for me. I've felt it coming for a while now. That's why I knew you were the one.'

'You sure about that?'

'Aye, demon, I am. I've felt death's grip tightening ever since I met you. I knew it was a sign. Promise me, when you're back on the other side, you will close the gate. There's things in here no mortal should get their hands on.'

'Such as…?'

'Breed, really.'

'Alright, alright.'

I took one last look at the battlefield, at the thoasa, arrachids, ogren, amphibanes, and humans lying side by side amid the demon horde. The sacrifice was immense. I'm not given to sentimentality but right then I did something that I'd never felt another living body had ever deserved of me.

I raised the hammer in salute to the dead and let all the lies, all the sneering and the hurt, boil out of me and pour into the hammer.

And then I burned the sky. Volcanic fire leapt from the hammer, up into the frozen vault where it turned the cold black to molten gold.

'Looks like I can do more than just boil water. Mother will be surprised.' He didn't answer. I looked round. Tosspot had vanished. The magic faded from the sky like a sunset. Red gold light struck the frosted field, striking glittering arcs from the ice and swathing the dead in the glory that the Mage Lords had tried to deny them. I stood in silent contemplation until the gold faded to silver and then, after a final nod to the Hammer's bier I stepped back into my own world and…

… Absolute, fucking chaos.

On seeing the carnage, my first impulse was to go back inside and wait until they'd finished killing each other, but as I was in possession of the real Hammer's hammer, I felt I should probably do something to help my friends.

But first things first.

I took a two-handed grip on the weapon and swung it into the nearest of the standing stones. A neat crack raced across it and it broke in half, instantly sealing the rift between worlds.

I might have taken a moment to congratulate myself on a job well done but a shot winged past my head and buried itself in the mound with a soft thump. At least two companies of knights and greenshanks were fighting swarms of rock and dog rats. Clary and Tobias were hiding behind the stones on the mound, which was surrounded by dead imperials who had been charred to piles of ash and molten metal. The sorceress was standing protectively in front of Marius, who was cowering in the tunnel entrance.

'Breed!' shouted Tobias just before he sent a blast of crackling energy at the sell-spell.

She waved her spindly arms and a wall of dirt rose before her and absorbed the lightning.

'If you have any intention of using that bloody thing, would you please get on with it?' Tobias yelled, sweat running down his pasty face. I rested the hammer on my shoulder.

Tobias sagged against one of the stones. Clary caught him before he fell and lowered him to the ground.

'Clary, call your pets off,' I said. She didn't look convinced but gave a keening wail. The rats disengaged and scattered.

The knight captain raised his hand and the clanks stopped firing and reformed their ranks. He stepped forward and raised his visor. 'In the name of his Imperial Majesty, Durstan the Seventh I order you to lay down your er... weapon and surrender.'

I grinned. 'No.'

'No?' He didn't look like he was used to being disobeyed.

'You heard me, clank, I said no. I will not lay down the Hammer of the North's hammer,' I said it loud enough so that everyone could hear me, so that every jaw would drop, which they did. The smell of fear-piss and excitement bloomed in the iron air.

'Listen to me, you fucking animal,' said the knight, oblivious to the wincing gasps from those around him. 'You will lay down your arms and surrender, or by the All Seeing Eye, I will put you down, and I don't give a donkey's fuck-piece whose hammer you've got.'

The knight pointed his sword at me to emphasise his point. I pointed the hammer at him. The blast must have boiled every drop of liquid in his body so quickly that he literally exploded, covering everyone within twenty feet in hot gobbets of Imperial fuckwit. One of his more dull-witted comrades bellowed a battle cry and charged me. I pointed the hammer at her and she pulled up so sharply that she fell on her arse.

'Breed, no! Enough! I order you to desist,' Tobias shouted. He looked pale and scared, and well he might.

I tugged the cuff off my wrist and tossed it to him. 'Sorry, priest, I'm done playing servant. Anyone else want to try their luck?' I shouted. A couple of the knights weighed their swords but wisely stayed where they were.

Marius shoved the sell-spell in the back.

'What?' she said.

Marius chinned in my direction.

'Are you deranged? That's the Hammer of the North's hammer. You aren't paying me enough to take that on. The Empirifex couldn't pay me enough.' She looked at me and pointed towards Valen. 'Do you mind if I…?'

'Not at all,' I said.

'Most kind,' she said and melted into the ground.

I turned to Marius. 'Right, you. Get your arse out here.

He thought about it before stepping forward all nice and sheepish.

'What do you think of the prophecy now, eh?'

'This proves nothing!' he said, but his tone lacked conviction.

I pointed the hammer at him.

He shrieked and ducked. 'Please don't kill me!'

'Say it then.'

'Tobias was right.'

I cupped my ear. 'Sorry, what was that?'

'TOBIAS WAS RIGHT!' he bellowed.

I scanned the faces of the knights. 'You all heard that, right?' Nobody answered. I raised the Hammer and without looking, although I'd clocked it a moment before, fried a gull that was passing overhead. Its cindered corpse fell from the sky. 'I said, you all heard that, right?'

A chorus of affirmation followed. Satisfied, I turned to Tobias. 'Well, that's that sorted.' I was rather pleased with myself.

I should have known better.

No sooner had the words left my mouth than a shadow passed across the suns. The air turned cold, the sky roiled and clouds knotted overhead. A flash of lightning was followed by an earthshaking peal of thunder. The acrid stench of sulphur filled the air. The Imperials scattered and took cover where they could find it. Marius crawled back into the tunnel.

'Ah, Breed, you didn't forget about me, did you?' said the demon Shallunsard, who'd apported onto the scorched patch of ground where the knight captain had given his final speech. The last time I'd seen him in his own flesh he'd been naked. Now he was clad in burnished bronze armour, his horns were bound in rings of silver, and his wings were tipped with steel.

'No, of course not. I just had a few other issues to deal with first.'

'So I see.' His laughter shook the ground. 'You finally worked it out, then?'

'I did, no thanks to you. Why didn't you tell me?'

'I couldn't. That is the irksome nature of one of the many geas I am bound by. You don't think they just locked me in my stronghold, do you? Actually, knowing you, you probably did—if you even thought that far, which I very much doubt.'

'I have my own troubles, why should I give a donkey's fuck-piece about yours?'

The demon shook his head. 'Ah, Breed. So ungrateful, and after everything I've done for you. Now hand it over; there's blood-letting to be done.'

He held out his hand. My palm itched. Part of me wanted to give it to him and be done with this, but a more stubborn and, it has to be said, suicidal part of me didn't.

I have a knack of making bad decisions, a gift for choosing the wrong path, or rather, not choosing a path at all and just running blindly from one disaster to the next as though all the demons of hell were chasing me. Most of the time it's bloody good fun. But there comes a time in everyone's life when they have to make a decision. I looked at Tobias. He looked at me like the soft, soapy cull that he was.

'What about him?' I asked the demon.

'Why do you care?'

I looked at Clary, saw only myself reflected in her eyes. She was holding Tobias's hand.

In truth, I wasn't sure that I did care. I'd never been in the position where I'd had anyone to care about. I swung the hammer off my shoulder.

The demon's fingers twitched impatiently. Tobias tried to get up to speak but Clary held him back. I didn't hear what he was saying. I was too busy concentrating on a spell. One thing I did notice was the shocked expression on Shallunsard's face when I not only hit him but unleashed all of the magic I'd found within me when I'd picked up the hammer. Then I had burned a dead sky. Now I burned the demon.

I caught him square in the chest, though it felt like I'd hit a mountain. The shock almost tore my arms from their sockets. I planted my feet and roared.

I didn't care.

I didn't care about anything and that was the truth, and the key to my paradox.

I opened my eyes, peered through the smoke. There was a small crater of glassy ground surrounding the demon but the bastard was still standing. I have to say, I was more than a little disappointed. I'd hurt him, as the ichorous black blood oozing from the rent in his breastplate proved, but I hadn't dropped him. Nevertheless, I stood my ground even though my every instinct was telling me to run.

'We made a deal, Breed,' he snarled.

I shrugged. 'You tricked me.'

'I did not! Well, not much, and not about the deal we struck with regards to the hammer, or killing him.' He pointed to Tobias, who gave me *a look*.

'I didn't do it, did I?' I said to the priest.

'Give me the hammer!' the demon demanded. The ground shook, lightning lashed the clouds, it was all very dramatic, but I knew it was bluster. He was unsteady on his feet and bleeding.

'No,' I said.

'You dare say no to me. Don't you know who I am?'

'Yes, of course I do, I just don't care who you are. Your time is over. It was over centuries ago. Now fuck off while I'm feeling generous.' By generous I actually meant fit to drop. I was exhausted; those spells, half formed and ill conceived though they were, had utterly drained me. Now I knew why Tobias fell over quite so much.

'I'll make sure you live long enough to regret that decision, halfling. I will destroy everyone you have ever loved, everything you have ever cared about, and then I will destroy you.' The demon roared to the sky, blinding, coruscating lightning lit along his outstretched wings. When I could see again, he was gone.

I had to laugh. 'Everyone I've ever cared for, eh? Good luck with that.'

The blast of lightning had knocked everyone else off their feet. The leaden sky growled like it had eaten something that didn't agree with it. Tobias was looking at me, his expression a mixture of shock, anger and surprise. I rested the hammer on my shoulder and turned to Marius and the remaining knights who were creeping out of the tunnel.

'Right, you fucks, pay heed.' They all very sensibly looked extremely attentive. 'Here's what you're going to do. You're going to go back to Valen, and if any of you so much as think about *glancing* over your shoulder, don't, or I will turn you into a cinder. When you're back in your pig pen of a city you will tell the Senate and the Synod that Brother Tobias Vulsones of the Order of the Scienticians of Saint Bartholomew was right. I'm looking at you, Marius, you miserable, back-stabbing bastard and if your father has a problem with that, tell him to talk to me.'

It took some longer than others to digest my words but with a little encouragement from their brighter friends, they all eventually seemed to get the message. Marius allowed himself to be ushered away by the Imperials, who all seemed very eager to get away from the angry thoasa with the hammer, demonstrating their excellent survival instincts.

As I'd expected, Tobias and Clary stayed where they were.

'Nice thing with the rats, Clary,' I said when the last of them were out of earshot.

'Thanks. Where's Rubin?'

I didn't know how to tell her what had happened. They'd grown quite close and she was just a kid. 'He decided to stay with his friend.'

'He's dead, then?'

A kid who knew more than most.

'Yeah.'

She nodded. That seemed to satisfy her. She made a funny little squeaking noise and a fat white rat squirmed its head out of her pocket. She sat down and started grooming it.

'So I was right. You were the one,' said Tobias. He pushed himself up against the stone.

'And, so? What do you want? Only, I'm all out of thanking humans for their amazing insight. Those paintings in the Hall of Heroes, they're lies. Did you know that?' I was more angry than I'd realised. 'The Hammer, the real Hammer, was a thoasa, *a fucking warspawn*. Tell that to the order and the Synod when you see them next, if you dare.'

'I... I had no idea, Breed. Although, I suppose it makes sense.' He rubbed his head with his stump. 'I don't blame you for being angry. Humans have treated you and your kind poorly.'

'Damn right you... *they*, have.' He looked like I'd just slapped him and blushed to his roots. 'It's alright, priest. Your secret's safe with me.'

He sighed. 'It... it shouldn't be a secret, but my father insisted upon it.'

'If you want my advice, see how this anti-warspawn thing turns out before you tell anyone you're touched, eh?'

'Aye, perhaps. Though I doubt that is the worst of my problems. What are you going to do now? Have you chosen a side?'

'I have: my own. As to what I'm going to do, that's easy. I'm gonna keep out of it, let the humans and the demons rip each other to pieces. You should do likewise.'

Tobias smiled and shook his head. 'I don't think so, and you don't mean that.'

'Yes I do.' I fingered the bead I'd taken from the Hammer. 'I know how this story ends.'

'What do you mean? Ah, yes. The Hammer.'

'Yes, *the Hammer*. I'm not like that stupid bastard. I'm not going to sacrifice my life for anyone, especially not humans.'

'I don't blame you. I'm not that keen on them at the moment either.'

I shrugged. 'Up to you. You going back to Valen?'

'Yes. I have to try and reason with the Synod and the Senate. After seeing the demon not even Marius will be able to deny what's happening and how much we need the warspawn, how much we all need each other if we're going to survive. Of course actually having proof would help. I don't suppose you'd…?'

I laughed. 'Not a chance.'

'Didn't think so. Still, it was worth a try.'

We both laughed and when the laughter died we stood there… and stood there.

I broke first. 'You'd best get going, see if you can catch up with the others, vent your brother before he gets back.'

'Breed!'

'I'm joking. Good luck convincing your father and the Synod.'

'Thank you. I think I'll need it.' He half turned. 'Just out of interest, when did you break the geas?'

I winked. 'Look after yourself, priest, try not to get hung.'

'And you, Breed. Take care of yourself.' He said it like he meant it, the soppy cull.

'Always. And tell your friends not to come looking for me.'

He nodded and followed after the others. I noticed the confidence in his stride and the way he carried himself, shoulders back, head up, just a touch of swagger. He reminded me of me.

Clary popped the rat back in her pocket.

'You can stick around if you want,' I said, not really meaning it. 'It's probably safer away from Valen for the likes of you and me.'

'Safe?' She squinted up at me, dark eyes bright with mischief. 'Where would be the fun in that?' she said and then did something nobody had ever done that I hadn't paid first. She *hugged* me. It felt uncomfortable.

'Alright, alright, that's enough of that.' I pried her off. 'Now get lost, and stay away from rat boy; he's a bad influence.'

She grinned and scampered after Tobias.

I watched the procession of knights head towards the city followed by Clary and Tobias, watched them until they were swallowed by the shadows of Valen's mighty walls. I didn't have the first clue what I was going to do now. I briefly considered going back to Appleton and killing Mother and Jing, but after seeing the Hammer that seemed petty and pointless, a bit like me. I sat on the broken stone by the mound. I had a hero's weapon, but I was about as far from a hero as you could get.

A cold wind scythed across the fields as darkness closed the wound at the world's edge with glittering, night-strung stitches. I picked the brightest of those low-slung stars to be my guide, hefted the hammer onto my shoulder, and started walking.

F🦊X SPIRIT

Foxspirit.co.uk

'After nourishment, shelter and companionship, stories are the thing we need most in the world.' Phillip Pullman

Skulk: *noun* – a pack or group of foxes

Fox Spirit believes that day to day life lacks a few things, primarily the fantastic, the magical, the mischievous and even a touch of the horrific. We aim to rectify that by bringing you stories and gorgeous cover art and illustrations from foxy folk who believe as we do that we could all use a little more wonder in our lives.

Here at the Fox Den we believe in storytelling first and foremost, so we mash genres, bend tropes and set fire to rule books merrily as we seek out tall tales that excite and delight us and send them out into the world to find new readers.

With a mixture of established and new writers producing novels, short stories, flash fiction and poetry via ebook and print we recommend letting a little Fox Spirit into your life.

@foxspiritbooks

https://www.facebook.com/foxspiritbooks

adele@foxspirit.co.uk

Printed in Great Britain
by Amazon.co.uk, Ltd.,
Marston Gate.